# BEYOND TOMORROW'S SUN

Also by Ronald McGuire

*Beyond the Rivers of Time*
*Nightmares & Lullabies*
*Pax Liminalis*

# BEYOND TOMORROW'S SUN

Ronald McGuire

Beach Book Press

To Matthew, Andrew, Patrick, Dylan, Peyton, Parker,
Nathan, Ryan, and now, Callan.


"Do not pray for an easy life; pray for the strength to endure
a difficult one."
– Bruce Lee

"The price of anything is the amount of life you exchange for it."

~ Henry David Thoreau

# 1

# Now or Never

It was a long night of verbal abuse, accusations and counter accusations, punctuated by threats of physical violence. When it was over I was physically unharmed, but I was more frightened than I'd ever been. My uncle eventually got too drunk to maintain the basic thread of the argument. Once he passed out, I spent some time organizing my camping gear, then grabbed a few hours of sleep before I had to go to school.

It wasn't much of a school, one teacher and a handful of students whose attendance was irregular, at best. But it was a refuge for me, whether I stayed awake or not. All morning, I sat fidgeting at my desk until the teacher admonished me to either stop or go home. My anxiety got worse as the hours ticked by, but I couldn't go home. I needed access to the media center. The time had come. I was going to leave for good after I made one more run to the reclamation center to top off my recycling credits. My e-bike, with its long-range batteries, regenerative pedals, and fat knobby tires, had triggered my uncle. He'd been angry about the purchase since he discovered it tucked away in what was left of the garage. He knew I was holding out on him, but he had no idea how much. As far as he knew, I'd made one good score and burned all the credits on the bike, without sharing any of it with him. He was right about the not sharing part.

I had the bike and my pack loaded with all of my camping and survival gear. The equipment wasn't heavy, but I didn't have much space left. I wasn't sure how much more I could carry. I didn't like the idea of leaving behind the wealth of material hidden at the factory ruins, but I liked the idea of staying with my uncle even less. The cache of metal, plastic and glass parts I'd stumbled upon was huge, left forgotten after the war in an underground warehouse. It was a lifeline for me, one I leveraged to purchase all of my equipment, piece by piece to avoid drawing attention. With the exception of my bike, I'd managed to keep my spending hidden. But my most recent visit to the rec center had netted me my biggest payday ever, the bulk of which I'd spent the previous day at the surplus store.

Mr. Figgins had been shocked by the quality of the objects I turned in on my last trip. He made it a point to tell me how important they were, how rare and valuable the metal. I'd never heard of palladium before. I wouldn't tell him where it came from, and he eventually settled for telling me he'd buy as much of it as I could get. I knew my rights; the cache was mine by salvage claim. All I had to do was keep it hidden and squeeze as much value out of it as possible. It was easy when I first found the underground parts depot, but the more I turned in, the nosier Mr. Figgins became.

My plan was to make one more run, get what I could carry, collect as many credits as possible, then put all the bad things in my life behind me. I wanted to see what was at the end of the old road. It either sprang up from the dusty basin beyond the hills or terminated there in a crumble of concrete and caliche, depending on your perspective. The road ran east, all the way to the ocean, or so I hoped. The sea was a vague memory from better days, when my parents were alive. We lived near the coast and made frequent trips to the beach, but my memory of those times was fragmented. I was ashamed I had forgotten what my parents looked like. My uncle had taken away the few photos I had of them. He said it was punishment for some wrongdoing, but the truth was, Uncle Geo needed money, and the digi-frame holding my childhood memories was worth at least a bottle or two of whatever rotgut booze the fool was drinking at the time.

The GPS on my e-bike showed a blank space where the road appeared to end in the middle of nowhere, far short of the sea. From the moment I'd spotted the emptiness on the map, I'd wanted to find out for myself what was there. My imagination took fire with the possibilities.

The school once accommodated 200 students. It was constructed a century before I enrolled. It lacked most of the services found in modern schools in the population centers of the country. I wasn't getting much of an education, but I read, constantly, anything and everything I could get. Despite its failings, the school had a modern media center, with access to digital versions of nearly everything ever published.

When school ended, I hurried to the media center to download as much content as my reader would hold. How-to books, survival strategies, military manuals, anything I thought would help me on my journey. I finished my downloads and was running to my bike when I decided to change my plans. Instead of going directly to the ruins, I made my way into town, back to Mrs. Carter's Army Surplus store, where I'd purchased my equipment and supplies over the previous year. Mrs. Carter never questioned where I was getting all the money, she was glad I was spending it at her store. Customers were rare as rain, and she hadn't rented any of the rooms above her shop in years. If she accepted my proposal, we could both come away rich.

I found her in her usual spot, sitting behind her counter watching the news. I never understood her fascination with it, the news was always depressing. But I found her routine reassuring. I also appreciated the fact her air conditioning, unlike my uncle's and most others, still functioned. When I got there, I always paused to enjoy the cool air, a relief from the blazing sun.

When I walked in, she greeted me with the same exuberance as always, and said, "Look who it is! Twice in 24 hours, to what do I owe the pleasure?"

I'm sure the dark circles under my eyes were a dead giveaway I hadn't slept much, but she was happy to see me. Everyone in our dried-up little dust-bowl of a town knew about my uncle. I'd given up lying about my life, and people stopped asking. At least I didn't have a black eye or bloody nose this time.

"Hi Missus Carter," I replied. "I was wondering…I mean, I was thinking…you know those credits I used…"

"Charlie, you know I don't give refunds. If you changed your mind about something…"

"Oh no, ma'am, not at all, I was thinking you could help me out with something. It could help you, too. A win-win, if you know what I mean."

"A win-win…I'm listening, but this better not be illegal, you know I'm too old to start robbing banks. I don't wanna spend my last days in a prison cell, not on Earth, not in orbit, no place, uh-uh, not for me," she said.

I always liked Mrs. Carter's sense of humor.

"This isn't illegal, but it does have to be a secret, and we'll need your hover truck. If you help me, I think you'll be able to spend your last days any place you like."

"You don't say? I'm all ears, spill it. And don't leave anything out this time, you know what I told you about lies of omission."

"A lie of omission is a lie all the same."

"We're gonna break you of your habit one of these days, ain't that right?"

I didn't answer her. Instead, I launched into the story about the stash at the factory ruins, how the 600 credits I'd spent in her store the previous day was a minuscule fraction of the horde I'd kept hidden for over a year.

"If you help me load up your truck and take a load to the rec center, you can have everything else; I won't take any more. It's yours, millions of credits, you can have it all. I need one big payday, then I'm done."

"I don't know if I like the sound of this. Why make this kinda deal? If you've got half what you say, why not keep it all and live off it yourself?"

"Because I'm leaving. I can't stay here anymore. My uncle…"

"Charlie, you're not gonna be a kid forever. Stick it out, wait until you're eighteen, then you'll be the one set up for life."

There was no way she could convince me to stay, but it was nice of her to try. I wasn't one for exaggeration, but I got the feeling she thought I was stretching the truth or, as she said, leaving something out. I was a terrible liar, so I had to be careful about the truths I told. Like most people living in a reclaimed zone, she was a mixture of pragmatic and opportunistic, and generally bored. Besides, I wasn't her kid, so I wasn't her problem. She could take the money and I could hit the road, a win-win for sure.

"I can't do it. Five more years, I can't. He's…please, Missus Carter." If I had to beg, I would beg. I was desperate.

"Tell you what kiddo, let's hop in the truck and take a ride and get a look at this treasure, then we'll decide what to do next, sound fair?"

"Fair enough."

"Good, you take your bike 'round back and load it into the truck. I'll grab a few things and meet you out back."

"Thanks," I said in a rush, "you won't regret it."

"Go on, I gotta lock up after you."

Once I had my bike loaded, Mrs. Carter appeared through the back door of her building and unlocked the cab of the hover truck. She carried a small black box with a biometric lock on it, which she placed in a compartment in the dashboard.

"What's in the box?"

"What we in the business call a just-in-case," she said. She punched the start button, the truck rose up on its cushion of air, and we were off.

We left town through the no-man's land of empty houses and torn-apart buildings, blocks of decayed wood and concrete bordering what remained of Greenfield. The hover truck kicked up a trail of gravel and dust and sent it drifting across the arid plain, but it was a smooth ride.

***

The drone followed every twist and turn of the truck, never falling out of range. Video from the drone was relayed to a receiver in the Sheriff's cruiser. It was an old-style electric utility vehicle, where Sheriff Figgins and his brother Harry watched like buzzards drifting over a body. They kept their distance and inferred the truck's destination long before it arrived at the ruins.

"There's no way," Harry Figgins said, "I personally picked this place clean decades ago. Something's not adding up. You think they're onto us?"

"Relax," Jack said, "the kid's not too clever and the old lady doesn't have a clue. Whatever he's hiding, we're about to see it."

"What about her?"

"You worry about the kid, I'll take care of her."

"I'm not in this to hurt anybody," Harry said, "I want to see what he's got, then we come back for it later, nobody gets hurt. For all I know I've already bought his best stuff. Three pounds of palladium. I've never seen so much at once. How much more could there be? Kid didn't know what he had when he dumped it on my desk."

"Brother you may be smarter than me, but sometimes you're dumb as a brick. They've got a truck, a big one. They're not out here sightseeing, they're out here to load it up, likely plannin' to pay you a visit at the rec center today. What if they haul off every last bit of whatever he's got stashed out here? Then what? We go to all this trouble for nothin'? Even with your lowball payouts, we might stand to lose a fortune. What if he fills the whole truck with palladium, or something worth even more? What happens if you don't have enough credits to pay him? I'm not takin' the chance."

"All I'm saying is, nobody gets hurt."

"And I heard you the first time."

The hover truck cut through the ruins and came to a stop at the end of an expansive concrete slab, next to a space thick with dead brush and tangled vines. The drone returned metrics with the video and measured the slab at 60 meters long and 30 meters wide. Harry pointed at the screen. "I know this spot, but I've never seen it from above. Look at this end," he said, pointing at the opposite end of the slab from where the hover truck had stopped, "looks like the outline of an old ramp, the sunken space between…"

"Sure does," Jack replied, "but ain't no use to us, all filled in. Maybe focus on the business end of this operation," he said, pointing at the two people exiting the truck, "where the money is."

"Who's the dumb one now? My point is, I never knew they had facilities underground. Never occurred to me. This could be bigger than we thought."

"The bigger, the better," Jack said. A red light flashed on the screen and a thin red circle appeared around Mrs. Carter. "She's armed, didn't expect the old gal to be trouble. Wait, look at 'em, they disappeared," he said snapping his fingers, "right through the bushes."

"Emergency exit, fire door, something else, there must be a bulkhead or staircase down there. How the hell did I miss it?"

"Like I said, dumb as a brick sometimes," Jack said, "let's go see this mystery for ourselves."

Jack pulled the cruiser alongside the parked hover truck. When they exited their vehicle, Jack left his door open and set the drone into its landing pattern. Harry slammed his door shut and walked around the front of the vehicle to join his brother.

"Hey big shot, nice stealthy move there. They know we're here."

"Well damn, you got me there."

***

I was switching on a few of my camp lanterns when the sound of the door slamming echoed down the stairs.

Mrs. Carter was speechless when I showed her the contents of the underground storage facility. It was a massive cache of both pristine and oxidized parts left over from the heavy equipment factory. I could tell she was impressed. When we heard the noise outside, she stopped staring at the row upon row of pallets stacked high with rare metals and other materials and looked over her shoulder.

"You sure nobody else knows about this place?"

"Not anymore," I said.

"How well do you know it?"

"I've been through all of it…"

"Is there another way out? And if there isn't, can you make your way around in here without the lights."

"Yes, I mean no, there's not another way out, it's blocked, and yes, I think I can manage in the dark."

"Okay, here's the plan. Turn off all the lights but one," she said, pointing at one furthest from the door. "We'll get over to the corner, out of the light from the door. Once whoever it is comes inside, I'll distract them and you scoot up those steps quick as you can, you got it?"

"What about you?"

"Now you know why I have a just-in-case, get moving."

I ran down the center row shutting off all but the last lantern and made my way back to her. We tucked into the darkness of the corner as the first of two men entered the storage facility. I didn't recognize him, but I recognized the pistol in his hand and the uniform he wore. My heart sank when I saw the second man, Mr. Figgins. One of the few people who had ever been kind to me was betraying me. I never considered he would double cross me, but my last visit to his reclamation center should have been a clue. He was too excited, more than I'd ever seen him. I had to fight to control my anger at him for betraying me, and at myself for letting it happen. I started to rise when Mrs. Carter placed a hand on my shoulder.

"Okay you two," the man with gun shouted into the darkness, "we know you're in here, no point draggin' this out. Show yourselves or we'll lock you both in 'til you come to your senses."

"Lights," Harry said, pointing at one of the lanterns I'd switched off. The two men walked further into the interior and switched on one, then another lantern. When the second light came on, we weren't hidden from view any longer.

Mrs. Carter rose and drew her pistol from the holster concealed at her waist. She aimed it at the Sheriff. "Go Charlie," she said softly, "it's now or never."

I jumped up and ran for the door. The Sheriff and Mr. Figgins spun around. The Sheriff didn't seem to know where to aim first, but he settled on the more pressing threat, the woman with the gun. I scrambled up the steps, pushed through the vines and shrubs into the afternoon sun, then turned to listen. I heard Mrs. Carter's voice echo through the space below.

"Holster your weapon Jack, this ain't your place. I claim everything in here by right of salvage, passed to me fair and legal. You two can move along and nobody has to get hurt."

For a second, I thought things might work out, she might persuade them to move on, then I heard a laugh, and a chill ran up my spine. I assumed it was the Sheriff. I'd never heard such a cackle from Harry Figgins.

"You think you got the drop on me, old gal? Think again. Your little pea shooter don't scare me. You go on an' get yourself back to your little shop. We'll take care of things from here on out."

"Not a chance fellas, what's mine is mine, you oughta know…"

Her voice was cut off by one gunshot, then a second. I heard her cry out. I started to go back down to her, then I heard her scream, "Charlie, run!"

Then more gunshots, different from the first, returning fire, Mrs. Carter buying me some time. There was nothing I could do to stop a gunfight. I ran to the hover truck and dragged my bike from the back. I heard two more shots from the sheriff's gun, then the sound of someone clambering up the steps. He cursed when he slipped on the rotted debris I'd left in place to help hide my coming and going. I climbed onto my bike and looked over my shoulder and saw Harry Figgins clawing his way over the last step and through the curtain of dead vegetation sheltering the stairway. I opened the accelerator to full power and the bike lurched forward, then slipped sideways on the sand and gravel, threatening to bring my escape to an abrupt end. I kicked the ground with one foot as hard as I could and brought the bike upright, then I was away, speeding toward the stony path I used as a shortcut back to town. If I could get into the hills, I could find some cover. If not, there was no way to outrun a bullet, and I knew it.

***

Harry Figgins was overweight and smoked like a chimney. He covered no more than a few paces before giving up the chase.

Jack joined his brother. They watched the witness to their crime speed away into the hills. Jack raised his sidearm and took aim.

"No!" Harry shouted. He slammed his hand down on his brother's arm, ruining his shot. "He's a kid, damn you. I told you…"

"I know what you told me, but it was self-defense down there, and this is self-preservation," he said, pointing in the direction of Charlie's escape. "He'll be the end of both of us. I can explain away what happened down there, but not with a witness on the loose. Tell me, genius, what do you propose we do about it?"

"I don't know," Harry said, "but I'm not killing a kid, not for all the money in the world. This is on you. You figure it out."

Jack's eyes followed the dust trail heading into the hills. Before Charlie was out of sight, he laughed and said, "I reckon it don't matter no how. Nobody's gonna listen to him, no matter what he says. Come on, brother, we got work to do."

# 2

# You and Me Against the World

I spent a lot of time on the part of the ancient road close to Greenfield. I would ride for hours, weaving between the broken places, jumping over the smaller gaps, burning daylight in the hope my uncle would be out of the house or passed out cold by the time I got home. I would peddle myself to exhaustion, then coast on the batteries for the long ride home, a ride I had no intention of ever taking again.

I made my escape from the ruins through the dry rocky hills and didn't look back until I saw the broken old road in the distance. When I was certain no one was following, I rode down to the plain, across a cracked and blistered lakebed, and started my journey east. I didn't know where the road would take me, other than east. I knew it led away from home, away from my uncle, and away from the two men who had killed Mrs. Carter and tried to kill me. Everything bad was behind, and what lay ahead, whatever it was, had to be better.

My vision was blurry, and I tasted salt on my lips, but I pushed on. I couldn't stop myself from crying. I rode as far as I had ever ridden before, driven forward by my anger. When my legs began to burn and cramp, and my back started to ache, I let the batteries take over for a while. I coasted on the bike's energy and felt the hot wind for the first time, gradually coming back to my senses after losing myself in pain and fear. When the batteries died, I peddled again, keeping up a punishing pace, my exertion rebuilding the charge in the lithium-polymer bricks inside the bike's frame. I knew the longer I could peddle, the longer I could coast. I was exhausted but I kept going, leaning into the effort of guiding the bike across the uneven remnants of pavement.

Dust and rocks gave way to low brush and the occasional gnarled tree. When I spotted a stand of small trees I could use as a hideaway for my camp, with the sun casting shadows along the mountains in the distance behind me, I decided it was time to stop for the night. I checked my GPS and was surprised to find I'd traveled over eighty kilometers. I'd never traveled so far from town. Despite my circumstances, I was relieved by the realization no one would have any idea where I was.

I'd slept outdoors before, and I'd left home more than once. This time things were different. This time I was prepared for a long journey, with food and proper equipment. I was never going back. I was certain Mrs. Carter was dead, as I would have been if I hadn't gotten away. I couldn't understand her sacrifice. She made a choice and paid for it with her life. I couldn't help wonder if it was for me or for the money she stood to make. Either way, I made a promise to myself I would never forget what she did for me, whether she meant to or not.

I set up my insta-tent, the spring-loaded set of hoops and rods popping into shape at the push of a button, then gathered up dried scrub and dead wood for a fire. I dropped a thermtab into the pile and it took light, pushing away the shadows growing around me. I sat down by the fire and all the anguish of the day and all the days before it rolled at me like a giant wave. I started to cry again, until the wave crested, then crashed down on me. I don't know how long I sat there, oblivious to everything around me, reliving my last fight with my uncle, hearing Mrs. Carter scream, seeing the look on Figgins' face; all of it took me out of myself for a time. When it finally passed, I knew I needed to take stock of my situation.

I wasn't worried about animals. The big carnivores had been extinct since before I was born. The remaining scavengers would keep their distance, there were easier meals to be found. But people were a concern, for obvious reasons. I set up my perimeter alarm, then returned to the fire to eat.

I boiled water and poured it into a foil pouch of freeze-dried pseudo-beef stew and started eating, enveloped by the warmth of my fire. I could get used to living on the road, I thought, but when I was old enough to join the military, I would do it. Space Force would punch my ticket off Earth and I'd never have to see my drunken fool of an uncle again. If anyone did try to kill me again, by then it would be a fair fight.

I used to enjoy seeing my Uncle Geo during the holidays, or when he would stop by to visit with my mother, his sister. He also dropped by, if my dad was gone, when he needed money. My mother was an easy mark. Then my parents died, and Geo became my guardian. Things weren't too bad the first few months, better than an orphanage. Losing his job changed my uncle. He never recovered from the shame of it, or maybe he'd always been looking for an excuse to drink his life away.

I knew the road lead east. I hoped it ran all the way to the ocean. I imagined swimming in clear cold water, wave after wave of rolling surf. I remembered a seaside harbor, the coming and going of ships, people on vacation or earning their living from the sea. I imagined the sounds and the smells and wanted to experience it again, to make new memories.

I woke up to the soft bleeping sound of my perimeter alarm. I had no idea how long I'd been asleep. It must have been a couple of hours because the fire had burned down to a glowing pile of embers. I tossed a handful of sticks onto the coals, then ducked behind my tent, crouching in the darkness. I retrieved my knife from its hiding place and slipped it from its sheath. The fresh wood took flame, expanding the circle of light. I couldn't turn the alarm off without exposing myself to the light, so it continued bleating softly overhead. I turned my head and listened intently, seeking the source of the noise, waiting for whoever was out there to show themselves.

I didn't have to wait long.

A pair of green eyes, low to the ground, peered out from the shadows on the other side of the fire. The eyes moved closer, and a dog stepped into the light. It was big, shoulders as high as my hip, with a deep chest and a short brindle coat stretched tight over long curved ribs, outlined by the firelight. It was plain to see it hadn't been on a steady diet. It moved tentatively, its legs like coiled springs, ready at a moment's notice to bolt back into the shadows. It sniffed the air, searching out what was left of my meal. It moved with an impressive stealth for such a large animal, closing in on its prize.

I could see a collar around its neck. I'd always wanted a dog, but pets were never a possibility in my uncle's house. I would never subject a dog to that life. I stepped out of the shadows to greet it, but in a flash the dog spun around and disappeared back into the night.

The dog was afraid of me, but I wasn't afraid of the dog. Its fear of me made me sad, but I could relate to how it felt. I picked up the remainder of my dinner and tossed it into the darkness in the direction it had run. I reset the alarm and when I didn't hear anything else for several minutes, I turned in for the night.

I woke up at dawn and got underway with the rising sun warming my face. The landscape continued to change as I rode. Low scrub and bent broken trees began to give way to healthier vegetation. Late on the second day I paused to check my GPS against my surroundings. I had come to a place where I once again had long unobstructed views to the north and south. A line of low hills far to the north I originally thought ran parallel to the road was growing closer. When I stopped, the low buzz from the bike's motor stopped too. While I tried to work out where the hills and the road might merge, a noise coming from somewhere off the road caught my attention. I laid my bike down and went to investigate. I pushed through low brambles laced with thorns and was thinking of backtracking and trying a different approach when I saw the source of the sound through the brush. I couldn't believe my luck. Before me, sparkling in the sun, was the first natural flowing stream I'd seen since arriving in Greenfield. The stream ran clear and cool. I filled my water bags and added sanitizer tabs. "I hope the dog finds this, too," I thought.

Each night, I left food out for the dog beyond the range of the proximity alarm. Each morning, I checked and found the food had been eaten, but after four nights with no other sign of the dog I decided to leave the food close to the fire. If it wasn't the dog eating the food, I didn't want to keep wasting it on whatever else was out there. I set the alarm as usual and crawled into my tent. It seemed like only seconds passed before the alarm tripped. But the early dawn sky told me I'd slept soundly through the night for the first time. The weather was turning cooler, a light dew had settled on the earth, adding a hush to the already quiet world.

I peeked out from under the tent's flap and saw the dog eating. I moved in slow motion, gradually pulling the flap aside so the dog could see me. The dog stopped eating, but it didn't run away. Instead, it stared at me for a moment then went back to eating. When it finished, it curled up near the ashes of the fire. I climbed out of the tent and the dog stayed put, but it watched my every move.

I stretched and yawned, then reached back inside the tent for my canteen. The dog's head rose and it watched me drink, licking its lips to let me know it was thirsty. I filled a collapsible bowl with water, placed it on the ground a short distance from the dog, then walked back to the tent. The dog went to the bowl and lapped up the water, licking away long after the final drop was gone. I could see a name woven into the dog's collar.

"Hello Katie. Think you and me can be friends?"

At the sound of her name, the dog's ears pointed up like arrows and her tail began to wag, slowly at first, then with an increasing rhythm. Her light brown brows formed little arches, and she cocked her head to one side, listening. "Katie, Katie, Katie," I said, which sent the dog into a frenzy of jumping, spinning and barking. The ice was broken. She ran toward me, fell to the ground at my feet, and rolled onto her back.

I knelt down and touched her chest, rubbing her brindle coat, feeling the dust and grime of the world embedded in her fur. I felt her heart pounding, keeping time with her panting, her tongue hanging out to one side. She stretched her head out so I could scratch her long neck.

"All right Katie," I said, smiling, "looks like it's you and me against the world."

# 3

# Rules of the Road

The next morning, Katie decided to travel with me. She couldn't travel as fast as I could ride, and her slower pace allowed my sense of urgency to fade. Aside from keeping me company, she found lots of ways to be useful. Her nose and ears were more sensitive than the perimeter alarm, and they didn't need to be switched on. She was always on alert, even when she slept.

For our first few days together, she slept outside between the tent and the fire. Then it rained one night, something I hadn't experienced since before my parents died. Rain was rare in the reclaimed zone. Some people measured their lives against its falling. I used to imagine what it would be like.

When the sky opened up, I got out of the tent, undressed, and enjoyed the downpour. I loved the feeling of the cold drops pelting my face, the water flowing across my chest and back. I stretched out my arms and let the water wash the collected filth away from my body, rivers of grime washing back down to the earth. I spun around in the rain, a song in my head. I couldn't remember all the words, but the beat was there. Something about the rain and the dirt and the flashes of lighting in the distance, all of it came together in a single feeling. For the first time in my life, I felt free. I stopped moving and stood in the rain with my eyes closed, smiling up at the downpour.

I stayed there for a several minutes while Katie stared at me with her ears tucked down and eyes narrowed. She looked miserable. I grabbed a tube of soap and managed to get her to be still long enough to give her a decent bath.

Afterwards, we mutually decided it was okay to sleep in the tent together. I was happy to have her with me, comforted by her closeness. I didn't mind it when she snored, her deep chest rumbling against me. A dog curled up next to you was the best heater you could get on a cold night. I woke up laughing when she got too warm and stretched out, pushing her legs against me, shoving me to the side of the tent.

The further we traveled, the closer the hills to the north came to the road, and the more alive the land became. Tall trees lined the road for long stretches, marching off into the distance. Occasionally Katie would disappear for the day and return when I made camp, bringing with her a rabbit or other animal she'd manage to catch. Her hunting helped us extend our food supply, but it wouldn't be enough to keep us both going for the long haul.

There were crumbling ruins at irregular intervals along the road, usually at points where other roads intersected the road we were following. I stayed away from the buildings, assuming they'd been picked over years earlier, or were inhabited by who-knew-what. They weren't worth the risk, until our food supply ran low enough to worry me.

One morning, we came to a place where the road passed over another running north–south. The overpass was broken apart, there wasn't enough of it left for us to cross. I scanned the area below the embankment and saw a structure less than a kilometer up the northbound road. A one-story building, with remnants of a large sign clinging to the side. Through my binoculars I could see the front of the building was all windows, with some of the glass still in place, except for the doors, which were missing. I could see booths and tables inside. We'd found a restaurant.

"We gotta check this one out Katie, there might be something left in there, you never know."

Katie let out a low grumble, not quite a growl.

"Yeah, I know, rule number one, stick to the road. But if we gotta leave it anyway, might as well do some scavenging. Come on, let's go have a look."

We backtracked to a point where we could make our way down, then headed to the building. I set my bike against a rusty metal column out front. I didn't lock it up, in case we needed to make a fast exit.

"Stay here Katie, you gotta keep watch."

Katie sat down and let out a short whine.

"Yes," I said, "it's a bad idea, but we're gettin' low on food and I don't plan for us to starve. Stay here."

I kept my pack on and drew my knife, then entered through the front of the building. Everything inside was covered in a layer of dust. I looked over the floor for any signs of recent disturbance. All I saw was a flat expanse of grime with bits of broken glass and a few shards of ceramic scattered around. There was a long counter fronted by a row of stools, fixed in place by bolts into the floor. Out of habit I calculated how much the metal posts would be worth at the reclamation center, then pushed the thought from my mind. That was the past, I had to stay in the present. I stepped further into the building and could see empty space behind the counter. The sinks, grill tops, and other implements of a restaurant were gone. Someone had picked the place over but left a lot of material behind. It didn't make sense but I was encouraged by what I saw. If valuable recyclables remained, some food or other useful items might remain as well. There was a set of doors behind the counter, each with a small window. I approached the doors, trying not to make any noise, and looked through one of the windows.

What I saw inside made my heart race.

Along the back wall, two sets of shelves bordered two more doors held shut by a handle and lock mechanism I'd never seen before. One of the shelves was empty, and there was a broken-out window in the top of the wall next to it. The other shelf was loaded with canned goods. I couldn't read the labels from my position, but if half the cans contained edible food, we would eat well for several days, longer if we stretched it. I knelt down and looked around the dining room, then out at Katie still seated next to the bike. She was focused on me like a laser. I peeked through the window again. "It's now or never," I said, and eased the door open. I winced when it made a soft creaking sound as the hinges rubbed against the dust. The hinges were spring-loaded, and when I stepped inside, I had to hold the door to keep it from swinging back on its own. I guided it back to the closed position, again wincing at the creaking sound it made.

When it was closed, I looked around for any signs of recent disturbance or anything suspicious. It was like the rest of the place, covered in undisturbed dust. I went to the shelf and picked up a can labeled "Peaches." I slipped off my pack and placed the can inside and started reading the other labels. I couldn't believe my luck, everything from beans, to corn, even cans of real meat stew. I couldn't take it all, so I selected the best of what was there and hoped it was still good.

I was loading cans into my bag, thinking of the meal we would have later, when Katie started barking. It wasn't her usual sound. I could tell it was an alarm. I slung my pack onto my back and heard a loud thud as one of the doors impacted the wall. I spun around, thrusting my knife out toward the person who had entered the kitchen behind me.

The man was thin, his clothes not more than rags, his face unshaven with a straggling beard, his leering grin revealed dark gaps between his crusty teeth. I could smell the stench of him from across the room. I would have known he was coming if the door had been open.

"Stay away from me!" I shouted, "Katie!"

"Boy, your dog ain't gonna be no help to you. Matter fact, she gonna be some fine eatin' once you and me settle our differences."

"I got no fight with you mister, you get outta my way and me an her will move along, no harm done."

"Oh, but you's trespassin' here boy, you done snuck up into my place and tried to steal from me, ain't it a fact?"

"This ain't your place, that much I know. You come up on it like me. Makes it mine by right, but I'm leavin', and you're not gonna stop me. You can have the rest, but you hurt my dog and you and me, we got us a fight."

"Look at you, little boy, all tough with your knife, all alone out here in the wastes. You even know where you are, boy?"

The man began moving forward and to one side. I took a step back then realized his intent, to drive me further into the room. I remembered what I'd read once, about being ambushed. The best hope for survival was to attack the ambush, fight your way through it. I stopped backing up, then heard Katie's bark change. Her deep throated growls and barking became high-pitched, interspersed with yelps and whines. That was enough for me. I glanced over my shoulder at the empty shelf and up at the open window, pretending I wanted to climb my way out.

When the man lunged forward, thinking I was distracted, I dropped to one knee, gripped the knife with both hands, and thrust forward and up, closing my eyes when I felt the knife strike home. The man screamed and fell back, tugging at the knife, threatening to dislodge it from my grip. I opened my eyes and leaned forward, driving the knife deeper into his thigh, and turned the blade. Blood pulsed out over my hands in hot jets. He grabbed at my hands, trying to pull the knife away. I heard Katie yelp again, and my adrenalin surged. I pushed up from the floor, then pulled back on the knife, twisting it on the way out. The man screamed in agony again and fell to the floor, blood pouring out across the dusty tile. He tried to shout, "Kill the dog, kill the dog," but his strength was already leaving him. I looked at the blood-drenched knife and my soaked hands, then looked in the man's eyes and said, "It didn't have to be this way."

I ran from the room, through the dining area and back toward Katie and my bike. What I saw brought me up short. A girl, not much older than me, clothed in filthy rags, like the man who had attacked me. She had a rope wrapped around Katie's neck and the pole. She was pulling it hard, pinning Katie against the bike. Katie struggled, but she couldn't break free. She panted and yelped, fighting against the rope. I held the knife out toward the girl, blood dripping from the blade and my hand, and shouted, "Let her go!"

The girl took a long look at the knife but didn't let up on the tension.

"Is he dead," she asked, "did you kill him?"

"He's as good as dead. He ain't got much time left. You wanna say your goodbyes, now's your chance."

"Will it hurt me?"

"No, if you let her go, neither of us will."

The girl looked at Katie, then at the knife, then back at Katie. "I'm sorry," she said, then dropped the rope and ran away. Not into the building, but north, toward the hills, never looking back.

I jammed the knife into the sheath strapped to my calf and unwrapped the rope from the pole. I slipped the loop from Katie's neck. She licked my face as I checked her for injuries. She had abrasions around her neck, but they weren't deep. I could treat them later, after we put some distance between us and the dying man. I mounted the e-bike, and Katie ran back the way we'd come, faster than I'd seen her run before. I called out to her, "No Katie, this way!" and pointed east, toward the opposite side of the damaged overpass, "Let's go!"

I opened the accelerator and Katie turned to run where I pointed. We were back on the road within minutes. When I noticed Katie was tiring, I stopped and called her to me. I took out the first aid kit and a water bag, washed my hands, then started to treat her wounds. My hands were shaking, and I struggled to make them stop. My skin was stained a dark red and black from the blood, some dried and crusted under my fingernails. I was about to cry but I pushed back against my emotions until the fear turned to anger. "Never again, Katie, never again. We stick to the road and we stick together, you and me against the world."

From then on, we stuck to the easterly course and stayed on the road. The cans of food I'd manage to collect wouldn't last forever. I had to hope we would find something akin to civilization before we starved.

We passed more streams cutting through the landscape, with some forming into large pools in places where the earth was sunken or a tree had fallen to block the water's path. The road grew narrower as nature reduced it to a fraction of its former size.

Once, when we came upon a pond next to the road, Katie kept her distance and didn't drink from it. When I went to the water's edge, Katie began barking with the same fury she'd displayed outside the building where we'd been ambushed. She didn't stop until I stepped away from the water. From then on, I knew, if she drank, I could drink. I figured out then I needed to pay closer attention to her when she had something to say.

After several days, the immediate trauma of our close encounter began to subside. We fell back into a more normal rhythm. The worsening condition of the road slowed my riding, which made it easier for Katie to stay out ahead.

One morning, two weeks after the ambush, we came to a bend in the road. Katie froze in her tracks, crouched down with her tail back, ears up, one front paw off the ground. She was aiming herself at a fallen tree around the bend, partially blocking the way and obscuring the view. I ground the bike to a stop and listened. I didn't see or hear anything unusual. All the same, I'd learned my lesson. I laid the bike down, drew my knife, and knelt down next to her. She made quiet whimpering sounds, then a low growl I could feel rumble in my own chest.

"What is it, girl?"

Katie stopped her vocalization and glanced up at me, then returned her gaze to the fallen tree. It was the only cover nearby and had her full attention. I moved forward a step and Katie leaned her shoulder into my leg, telling me I should stop.

"Whatever it is, we gotta face it."

I had no intention of leaving the road again, especially in an area bordered by a bog on one side and sparse forest on the other. I moved forward again, and she crouched low to move with me. When we reached the fallen tree, I looked over it and could see what had upset her. The tree had obscured our view, but not her sense of smell. Beyond the tree, a section of the roadway was missing, leaving a pit a dozen meters across and several meters deep, partially filled with water.

The water wasn't deep. I could tell because it didn't cover the buzz bike lying in it, and it didn't cover the body of the rider trapped beneath the machine. There wasn't much left of the rider, bones and shredded clothes where scavengers had been at the corpse, and the elements had taken the rest of the toll. One side of the hole was open to the bog, with slick mud lining either side of the opening.

I stared at the body for a long time, thinking about my options, wondering what had happened, and why they were on the road in the first place. Were they like me, escaping a world of pain and sadness? Or were they an ordinary traveler, going from one known place to another? It was both strange and sad to think about how the body had once been a person, someone with a destination whose journey overlapped mine.

Based on the chunk torn out of the side of the fallen tree, and the position of the machine and the rider, it was obvious they had struck the fallen tree, probably in the dark, and landed in the gap with the heavy machine coming down on top of them. It was a terrible way to die, all alone in the night. I thought of Mrs. Carter and wondered if her last moments were any better than the rider's. There was no sign the rider had tried to escape. I hoped their death had been mercifully quick.

Buzz bikes were the most common form of transportation around Greenfield. While this one was different, with a sidecar attached and large saddle bags strapped to the back, I knew from experience the machine had a substantial storage compartment beneath the primary seat.

I took off my shoes, socks and pants to keep them dry and lowered myself into the hole. Katie remained at the edge whining and whimpering. She started barking when I moved the bike, causing the body to move beneath it.

"It's okay girl, simmer down. This won't take a minute."

Once I had the machine more or less upright, I unbuckled the straps attaching the bags to the sides, then tossed the bags up onto the road. I removed the cover to the storage compartment next and was happy to find it packed full, the contents dry. I placed several items inside the cover, set it on the road above me, then moved the rest in two trips before climbing out of the pit to examine my haul.

I sorted through the items, examining each, setting aside what I wanted to keep. The contents of the submerged bag were mostly ruined. There were several sealed-foil food packs I kept, though the labels had dissolved away. There was a better flashlight than the one I already had. The batteries were dead, but I kept the flashlight anyway.

The other bag was more interesting.

The contents were in good condition, including the stash of money wrapped inside a pair of socks. It wasn't a lot of money, but it was more than I had, which was exactly none, so I was pleased to find it. Cash wasn't used much, but where it was, it was worth more than credits. There were also more food packs, this time with labels intact.

The storage compartment contained some clothes, a shaving kit, and a couple of bars of soap. Everything was clean and dry, so I kept most of what I found. I lifted a rolled-up towel and discovered it, like the socks, had items hidden inside. I unrolled it and found a battery pack for the flashlight, a folded map, and some more money. I was excited by the treasure we'd found, but Katie wanted nothing to do with any of it. She walked back to the e-bike, sat down next to it and stared at me in a way I couldn't help but think of as disapproval.

"Rules of the road, Katie, finders-keepers. He doesn't need this stuff anymore."

Katie whimpered and laid down, looking back at me from beneath her furrowed brow.

When I gathered up my bounty and carried it back toward the bike, she walked away a short distance, then sat down. I laid the bundle down by the bike and walked toward her.

"It's okay girl, we need this stuff. We're running out of food. Come on…"

When she walked away again as I approached, I realized the problem.

The corpse had been decayed for a long time, but some essence of it must have hung in the water, and the water had come up to my knees.

I smelled like death.

I returned to the edge of the hole and retrieved the storage compartment cover, then walked back up the road, Katie keeping her distance. I stepped into a pool of water in the bog and began scooping and pouring, using a bar of soap to wash my legs and feet.

I finished and approached Katie again. She gave me a sniff before wagging her tail and trotting back toward the bike. I dressed, then we made our way along a strip of stable earth next to the gap containing the body before I began to ride again, more cautious than before. My thoughts were focused on the rider. I had no way to bury him, but I made a vow if we came upon other people before we were too far from the body, I would try to get them to help me. Whoever the person was, they deserved a proper burial.

An hour passed before I thought to look at the map. I stopped and Katie came back and watched with her typical tilted-head posture as I unfolded the map on the ground. Printed maps weren't used much anymore, given how expensive they were. GPS systems were cheap and had a complete set of maps for every remaining habitable zone in the country.

When I had the map spread out, I oriented it to north, then myself to the map.

The rider had been marking off each section of their trip. A circle around a town to the north, in the foothills of the mountains, appeared to be their starting point. Based on the distance between the marks, I estimated they'd been on the road for no more than a week before their accident. They had taken up the same route we were on, but the map had details where my GPS showed only an empty space. Based on the lines and x's, they were close to their destination, a city less than 60 kilometers east of our location, and a few kilometers beyond the city lay the ocean, our ultimate destination. But the city on the map bore a symbol every school kid learned early in their education. A yellow triangle with a black border and three black wedges around a black dot in the center.

The trefoil symbol for radiation.

The city ahead was radioactive. According to the map, Katie and I were already well inside the exclusion zone. Such a large zone meant the city had been destroyed in the war. But the terrain around us told a different story. It didn't look like any of the pictures I'd seen of radiation zones or bombed-out cities.

"This explains the big empty space in my digi-map," I said to Katie. "The way I see it, we can turn around and see if we can find another road to travel, or keep goin' the way we're goin' and see what we see. What do you think?"

Katie did her usual, perking up her ears and twisting her head to show she was listening.

"I say we stick to the road and keep moving east. We're no more than a good day's ride away from the coast. Besides, we'll never know what's out there unless we keep going. And if Mister Buzz Bike Rider thought it was okay, then I say we take a look for ourselves."

I picked a spot on the map a short ride from the edge of the city where we could stop for the night, where the road crossed a river. Katie had already started moving again by the time I was back on my bike.

When we arrived at the river, I knew I'd made the right decision. The water was crystal clear and shallow, a gentle flow over a gravel bed between grassy banks. Katie walked into the current and drank her fill. I set up camp next to the crumbling concrete of the bridge abutment, then bathed in the river. I hadn't had a proper wash since the night it rained. No matter what we found the next day, I didn't want to look, or smell, like I'd crawled out of the wastelands, even though I had. I set aside some of my new-found wardrobe to wear the next day, a blue gingham shirt, jeans, and a pair of socks. I would have to roll the pant legs and shirt sleeves up to make them work, but at least they were clean. I followed Katie's example and drank my fill from the river, then rinsed and refilled our water bags. I lit a fire and we settled in for the night.

The next morning, we rose early and made our approach to the city. The previous day's ride had recharged the batteries, but as we grew closer to where the city should be, the road became so overgrown I had to dismount and walk beside the bike, picking my way through what had become a lush forest. When the road had all but disappeared beneath the forest floor, I lost sight of Katie and moved faster. I pushed through a line of thick undergrowth and was brought to a stop by a concrete barrier, about waist high and 20 meters wide.

On the other side of the barrier, the road was reborn, pristine, without a crack or a crevice, not so much as a weed. The forest ended at the barrier. Open space with clean, flat pavement lay ahead of us. The dark pavement, marked with crisp white and yellow lines delineating the lanes, ran in a gentle arc over a grass-covered hill, disappearing over the near horizon less than a two hundred meters in the distance.

Katie had already skirted the barrier and was waiting for me on the other side. I made my way around it, then started up the road, Katie trotting along ahead of me, faster and farther ahead than usual. She reached the top of the hill, sat down in the road and looked back at me, then turned to stare at something on the other side of the hill. I caught up to her, then stared along with her.

The city sat below, with the ocean glittering in the distance beyond it. I had not seen the ocean since I was a small boy, and for my entire journey it had been my destination. I had no reason, other than fond memories, to set it as my goal, but now my goal seemed unimportant. While I was in awe of the majestic blue and green stretched out as far as the eye could see, the city below the hill fascinated me and held my gaze.

It was not the ruined city I'd been expecting. It was alive and thriving. Buildings rose into the sky, surrounded by trees, with open avenues dividing everything up into neat little blocks. There were auto-cars, buzz bikes, drift carts, all manner of machines moving along the open spaces. I could see neighborhoods with houses bigger than any I'd ever seen. It looked like they all had swimming pools. Further up the coast from the city I could see a vast facility, dozens of buildings of all shapes and sizes, with long tracks leading to circular concrete pads. The rocket on one of the pads was a dead giveaway, I was looking at a space port. I knelt down next to Katie and shook my head in disbelief.

"I sure didn't see this coming. What say we go down there and see what this is all about?"

Katie surprised me with a loud bark, then started down the road toward the city below. She stopped and looked back and barked again. "Okay, I'm coming," I said. Katie already understood English when we met, and my understanding of Dog had gotten better with each passing day.

I rode down from the grassy hilltop at a casual pace. I didn't want to look like I was in a hurry. To anyone who happened to see us, I was an ordinary kid out for a bike ride with his dog.

The closer we got to the city, the more orderly and manicured the land became. We turned onto a street lined with trees so large they grew together over the roadway, forming an arched ceiling overhead, dappled with sunlight. I could smell the ocean, carried in by a cool breeze. Squirrels and other small animals scurried up the trees or into the ornate gardens fronting the homes.

The houses looked big from the hilltop. Close up they were enormous. Most had large, covered porches on front, held up by thick white columns, with wide walkways running up to the front doors. It was repeated so often I wondered if all of the houses had been built at the same time, and by the same person. I thought of my uncle long enough to dismiss the idea of Geo finding work in the city. I had no reason to help him, and I didn't want to remember him.

I struggled to make sense of the place. Nothing like what I was seeing existed in Greenfield. We moved through the neighborhood until the homes gave way to cafes and shops populated by well-dressed smiling people, some of whom took passing notice of us, a few of them pointing and commenting to each other.

It was unnerving. When we turned another corner onto a bustling street filled with vehicles of all sorts, the sidewalk was a safer bet. I pushed the bike instead of riding. Katie acted right at home in the foot traffic and weaved her way along ahead of me, as if she had some place she wanted to take me. When she got well ahead of me, I hurried forward, not wanting to lose sight of her.

I caught up to her at an intersection where she was waiting for me by the curb. I started to cross when Katie leaned against my leg, stopping me. The light was about to change and a large robo-transport was approaching. I'd never seen one up close before, so I was content to wait for it to pass.

That's when the girl appeared, and when things got a little crazy.

# 4

# You're Either Here, Or You're Not

Becca hated her new school. The buildings were nice enough, but everyone called her Rebecca, and she hated being called Rebecca. When she complained, some of the students made fun of her for it. Some of them called her Becky, which, to Becca, was worse.

Her parents loved the school. It had beautiful lawns and gardens with fountains, red brick buildings with bright white peaks and gables, and all sorts of facilities to nurture a young person's mind and body. Her old school didn't have all those things, but she liked her classmates and teachers there, especially her math teacher.

The fact her parents could afford the school's astronomical tuition gave them a sense of pride. Their work was making them wealthy, so they committed to nothing less than the best for their little girl. Becca despised it all the same. Every day she would bolt from the campus, running down the tree-lined streets until she arrived home, covered in a sheen of sweat, her heart racing. Her mother preferred for Becca to wait for the auto-car to come and fetch her home, but running made Becca feel better, so she never waited.

Her parents had an assistant, Julia, who looked after all the things they were too busy to deal with, like managing household projects, or making sure Becca finished her homework. Early on, Julia thought Becca would be another spoiled brat, given her parents' constant indulgence. Then she got to know Becca, and her opinion changed. Eventually she figured out Becca was an assertive, perhaps willful, self-determined child, as Julia herself had been. Julia had yet to start a family of her own and before long she and Becca grew close. She became more like family to Becca, like an aunt.

Becca's parents had invented something important. Becca didn't know much about it when she was younger, but she knew it had made them loads of money. But because all their money got her pulled out of her old school and stuck in a school she disliked, years passed before she cared about their invention.

Her mother would explain it to her, going on at length about the fabric of space-time, quantum physics, and an ancient mathematician named Einstein. A bit much for a fifth grader, but her parents believed she was a genius and would understand eventually. Her father took a different approach to explaining their invention. He didn't try to explain how it worked. Instead, he focused on what it did. Where her mother tended to be a lecturer, her father was more of a storyteller.

He told Becca they had invented a machine to enable the movement of objects from one place to another in a matter of seconds. As long as they had a machine in both places, they could use one to send anything they wanted to the other. He described it as stepping through a door in one house and landing in a room in another house. The house could be anywhere, so long as one of their machines was there.

It sounded like fun to Becca. She started to imagine stepping through one of the doors in their big fancy house and arriving back in their old house. The little cottage by the pond, a short walk from the ocean, became like a dream to her. Her memory of it was fading, and she wanted to hold on to it. Now they could no longer walk to the ocean, and the pond had been replaced by a swimming pool.

One day in autumn, after the thick blue fabric cover had been stretched tight across the pool, Becca's mother called her to the patio for a demonstration. She took a heavy ball from a bag, part of a lawn game her parents liked to play when they hosted summer parties. Her mother rolled the ball onto the fabric and said, "Try to think of the pool cover as the fabric of space-time. If we fold the fabric from one place and connect it to another place, one can move to the second place in a matter of minutes or seconds, depending on the original distance."

"Imagine the ball represents mass and energy," she continued, "notice how it bends the fabric around it. If we have the right combination of those two things, mass and energy, this folding process becomes possible, on a large scale and across great distance. It's a called an Einstein–Rosen Bridge," her mother said, "but most people call it a wormhole."

"Worms are disgusting," Becca replied.

"No, darling," her mother laughed, "it has nothing to do with worms, it's a name for a tube through the fabric. Come, let's go to the lab, I have something else to show you, a new prototype of our invention."

Her parents liked to bring their work home with them, so they had a large addition containing a laboratory built onto the back of their house. Until that day, Becca had never been inside the lab, it was strictly off limits.

Her mother unlocked the door and swung it inward, revealing a space crowded with equipment on one side, and a long metal workbench with two stools along the other side. There was so much to see, so many distractions, Becca stumbled into one of the stools, nearly knocking it over. "Careful, dear," her mother said, "pay attention, this is no place for idle curiosity."

Her mother took a rectangular metal device from a shelf and placed it on the workbench. It was a plain-looking box, not much larger than a suitcase. It had a switch on each side, one red and one green, and a piece of curved glass across the top. The glass was thick and dark and had an iridescent quality Becca had never seen before.

"The glass is pretty," she said, but in truth she thought the device didn't really look like much to her.

"Yes, it is, but this device is more than pretty, quite a lot more. This little box might one day change the world. This is one of four in existence. They're difficult to make, but in operation they're rather simple. With two such devices, each synchronized together, we can create an Einstein–Rosen Bridge, on command. We can create a wormhole, and more importantly, we can control it. The first step is to know where it begins or ends, depending on your perspective. By creating those two points, we can move objects through one point and they will travel to the other point."

"Can people use it? Could I go through a wormhole?"

"We're not ready yet. We've got two of these newest little gems, this one and one at our lab at the Institute, and we haven't tested them with people. But we'll get there, one day."

The idea of traveling through a wormhole, of instantly going from one place, a place you didn't want to be, to another place, perhaps one you missed, intrigued Becca.

She decided she wanted to go through a wormhole.

So, she did.

She assumed she would go where the other device was located, her parents' lab at their research facility. But assumptions are dangerous, especially when you're dealing with the fabric of space-time.

Becca's parents usually kept the door to their lab locked, but sometimes they forgot. Becca started checking the door when she got home from school each day.

After several attempts, the door opened. Since Julia was busy running errands, Becca had the house to herself. She entered the lab and found the machine sitting on the floor inside a glass cube at the back of the lab, a room within the room.

Becca's mother had explained green was the "send" switch and red the "receive" switch, so she flipped the green switch. The box made a humming sound, but didn't do anything else right away.

Becca was about to switch the machine off when a hazy yellow disc of swirling light appeared before her, rising up from the glass on top of the device. It pulsed and spun and took on the appearance of a tunnel heading away from Becca, with a black circle at the center of the languid spinning light. She stepped around the device and was surprised to discover…nothing. The tunnel of light didn't exist unless she was in front of the device, where the green switch was located.

Becca was fascinated. She couldn't make sense of how the wormhole could exist in the first place, much less how it existed from a single perspective. She wondered if it was an illusion. She reached her hand out and let her fingers fall into the slow spinning vortex. It felt like something pulled on her hand, stretching it to an unthinkable length, so she pulled it back, clutching her fingers. When she looked at her hand, it looked perfectly normal. She touched the light again, this time allowing the pull to draw most of her arm into vortex.

Since no one at the Hofmann Institute was aware of Becca's secret experiment, scientists on every floor of the research center carried on with their own experiments, oblivious to the fact history, of one sort or another, was about to be made.

One such experiment involved a new type of electromagnetic propulsion. It used a specific type of gravity wave to generate thrust, without the need for propellant. If they could make it work, it had the potential to revolutionize space flight. They were testing a scaled-down prototype on the third floor of the Institute at the same time Becca entered the swirling vortex of the wormhole spinning away inside her parent's lab.

Meanwhile, on the fourth floor, alarms began to sound as the receiving device signaled an incoming connection. It was housed in a glass room in the Kiel's' research lab, similar to the one in their lab at home. The team gathered around the glass room and everyone could see it was empty, with no sign of a wormhole. Then a sudden intense pulse of light flashed within the receiving room and disappeared as quickly as it appeared. People began to panic, especially Becca's mother. She knew all of their devices, save one, were there, at the Institute. The remaining device was at their home, and Becca was at their home, alone.

Becca found the strange distortion of her arm amusing. At first, she laughed while her arm was stretched and spun and blended with the light. She leaned forward and before she realized anything had happened, she wasn't at home anymore. She wasn't certain where she was, but it definitely wasn't home.

In the instant it took Becca to realize she had been transported from her home to the middle of a busy street, she felt something slam into her and knock her to the ground at the edge of the street. She spun around and landed on her backside. While it hurt, she was more surprised than injured. As abruptly as she appeared in the street, a boy she had never seen before appeared there and saved her from being run over by a robo-transport. The boy landed on the ground nearby. He was a mystery to Becca. It was as though he had stepped through a wormhole too, and popped out exactly where he needed to be at precisely the right moment. The boy who had saved her life walked toward her. She saw a tendril of smoke drift up from his burnt pant leg. The boy knelt down beside her and grinned, then reached out his hand.

***

The flash of swirling multicolored light in the middle of the road was so fast you'd miss it if you blinked when it happened. In the same instant, a girl about my age, but taller than me, appeared in the middle of the road. The girl was facing away from the oncoming traffic and didn't see the transport bearing down on her. I didn't think through what I did next. I shoved the e-bike aside, ran into the street, and pushed the girl out of the transport's way. I rolled out of the vehicle's path, but I wasn't fast enough. Heat from the transport's maglev impeller grazed my leg long enough to scorch my pants and leave a burn on my calf. The machine whooshed to a stop well beyond where the girl had been standing, its alarm blaring out, bringing all the traffic in both directions to a halt.

"Not too bad," I thought when I examined my burned leg.

The transport's alarm drew a crowd to the scene, and people were getting out of their vehicles to see what was happening. The girl was still sitting on the pavement, her reddish-blonde hair in disarray around her freckled face, looking confused and scared. I walked over to her, knelt down in front of her, and reached out my hand.

"Hi, I'm Charlie. Are you okay?"

The girl stared at me, then my hand, then back at me. While I waited for her to answer, a crowd formed around us and people began chattering away about what they'd witnessed.

"What are you doing?"

"You two sure are lucky."

"Are you hurt?"

"What's your name, kid?"

I helped the girl stand and Katie pushed her way through the crowd then let out one loud bark. Everyone fell silent, which made the girl laugh. Katie sniffed the girl's hand, then sat down next to me. "This is Katie," I said, "she doesn't talk much, but when she does it's a good idea to listen. I think she likes you."

"My name's Becca," she said. "Nice to meet you both."

"Are you hurt?" I asked.

"No, what about you?" she replied, pointing at my scorched leg.

"It's nothin'," I said, "I've had worse. How did you get in the middle…"

"Oh, for the love of Pete, Becca, what have you done?" a woman said from behind the crowd of gawkers. The woman pushed her way through the gaggle and looked at Becca with a mixture of humor and concern.

Becca hugged the woman and said, "Miss Julia, this is Charlie. He saved my life."

"Is that so?" Julia asked.

"He did," someone in the crowd said. Other witnesses chimed in. Before long someone said, "The boy's a hero."

"Becca," Julia said, "I think your parents might want to meet this young man, don't you?"

"Yes, ma'am, I think so too," Becca said, "and his dog."

"Uh-huh, and his dog…wait," she said, zeroing in on Katie. "This is Katie, Mr. Bimmy's dog." Katie's ears perked up at the sound of her name, but she didn't move from my side.

"Young man," she began.

"His name is Charlie," Becca insisted.

"Charlie," Julia started again, "what are you doing with Mr. Bimmy's dog? I haven't seen her around since I don't know when..."

"I'm not doing anything with her," I said. "She was hungry, I fed her. I fed her, she stayed with me. We like each other. We've been on the road together for a while."

"I take it you're new here, aren't you?"

"No, Miss Julia," I answered, "I'm just passing through."

Julia and several people in the crowd began to laugh.

Julia leaned down, looked me in the eyes, still laughing, and said, "Honey, you're either here, or you're not. Nobody, and I do mean nobody, just passes through Arcadia."

# 5

# **Fear**

A security detail arrived and took me to a tall building with a strange structure on top. I was led to a small room with a table and two chairs. One of the officers asked me a few questions, 'What's your name, how old are you, where are you from,' all the basics. She told me to wait in the room, then left me there with the door closed. I waited so long I started to doze off. I snapped awake when the door opened and a man in a dark blue suit entered. He didn't sit down.

"Charlie," he said, "I'm Commander Alan Post. I'm in charge of security for Arcadia. You've created quite the stir for our little town. You certainly know how to make an entrance. There are some people here, myself included, who'd like to speak to you, try to understand how you came to be here, maybe discuss what to do next. Think you're up for it?"

"Sure, but like I said, I'm passing through."

"I heard. You have to understand my position. This is highly unusual, on so many fronts. The folks who want to talk with you, you might say they have a special interest in this and, to be honest, they're important people around here. What say we go meet them?"

"Okay, but could I get some water please?

"Of course, come with me."

We left the room and went to a much larger room with a wide window along one wall. There were several people waiting. There was the girl, Becca, seated next to two adults. I assumed they were her parents. And there was another couple at the far end of the room, a man and a woman. The man stood out for his jet-black hair, cut close, and his tan skin and dark eyes. The woman seated next to him had more familiar features, but unlike the man, she had a slight smile on her face. They had Katie with them. Katie was on a leash and when she saw me, she bolted toward me, pulling the leash from the man's hand. I knelt down and she threw herself into my arms.

"Okay, okay, reunion's over. Have a seat, kid." Alan said.

"His name is Charlie," Becca said, with emphasis.

"Charlie," Alan said, "please take a seat. These nice people would like to ask you some questions."

I took a chair at the end of the table with a clear path to the door. Katie went under the table and lay across my feet with a rumbling sigh. I looked down and laughed at her, then looked around the room.

"Hi Becca," I said. I was calm, I didn't think I had anything to fear. Everyone had been nice so far, and I figured there wasn't much worse they could do to me than had already been done. "What can I do for you folks?"

The man who had held Katie's leash said, "Charlie, thank you for bringing Katie home to us. She's important to our family, especially our son."

I was stunned. I felt my composure start to crumble. It never occurred to me someone else might have a claim to Katie. "Um, well, you're welcome, I guess. I mean, I kinda feel like she's mine, we've been together, on the road, she…I mean I…" I felt my face start to burn and fear rising in my gut. I pushed back against it, not wanting to show my emotions to a room full of strangers.

A young man in uniform entered the room with a tray full of bottled water. He set the tray down on the table and left.

"Can I have some, please?" I asked.

"Of course," the man who claimed Katie as his own said. He picked up a bottle and moved to the chair closest to me. He handed me the water then turned his chair to face me. "Charlie, what we want to talk to you about…Katie is special. She's our son's service dog. It worries us she's with you and not with him. Our son was supposed to be here, in Arcadia, many months ago. Tell me Charlie, where did you find her? Please, tell us the truth. It will be much easier for all of us, including you."

"One thing you'll always get from me Mister…"

"Bimmy, Henry Bimmy, and this is my wife, Rose. You can imagine how worried we are about our son…"

I downed a gulp of water and continued. "The truth," I said, "you'll always get the truth from me. If I can't tell you the truth, I won't tell you anything at all, I promise."

"All right then Charlie, tell us how you and Katie came to be together out there," Henry waved his hand toward the west, "in the wasteland, far from civilization, a kid alone in the middle of nowhere."

"And why Arcadia?" Becca's father asked, "What brought you here? How did you even…"

"One thing at a time George, let the boy speak," Mr. Bimmy said.

"Yeah, daddy," Becca said, "let *Charlie* speak."

I took another drink of water, then a deep breath, and asked a question, rather than answering theirs.

"Does your son have a buzz bike?"

"Yes, how did…"

"Is it red?"

"Yes, Charlie, a red buzz bike, with…"

"With a side car, for Katie," I said, finishing Henry's sentence. I felt my face burn again and my lips began to quiver. I knew then I couldn't stop it. A tear slipped down my cheek, followed by more, drawn out by the gravity of what I was about to say. "I'm real sorry," I said, "but I think, I mean, I know, your son is dead."

"How," Rose asked, leaning forward, her smile gone, her words flying at me, "how do you know this?"

"I found him on the road. He'd been dead for a long time. I'm sorry, I couldn't…I mean, I didn't mean to…," I was losing my self-control. I looked down at my chest, tugged at the shirt I was wearing, and said, "This is his shirt. I took it. He couldn't use it, we needed the food, I didn't know, I…I'm so sorry…"

Henry placed a hand on my shoulder. "It's okay," he said, "everything's going to be okay. The shirt doesn't matter. What matters is the question I'm about to ask you. Catch your breath, let me know when you're ready."

"I know what you want to know," I said, "you want to know where he is."

"You're right Charlie. You're a smart boy. Can you tell us where he is? We'd like to bring him home."

I swiped at my tears and asked, "What was…is…your son's name?"

"Marcus."

"Marcus had a map. I didn't know people used those anymore. It's in my pack. I can show you…"

"I'm on it," Alan said and left the room.

Becca whispered to her mother, who took a pack of tissues from her purse and handed it to Becca. Becca placed it on the table in front of me. "It's okay to cry," she said, "it'll make you feel better."

"I don't know, Becca, but thanks all the same."

"It's all gonna be okay, wait and see."

I smiled, but I didn't feel it. I didn't think anything was ever going to be okay. How could it? Sitting in a room, surrounded by strangers, wearing the clothes I took from a dead son. My confidence collapsed into a heap of fear and self-doubt. When Alan returned with the map, I started to formulate a plan.

He spread the map out on the table. He examined the markings, then looked at me. "You're up, kid, what can you tell us?"

Henry and Rose looked down at the map with me as I traced my finger along the route Marcus, then Katie and I, had traveled. "I came from Greenfield. It's not on this map, and it's not really green, but if you follow the road west until it ends, you'll be close to the town. The road doesn't go all the way. Katie showed up somewhere around here, I think. I'm kinda guessing. But I know we found the buzz bike…we found Marcus in this area. He was marking the map as he went, see? We must have been right about here, three or four kilometers east of his last marker, when we found him. Maybe he was riding at night, I don't know. There's a tree across the road, and a big pit in the road right after it. He's there, in the pit." My hand shook when I touched the map where his body was. Rose reached out and took my hand and held it. I looked up at her, and for the first time I looked into her eyes. Her face was sad, but her eyes were kind, reassuring.

"Sweetheart," she said, and placed a hand on my cheek, "can you take us there?"

"It's a long ride, and the road is pretty much gone from…"

"We'll handle the transportation," Rose said. "Won't we, Commander?"

"Of course," Alan said, then addressed me. "You ever flown before?"

"Flown?"

"In an airplane, aero-car, a balloon, anything?"

"No."

"There's a first time for everything, I hope you've got a strong stomach. We'll take my cruiser, it has room for four."

"We'll go home," Becca's father said, "we can take Katie with us.

We'll wait to hear from you."

"Maybe Katie should come with us," I said, "her senses are better…"

"No, she won't be any help to us in the air and there's no room for her," Alan said.

I looked at Katie, and I felt she understood we were about to be separated. She panted and whined but didn't struggle against the leash when Becca and her parents left. Becca stepped back into the room. "Be careful, Charlie, see you later." She spun on her heels and trotted away to catch up to her parents.

Alan entered the coordinates from the map into a device on his wrist and said, "All right, follow me."

The Commander led us to a bank of elevators, which we took to the roof. The structure I'd seen was a flight deck, spread out over the building like a giant metal hat, overhanging the sides in all directions. We got into the Commander's cruiser, a black aero-car, me in the front passenger seat. I had an expansive view of the surroundings. Commander Post transferred the coordinates to the flight computer, and we launched. Our sudden vertical launch made me feel nauseous, and I understood the Commander's concern. I was certain I would be sick but when we reached altitude and began straight and level flight, I started to feel better.

I'd never been so high before or moved so fast. The buildings and roadways of the city grew small, then receded behind us. The city gave way to the forest, which began to thin into more sparse terrain. We flew in silence until Alan pointed at the flight computer. "Approaching coordinates, look familiar?"

"Yes sir, I can see the road but I don't see the…I think it's a marsh, or a bog, I'm not sure. It should be on the North side…wait, there it is, see it? All those dead trees. Can you go lower?"

Alan dropped the aircraft lower and adjusted the flight path to parallel the southern edge of the roadway. I leaned forward to get a better view. I didn't want us to land too close. It would upend my escape plan. I waited until we were directly over the fallen tree where I'd found the buzz bike and its dead rider and shouted "There, right there, you flew over it!"

Alan grabbed the controls and swung the vehicle around in a tight turn, then brought it to a hover over the road. "I can't land there," he said, "looks like we're in for a trek."

"Get us down there," Rose said. "Walking is the least of my

concerns."

Alan maneuvered the aero-car to a patch of open land a short distance from the crash scene and set the vehicle down, kicking up a cloud of debris as we landed. I was first to exit and ran to the road and up to the fallen tree. I was standing by the pit, looking down at the skeleton I knew was Marcus Bimmy, when the others caught up to me.

***

When Rose Bimmy looked into the pit and saw the remains of her son, she gasped, then placed her hand over her mouth and fell to her knees. She began to sob. Henry knelt beside her, placed one arm around her shoulders and said, "We have to be certain." He looked up at Alan and asked, "Do you have it?"

"You don't have to do this, I can…"

"No," Henry said, "I'll do it."

Alan nodded and handed a small cylindrical device to Henry. Henry lowered himself into the water, then approached the remains of the rider pinned beneath the wrecked machine. He pulled back waterlogged shreds of cloth and found what he needed, a bit of soft tissue still clinging to bone. He used the device to take a sample, then started the sequence analyzer. He moved back across the pit and handed the device up to Alan.

"Shouldn't take a minute," Alan said, "I'll patch the signal through the cruiser."

Henry returned to the body and looked down at what he knew were the remains of his son. He didn't need the proof. He looked at his wife, still kneeling beside the pit, and nodded his head once, to let her know. Henry then lifted himself out of the muck and mud and said, "It's okay Commander, it's him."

"I can't authorize a recovery unless…"

"It's fine," Rose said. She took her husband's hand, and he helped her stand. "We've waited this long, a few more minutes won't make a difference."

"Where's Charlie?" Henry asked.

"Charlie, get back here!" Alan shouted, then muttered, "we don't have time for this nonsense."

"He's scared, Alan. Shouting at him won't help," Rose said.

She was interrupted by a voice from the Commander's comm link, "DNA is a match, Commander. What are your orders?"

"Dispatch a recovery team," Alan replied, "and send a drone to my location. The kid's gone missing."

"We don't need a drone," Rose said. She placed a hand on Henry's arm. "Henry will find him."

Henry nodded. "I'll do my best."

Henry walked in a wide arc around the side of the pit until he found what he was looking for, scuff marks and disturbed earth leading off the shoulder of the roadway into the forest. He moved into the trees and continued to scan the area. The boy had left behind ample signs of his passing, written in the forest floor and the branches of the undergrowth. When the trail ended near a large hemlock tree, Henry stopped and looked around. He could find no other sign of movement. He was certain the boy was in the tree.

***

While the adults focused on the body in the pit, I walked backwards, beyond the fallen tree, then slipped away into the forest along the southern edge of the road. Once again, I had no idea where I was going, but fear drove me to run.

Now I was cornered. I thought I'd have more time before they noticed I was gone. I'd forgotten my own rule: never put yourself in a corner, always have an escape plan. In a panic, I climbed into a tall evergreen tree, climbing as high as I could through the thick growth, using its plentiful branches like a spiral ladder. I barely caught my breath before the man named Henry Bimmy appeared below me. He didn't look up, and I thought I might get away after all, but he didn't move on. He sat down on the forest floor with his back to the tree, crossing his legs beneath him. When he started to speak, my hopes for a quick escape were dashed.

"You know, Charlie," Henry began, "fear is natural. Fear keeps us safe, keeps us alive. But sometimes we fear what we don't know. We fear without understanding our fear. In such times, fear is our enemy. It can harm us more than help us. In such situations, we must put aside our fear, and replace it with something else. Logic, hope, strategy, there are many things to replace fear, Charlie. It is in these moments, when we overcome our fear, we find our courage. Do you understand what I'm saying to you?"

"Leave me alone!" I shouted, my voice cracking from the strain, more tears falling, "I'm sorry I stole from your son, you can have it all

43

back, let me go!"

"And what will you do? Wander through the forest naked and alone? This is not courage, Charlie, this is fear, fear that will not help you, not in this circumstance. You have nothing, no transportation, no food, no water, and you would give up your last few possessions, out of fear? Think about it, Charlie, where will you go?"

"You're gonna lock me up, or send me to an orphanage, or...I don't know, but I made it on my own so far, I can do it again!" I knew Henry was right, I had no place to go and no way to get there if I did. I felt my grip on the tree begin to weaken. A chill settled over my body and my strength began to ebb. I hadn't eaten since the early hours of the morning. It felt like a lifetime ago.

"No one is going to lock you up, Charlie," Henry said, "we don't put children in cages. Besides, you did nothing wrong. On the contrary, you're a hero, everyone knows it, except perhaps you."

I had lost the energy to shout. "I'm no hero," I said.

"Tell me something, Charlie, what is it you want? Not in this moment, but in life, what is it you want?"

No one had ever asked me such a question. "You'll laugh at me," I replied.

"And what if I do?"

I thought about how I would answer him. My hands and clothes were smeared in sticky sap and the branches had scratched my face and arms. I looked at my hands, touched my shirt and trousers, looked around at the forest, then began to climb down from my perch. I reached the forest floor and stepped out from the dark curtain of green hanging down from the tree. Henry remained seated and facing away from me.

"I want to get off this planet."

"That is no laughing matter. Do you have a plan?"

"Space Force. When I'm old enough, I'm gonna enlist and get off this rock for good."

"It's a good plan, I think. But you are too young, they don't take little boys."

"I know. And I'm not little."

Henry unfolded his legs, stood up and turned to face me. "I meant no offense, Charlie, I was merely pointing out the facts."

I felt the urge to run away, deeper into the forest. I was doing the math, calculating whether or not this person could catch me at a full sprint. I wanted to escape, to bolt the way Katie had bolted the first night I met her. Thinking of Katie caused a change inside me. I decided not to run.

"This is one of those moments, you can feel it, can't you? The struggle between fear and hope, fear and logic? The struggle within, this is you finding courage. Do you understand?"

I didn't feel courageous. But I understood.

"I have a choice," I said, "but I don't know what it is."

"It is a beginning, a good place to start. I will give you a choice, because you have shown great courage today. The choice is simple. Come back with me, let us help you. I can't say what it will look like, but if you take a chance on us, I promise we will help you. You can stay with us, in our home, for as long as you like. We have plenty of room."

"Why? Why would you help me?"

"Because I have been frightened for such a long time. You helped me face my fear today, Charlie. You helped me find my courage."

"What did you replace it with?"

Henry took a moment, I thought I saw a tear in his eye, then he smiled. "Love," he said.

We stared at each other, the silence of the forest between us.

"Okay," I said, "I'll come back with you until I can get myself sorted, but I don't want to be a burden."

"You've got yourself a deal."

# 6

# Shattered

Everyone rose when the judge entered the courtroom. I was so nervous, I didn't immediately take my seat when the judge said, "Please be seated." She looked at me and continued. "You're welcome to remain standing Mr. Weiss, but it's not necessary." Laughter rippled through the courtroom. I looked around and took note of those in attendance, the Bimmys seated next to me at the table in front of the judge's bench, the Kiels, including Becca, in the front row directly behind me, several of my classmates, and a few of my teachers. I added embarrassment to my nervousness and felt my face flush as I grinned at the people I'd grown close to over the preceding three years in Arcadia.

I turned back to the face the judge and said, "I'm sorry, nerves," and sat down.

"It's going to be fine," my attorney said, and I knew she was right. It had all been worked out in advance, the culmination of three years of effort on a number of fronts. At last, the effort was about to pay off.

"We have two items on the docket today," the judge said, "let's deal with the emancipation issue first, seems reasonable, don't you think Mr. Weiss?"

"Yes ma'am, I mean, yes your honor," I replied.

"Ma'am is acceptable," she said. She reviewed a set of documents then said, "Mr. Weiss, you've come before this court today seeking emancipation as a minor, correct?"

"Yes, ma'am."

"Miss Harris, I see due diligence was completed last month and Mr. Weiss's guardian, one Geo Wilkins, is aware of Mr. Weiss's desire to terminate guardianship?"

"Yes, your honor," my lawyer replied.

"I take it Mr. Wilkins is not present today and is represented by the sworn affidavit labelled document AFC647, voluntarily relinquishing his guardian status, pending the outcome of this hearing. Do I have those facts correct, Miss Harris?"

"Yes, your honor."

"All right then," the judge said, then removed her glasses and looked directly at me. "Mr. Weiss, Charlie, you understand what emancipation means. If I rule in your favor, all your decisions from this day forward will be yours and yours alone, as will responsibility for your life and all you do with it, the good and the bad. You fully comprehend what this means, and you're prepared for the consequences?"

I looked at Rose and Henry, then back at Becca and her parents, then turned to face the judge. "Yes, your honor, I understand. But I'm not alone. I've had a lot of help getting to this day, and I'll have all the help I need from now on, I'm sure of it."

Rose reached out and squeezed my hand and when I looked at her, she smiled up at me. I turned back to face the judge.

"Okay then," she said, "it is the ruling of this court that petitioner's request for emancipation shall be accepted and affirmed. Mister Weiss, you are hereby emancipated and the guardianship of Geo Wilkins terminated, effective immediately. Let's move on to the second item. I have a petition for adoption, and affidavits of petitioners from Mr. Henry Bimmy and Mrs. Rose Bimmy. I see also a completed court activity record for Mr. Weiss, and a sworn care and custody affidavit. We've got a completed home study, and I will accept the previously referenced document AFC647 and surrender of guardianship as sufficient to terminate any and all legal rights of Mr. Weiss's sole remaining blood relative. Is there anyone present here today who would object to this adoption on legal grounds?" The judge paused and looked across the room, then continued, "Hearing no objections I will move on. Mr. Charles Lee Weiss, are you ready to become a Bimmy?"

I smiled because I was happy, but also because the name Bimmy always made me smile.

"Yes, your honor, I am most definitely ready."

After our day in court, my friends and supporters joined me at the Bimmy's home, my home, for an Adoption Day celebration. Others from my school and friends of the Bimmys joined in and before long it was all a bit much for me. I was happy the day had come and my adoption by Henry and Rose was finalized, but I'd been calling them Mom and Pop for a long time by then.

I had one more thing to accomplish before the day ended.

I found Becca at a table with her father, George, debating whether or not science could turn the tables and help Earth recover from the impacts of the global war and the change in the atmosphere. It was a topic she and I discussed with some frequency, given my firsthand experience living in a reclaimed zone.

"We can't leave it up to your generation, daddy," Becca was saying, "it's up to us, my generation and the next, we are the ones who will have to figure this out, and it's going to take more than some clever recycling tech and…"

"Charlie!" George said, with more enthusiasm than expected, "Nice of you to join us. Have a seat, I'll be right back."

I grinned at Becca and took a seat next to her, "Who am I saving, your dad or you?"

"Both," she said. "I'll never convince him the Earth is beyond saving, and it was his grandfather's generation who got us here. Earth is drying up, like toast in the oven. It was already bad, then they had to go and start a war to make sure they ruined the planet. Meanwhile, the colonies are thriving and we're going to start throwing giant snowballs at Earth through a wormhole to replenish the atmosphere."

"Every little bit helps," I said.

"It's not enough, and you know it. They've been dropping ice onto Mars for a century and look where it's gotten them, a few more clouds and a population dependent on whatever water they can harvest."

"It's a start, and the Orbital Gateway is another big step."

"You bet it is," she said, "but until they get one into orbit over Enceladus, we'll have an Orbital Gateway to nowhere."

"Pop always says, one thing at a time."

"We're running out of time."

"That's why they're using the heavy lift system, to send both up at once."

"If anyone but my parents had cooked this up, I'd call it nuts. It's a three-year mission to Enceladus, plus assembly in orbit. A lot can happen in three years."

I sat back in my chair and spread my arms out and grinned. "I know," I said, "look how far I've come in three years."

"Yes, Charlie Bimmy, you are quite the impressive young man, aren't you," she said, returning my grin.

"Thank you for noticing. But there's something else I want to talk about."

"Let's hear it."

"I, Charles Bimmy, would like to take you, Becca Kiel, on a date. What do you think?"

Becca's laughter was so loud it brought nearby conversations to a halt as people turned to see what was happening. Once she stopped laughing, Becca surprised me by planting a kiss on my cheek. "Silly boy, you don't have to ask your girlfriend out on a date. You tell her when and where, and she'll let you know if she's available."

"Girlfriend? When did you become my girlfriend? I know we're best friends, I mean, I hoped one day we, I...help me out here, Becca."

"I have been patiently waiting for you to catch up to me for two years and finally you've managed to do it."

"Two years? You mean I've been your boyfriend for two years and didn't know it? How could I be so..."

"Blind? Naive? Stupid?"

"I'll accept the first two labels, but if I'm stupid, being my girlfriend is totally on you."

"Fine, I concede the point," she said. "What do you have planned for our first official date?"

"How would you like to go to the Gateway Mission launch with me?"

"How romantic."

"It's a night launch. There's a dinner involved."

"I would hope so, girl's gotta eat."

"And seats on the LORP."

That got her full attention.

"What? Civilians don't get access to the LORP! Did your mother..."

"Yes indeed, Miss Kiel, you are the girlfriend of the son of the Head of Launch Operations for Arcadia Station, and she thinks watching a night launch from the LORP is definitely a romantic first date."

"I've never...I mean, I've always...Charlie this may be the best idea you've ever had. Well done, Mister Bimmy."

"So, it's a date?"

Becca leaned in and kissed me again, on the lips this time. "You bet it is," she said, "now, boyfriend, how about you go get us a couple of sodas?"

"You got it, be right back."

On the way to get our drinks I was thinking about my new life, feeling foolish for having no clue about Becca and doubting her feelings for me, when Katie came bounding across the lawn and stopped in front of me. I knelt down to pet her and said, "Don't you worry Katie, we'll spend all weekend together, but today you have to share me with Becca." I pointed at Becca and said, "Go keep her company until I get back, go on!"

Katie barked once and did as she was told.

My father approached and asked, "How'd it go?"

"Pop," I said, "this is the best day of my life, bar none."

"I hope you have many more as good or better ahead of you."

"Me too, Pop, me too."

***

Rose Bimmy, Head of Launch Operations for Arcadia Station, had considerable influence. If you wanted to feel the launch when you watched it, you had to be outside. The closest viewing stand for the public was five kilometers from the launchpad. The absolute closest viewing stand, one they didn't let the public use, the Launch Observation and Research Platform, aka the LORP, was exactly 2.1 kilometers away. It was so close you had to wear protective headsets.

After dinner at our favorite restaurant, Becca and I were treated to a tour of the control center before being shown to our seats on the LORP. Once spacecraft construction had moved off the planet and into high-Earth-orbit, heavy lift launches had become rare. The viewing stand was filled with scientists, astronauts, and military personnel, some, like us, there for the spectacle of it all. Before he left us, the officer who led us to our seats said, "Have fun kids. When it's over, wait for me here. I'll come fetch you and take you back to the auto-park."

"Yes, sir," we both said before donning our headsets.

The moonless night provided a deep black background for the 50-story multistage rocket gleaming under the glare of the spotlights. Great white puffs billowed out from the colossal rocket's side and flowed away into the darkness, byproducts of the cryogenic fueling process. There was a large countdown clock on the ground below our seats. We could hear the control room chatter in our headsets as the time ticked away.

The final countdown began with the traditional "Ten, nine, eight, seven…" the clock reached one, then "Ignition…liftoff…we have liftoff of the Orbital Gateway, the first step in humanity's next great journey into the heavens…"

The mighty rocket roared, the ground beneath it trembled, its power shuddered through the earth. Becca grabbed my hand, squeezing it hard but never taking her eyes off the rocket as the thunderous power of the machine reached us in rolling waves of heat and sound.

Our eyes locked on as the rocket rose into the night sky, the trail of flame and vapor blasting behind it, acceleration increasing with every second.

"Approaching max q…prepare for main engine cut off…"

We strained our necks to stare up into the sky and follow the rocket streaking away from Earth. I was awestruck by the power and majesty of it all.

"Main engine cutoff…"

The darkness of the night was shattered by a colossal orange fireball. It spread out across the sky, followed by the sound waves from the explosion, light from burning debris and fuel reflected off the scant clouds drifting below. A shock wave plunged back toward the earth. Streamers of burning debris trailing flame and smoke showered down to the ocean in an ever-widening column.

Silence descended over platform. The chatter from the control room was replaced by a soft hissing sound. We continued to stare. I struggled to accept what we'd witnessed. Space Force hadn't lost a rocket in generations.

Becca released my hand and took off her headset. I looked down, then took off my headset. She looked at me, tears falling down her cheeks like the debris falling from the sky, burning and unabated. I took her hand again. "I'm sorry," I said.

She wrapped her arms around me and cried on my shoulder. I held her tight and didn't speak. Many people on the platform cried with her. After a time, she pushed away from me, then placed her hands on my face.

"Charlie," she said, "it's over, my parents' dream, the Earth, all of it, it died up there, what kind of future…how…we have to get off this planet, somehow." She buried her face in my neck and continued to cry. I knew how much hope she and her family had invested in the mission. I knew how much it meant to her, personally. Despite her skepticism, she believed it was the only hope for the restoration of Earth's climate.

Instead, it was a disaster, and I'd given her a front row seat.

"It's gonna be all right," I whispered, "whatever it takes, it will. I promise."

# 7

# Big News

The failure of the Gateway Mission gave Becca a renewed focus on her studies, which meant I saw less of her. Our time was compressed to lunches together at school and the occasional Friday or Saturday night date. Her hard work paid off, and a year after the explosion she was accepted into the astrophysics program at the North American Institute of Technology, the most prestigious university of its kind on Earth. She was overjoyed by the news, while I was equally devastated, though I managed not to show it, at least not to her.

The loss of the Gateway system was also a further blow to the already strained relationship between Earth and her colonies, particularly the ice mining planets. The Gateway would have relieved the pressure on the supply chain, and the miners who fed it. Instead, they were ordered to increase output, but provided no new resources by which to accomplish the task. Rumblings of rebellion had begun to emanate from the outer worlds, and these grew louder after the mission failure.

The weekend before Becca left for Tech, it felt like it was the beginning of the end for us. I didn't see Becca all weekend, which only darkened my mood. Katie stayed by my side, trying to understand my sadness, but her empathy did little to help.

My parents seemed to understand what I was going through. They made efforts to cheer me up, but it wasn't until Sunday evening, when my father challenged me to a game of chess, that I started to see things from a different perspective.

I had taken to chess with enthusiasm, to the degree I often had to prod him to play, rather than the other way around. It took less effort after my first win.

As always, Henry took his time staring at the board before he made his move. He never seemed to notice the timer ticking away, but never failed to beat the clock. This time, his pondering went on longer than usual.

"Strange you are so willing to sacrifice your Bishop. Have you been studying the game without me?"

"Of course, how else can I learn more than you know?"

"I've always said you were a clever boy. But I think you've been too clever. You want me to take your Bishop, thinking I might sacrifice my queen, but in fact, if your strategy is what I think, you'll have my King in three moves. Am I right?"

"Nope, you're wrong. Two moves, then he's mine."

"But you lack the confidence to call checkmate?"

"Two moves, not one. I'll call the match when I'm certain I've got you, not before."

"That is the correct choice," he said.

I'd been studying every book on chess in his library. I was certain I'd landed on a strategy he didn't know, a series of moves from a newer book I didn't think he'd read yet. The binding wasn't cracked and there were no bent pages as was the case with most of his books. But he didn't take the bait. He used his knight to take one of my remaining pawns, then tapped the timer.

"What the heck? You took a pawn when your queen is exposed… Pop, you're slipping."

I made my move, capturing his Queen, then tapped the timer.

Henry laughed quietly and moved his Bishop through the lane his Knight had cleared, capturing my own Queen, then tapped the timer and said, "Checkmate."

I fell back into my chair and slapped my hands to my head, "How did I not see it coming, such a rookie mistake."

"An inexperienced move, that is certain. Next time, read the entire book before you employ an unfamiliar stratagem. Chapter twelve, I think it…"

"Play again?"

"It's getting late, and we have an early start tomorrow. Call it a night…"

"Really Pop, a pun? Not funny."

"No pun," Henry said, "it's late, it's dark, it's night, and you lost. Go to bed and think about the tragic mistake you made."

"Let's stay up, I'm not tired."

"We both know this is about Becca. If you want to talk about what's going on in your head, I'll stay up and listen. Otherwise, I'm going to bed."

"Why is she leaving now? She could wait a few months, then we could leave at the same time."

"This is not how university admission works. You've had a year to prepare for it, and she's had a year to prepare for your enlistment. You would ask her to put her life on hold so you could leave first? How do you think she would feel?"

"I don't know. I guess it finally got real. I knew she applied for early admission, but seventeen? Who starts college at seventeen?"

"It is not uncommon for students from Arcadia to begin their university programs early. You are all talented, intelligent young people. You could still choose college over the military, if you want. We will support your decision."

"I didn't get accepted to Tech."

"You applied to one school. There are other schools, other programs. Not everyone can be an astrophysicist, it doesn't mean…"

"I don't want to go if I can't be with her…"

"A poor reason to go to college, Charlie, and a selfish one."

My father's rebuke, though gentle, stung me. I stared at the darkness beyond the window behind him.

"She's going away tomorrow. In six months, I enlist in Space Force. Off-world deployment is two years, minimum. If there's a war, deployment is for the duration. What if I never see her again?"

"A distinct possibility, but you have each chosen your respective paths, and you have both been open about those choices. Yet you continue to see each other, to the exclusion of all others. Have you considered what it means? What it means for your future, either apart or together?"

"I can't think about a future without her."

"Then don't. Focus instead on the life you want to make with her, after university, after your commitment to Space Force, no matter where it takes you. But never forget the years you've had together, those should be enough."

"Enough for what?"

"Enough to bring you back together, when the time is right for both of you."

The next morning, we met the Kiels at the Arcadia Transport Hub. Becca's parents could afford to pay for her to fly to her university, but Becca insisted she travel by maglev, to reduce her carbon footprint and to have a closer look at the land between her home and her school. She hadn't left Arcadia since moving there. Her parents thought it was a strange request for a student of the stars, but I understood. I knew she wanted to get a better look at the world outside the city than a flyover would give her. She'd listened to the stories of the world I had seen, the one I had escaped. But her entire route was through a habitable zone, nothing like the desolate land I had experienced. She wouldn't budge on the topic and her parents agreed under the condition she remain on the train for the duration. I told her the same, never get off the train, and she promised me she wouldn't.

We were in the passenger lounge, and I did my best to seem cheerful, but I had little to say. After ten minutes of silence, Becca said, "Come with me Charlie, we need to talk."

"Becca..." her mother began.

"In private," Becca said. She took my hand and led me onto the platform, out of earshot of our parents.

"What's going on?" I asked.

"You tell me, you're never this quiet. You knew this day was coming. Is this how you want to send me off, with the cold shoulder treatment?"

"No, Becca, I was...I don't want...I mean, I want you to be happy. I don't want you to go. But I do want you to go. I want...I want us to have a future together, and if we have to be apart for a while, I have to accept it. I don't have to be happy about it, but I'm happy for you..."

Becca placed a hand on my chest. "Stop blabbering and tell me what's really on your mind."

I laughed at first, then realized she was serious.

"Okay," I said, "I don't know when I'm going to see you again. If we go to war with the colonies, I don't know *if* I'll see you again. Pop says to focus on the future after college, after my enlistment, but it seems forever away. Doesn't it bother you? I'm going to miss you Becca. I'm not sure how to handle this."

"I'll miss you too, but I'm sure of one thing, we will be together again. We both promised. I trust you to keep your end of the bargain, and you can trust me to do the same."

"I love you Becca..."

"Stop, stop right there. You'll make me cry and I don't want to make a scene, I already cried at home with my mother. I know how you feel, you know how I feel, let's…"

I couldn't let her finish. I kissed her. It wasn't our first kiss, but we knew it could be our last. We held each other until the comm system made the "Now Boarding" announcement. Our parents joined us on the platform, then Becca hugged each of them before boarding the maglev train to begin her journey. She took her seat at the window and waved as the train began its slow movement out of the station, accelerating at a constant rate. We watched until it was out of sight.

My mother placed her hand on my back. I rubbed my eyes then turned to face her.

"Okay Mom, let's go home."

***

I made no secret of my sadness. My only solace was Katie's company. Her demands were simple and direct. We took long walks and played fetch at the park. Katie was six but hadn't lost any of her playfulness, nor had she lost any of her empathy. When my father suggested I use the auto-car to take Katie to the beach, I jumped at the opportunity. We swam until she tired, then sat staring at the vastness of the sea and its endless horizon. I would miss seeing it almost as much I would miss Becca and my family during my enlistment. The ocean eased my melancholy. By the end of the day, I knew I would be all right. I would realize my dream of joining Space Force, Becca would realize her dream of becoming an astrophysicist, and sooner or later we would be together again.

When I returned home at dusk, exhausted and tinged red by the sun, I felt better than I had since before Becca left. I felt at peace.

Until I saw my parents seated at the dining room table with a woman in the uniform of a Space Force captain. It was disconcerting, but my parents looked happy.

"Charlie, dear, take a seat," my mother said.

"I need a shower, I'm gross, I feel like a crustacean. Katie needs a bath too…"

"It can wait," Henry said, and motioned to a chair.

The officer waited until I was seated to speak.

"Charlie, I'm Captain Amanda Wilson," she said, "I'm here about your pre-enlistment exams."

"Did I fail? I thought I did pretty good, they weren't too tough."

"They're tough, it's a measurable fact. You think they're easy because they were easy to you. You scored in the top one percent of all enlistees in the history of pre-enlistment testing, quite the accomplishment."

"I don't understand, my grades are good, but…"

"Your father tells me you applied to one university. Why not more?"

"I've always wanted to join Space Force, since I was little. My reason for applying to Tech was…selfish. It wasn't a good reason, I'd rather not talk about it."

"Their loss is our gain. We are impressed by your scores. Our exams test more than knowledge, more than ability. We look for aptitude, adaptability, strategic thinking, creative problem solving, the list goes on. We care about what you know, and what you can do, but we also look for potential. Young man, you have extraordinary potential. I'm here to offer you an opportunity, one important enough for me to be here in person."

"I'm enlisting in the spring, after graduation…"

"Charlie," my father said, "hear the captain out."

"Sorry."

"That's okay, Charlie," the captain said, "we'll teach you customs and courtesies when the time comes, until then, we'd like you to focus on school and get your diploma. After you graduate, Space Force would like to offer you a provisional commission in the officer corps, subject to satisfactory completion of OCS, Officer Candidate School. What do think?"

"I'll be eighteen next year, I don't know anything about OCS, I never thought about it. Are you sure you've got the right person?"

The captain touched a tablet on the table in front of her. I saw my own image in the corner of the screen. "Are you Charles Lee Bimmy, formerly Weiss, resident of Arcadia, formerly of Greenfield."

"Yes ma'am."

"The same Charles Bimmy who, at thirteen years old, survived over two months alone in the wastelands."

"I wasn't entirely alone, but yes ma'am, I did."

"The same Charles Bimmy who, upon arriving in Arcadia, committed a selfless act of bravery and saved the life of one Rebecca Kiel?"

"She goes by Becca. I did what I thought was right."

"Then I'd say I've got the right person, wouldn't you?"

"Yes, ma'am. I guess you do. Um…Captain, what do I have to do?"

"Stay in school, keep your grades up, stay out of trouble. I'll send some documents for you and your parents to review, you sign them and send them back. Next spring you'll get your orders and travel instructions. Any more questions?"

"No, ma'am, I guess you pretty much covered it…"

"Excellent," the captain said. She picked up the tablet and her cap and pushed away from the table. Henry and I stood up with her. She stuck out her hand, "Can't wait to see you next year, Charlie, looking forward to having you aboard."

I shook her hand, followed by Henry.

"Captain," I said, confused, "I'm…I…what do you mean 'aboard'?"

"We don't train officers on Earth," the captain said, "we train them in space. You'll be on my ship, the *Helios*. It will not be an easy ride, but something tells me you'll do fine. You might even enjoy the training. As for Space Force, I'm sure you're gonna love it."

***

Seven months after the captain's visit, I knew she had been right. I did enjoy the training.

OCS comprised twenty-six weeks of technical and physical training, military indoctrination, and a crash course in Customs & Courtesies. We learned to fight in a weightless environment. Artificial gravity, and a gimbal-rigged command deck, took a lot of the feel out of space maneuvers. Understanding the limitations, and possibilities, of movement without the constraints of gravity was viewed as essential to the success of an officer. I took to it like I was born to be in space.

After she left, Becca and I had settled into a routine, messaging one another every evening. Our communication became less regular when I started training. The weeks passed quickly. I kept in contact with her and our families as much as possible, but time was structured down to the minute. Fifteen minutes of 'comm time' every day after evening mess often filled with other activities, including grabbing some sleep if you were unlucky enough to pull night watch while everyone else was slumbering away in their webbing.

Twenty-five weeks in and I could see the light at the end of the tunnel. I'd have two weeks of leave to use as I saw fit, and I saw fit to spend it with Becca. I was counting the days until de-orbit and our reunion. There were times I felt foolish for how worried I'd been about our separation, and now I was ten days away from being with her again.

At the beginning of my last week of OCS, midway through my watch, I was on the command deck with Candidate Eric Breuger. We were in orbit over Luna, preparing for a final exercise on the surface to wrap up our training, followed by a graduation ceremony at Artemis Station. Ship's time was matched to Space Force HQ on Earth, but there was no real sense of day or night. It took some getting used to but everyone adapted, some better than others. Breuger was my bunkmate, and I knew first-hand he hadn't adjusted, so I kept an eye on him during our watch. If he dozed off, we'd both pay the price.

I was at the nav station and Eric was on comms when a priority message alert began to sound, a red light flashing under the glass of his console. He started to read the message, then he leaned in closer and his face went ashen. He gripped the edges of his console and didn't speak.

"Breuger, what gives?" I asked. It looked to me like he was on the verge of tears. When he didn't answer I tried again, "Eric, buddy, what's going on? Talk to me."

"Gimme a second, Bimmy," he said. He put his hands on his face, covering his eyes, taking slow deep breaths, using a calming technique we'd been taught in our psych class. He composed himself, then looked at me with a face I hadn't seen before.

"My brother is dead," he said, "they killed him and his entire crew."

"What? Who killed him? What are you talking about?"

He pushed back from his station and pointed at the message displayed on the console. I walked over and read it, feeling my stomach churn as the words hit home.

It was an Alpha Alert, highest priority, sent to all stations, all ships. There had been unrest across the Sol system, every colony had a grievance. The colonies on Enceladus, Europa, Ganymede, and Callisto, all of the ice mining colonies, had declared their independence from the Earth Alliance. Their first act was to attack the military presence at each of their colonies, including the ships docked in orbit.

"Your brother's ship…"

"The *Agamemnon*," Breuger said, "docked over Ganymede, they delivered medical supplies, they were supposed to break orbit and head to Deimos. His ship was overrun, they spaced all but one of the crew, anyone who survived the initial assault. They made the last person alive send out a message, then they killed him. They killed my brother. The video is in the message, Bimmy, they made a record of it to…"

"Eric, did you watch it?"

"Yes, I didn't know…"

Breuger was falling apart. My training took over. I sent an alert to Captain Wilson, then triggered the ship's alarm calling all crew to their stations. I knew I needed to get Eric off the bridge before it was filled with officers and other trainees.

"Bimmy to Jones, come in, urgent."

"Acknowledged," Jones replied, "Bimmy, what's happening?"

"I need you on comms."

"It's not my station…"

"I don't care, I'll explain when you get here, Bimmy out."

"Eric, stand up," I said, and grabbed him under his arm, partially pulling him from his seat. When he was standing, I put my hands on his shoulders and looked him in the eyes, but all I got in return was vacant stare. I shook him and said, "Come on Eric, snap out of it, I need you. Pull it together, Jones is on her way."

"Jones…what are you talking about?"

"She's going to relieve you. If the crew sees you like this…"

"I don't give a damn about the crew, I…"

"Exactly why I need you off the bridge."

The door to the captain's quarters opened behind Eric and the captain entered the deck, still fastening the buttons on her tunic.

"You two better have a damn good reason for calling the ship to quarters," she said before looking up and seeing us.

"What the hell is going on?" she asked.

I snapped to attention, but Eric didn't move.

"Captain on deck!" I shouted, louder than necessary. I hoped it would get Eric to follow suit. When he didn't come to attention I repeated, "Captain on deck!"

Eric came to attention. Then he turned and saluted the captain.

"You don't salute on the bridge, what…Candidate Bimmy, report!"

"Captain, there's been an attack on Alliance forces, the colonies have rebelled, several ships have been destroyed or captured, casualty reports are incomplete, the situation is rapidly evolving. I've declared a medical emergency on the command deck, Candidate Jones is on her way to relieve Candidate Breuger."

"Breuger…," she said, "what's the emergency?"

"I…my brother, his crew…his ship…"

The captain looked at me, then at the hatch to the command deck as it swung open and Jones entered. I knew I could count on Jones. She came to attention and stood silently. The captain gave Breuger a long look, then said, "Candidate Breuger, you are relieved. Jones, you're on comms, Bimmy, my ready room."

The captain crossed the deck and entered her ready room and I followed. When the door closed behind me, the captain said, "Thirty seconds, Bimmy, go."

"Captain, Candidate Breuger received an Alpha message. It had an attachment, a video. The colonists who took over the *Agamemnon* killed the entire crew, but they kept one person alive to send a message. Then they killed him. That crewman was Candidate Breuger's brother. He watched the video. I could tell he was compromised. I alerted you, called the all hands, then ordered Candidate Jones to the bridge. Once I knew she was on the way, I declared the medical emergency. I needed to get Eric…Candidate Breuger off the bridge. I didn't think he was able to follow orders."

"Did you see this video, Candidate Bimmy?"

"No, Captain, I didn't think it was necessary."

"All right Bimmy, back to your station."

"Yes, Captain."

I did an about-face and walked out, the captain close behind. In the brief time we were in the room the bridge had filled. Every station was occupied. In addition, several members of my cohort were present, as well as a few of my instructors. Breuger hadn't left the bridge. I couldn't understand why he was still there. More confusing was the smile on his face. I went to my station, Breuger snapped to attention and shouted, "Captain on the bridge!"

Everyone snapped to attention, then Captain Wilson took up her post and turned to face us. She pointed at Jones and said, "Cancel all hands." She looked around the room and continued, "If you're on station, have a seat, except you, Bimmy. Everyone else, at ease."

I remained at my station and felt decidedly uneasy. I tried to stay calm and see how things played out. Whatever mistake I'd made, the punishment was about to be as public as it could get.

"This has been a drill," the captain said. "But not an ordinary drill, as those of you who played a role in the deception know. Candidate Breuger, well played, obviously convincing. Candidate Jones, you weren't in the loop but you handled the order from the bridge by the book, nicely done. Everyone, please join me in congratulating Mr. Bimmy on his promotion to Lieutenant, Junior Grade, effective immediately."

People applauded, a few whistled. I was more confused than ever.

"Lieutenant Bimmy, it is a tradition in Space Force to put the top ranked member of each OCS cohort through a test in their final week of training. If they pass, we promote them. If not, we use it as a standard training exercise. Lieutenant Bimmy, you passed, congratulations."

The captain walked toward me, a blue box in her hand.

"Attention!" she said, then opened the box. She handed the box to Breuger, then reached up and removed the epaulets from each of my shoulders as well as the insignia pinned to my collar. She handed them to Breuger and removed the gold bars from the box and pinned them to my collar, then placed new epaulets on my shoulders, each with a gold star in the center and single gold bar across the outer edge. "I'm proud of you, Lieutenant Bimmy, more than words can say."

"Thank you, Captain, I...I don't know what to say. I had no idea..."

"That is the point, Mister Bimmy. It would be my honor to receive your first salute as a lieutenant."

"It's against protocol...is this another test..."

"Tradition trumps protocol, so let's have it."

I snapped a salute and held it.

The captain returned my salute and said, "Have a seat, Lieutenant Bimmy. Everyone, let's review the scenario. This may have been a drill, but you've all heard the chatter, you know there's talk of war. A separatist movement led by the ice miners, it's no fantasy, it's real. We have to prepare for the eventuality of conflict. Who wants to go first?"

Around me the members of my cohort all raised a hand, as did I.

"Let's start with Lieutenant Bimmy," the captain said.

"I'm still in shock. Before we dive into the postmortem, I want to say Candidate Breuger should consider a career in acting, because wow, did he have me fooled. Way to sell it, Eric."

"What are friends for?" Eric replied.

***

After our graduation ceremony at Artemis Station, I took the next shuttle to the transfer dock orbiting Earth, then dropped down to the space port at Arcadia. Becca was on break from school and would be waiting for me.

I stepped onto the tarmac, closed my eyes and relished the surprising warmth of the late fall sun. I set off toward the terminal as fast as possible, but my body hadn't readjusted to Earth's gravity. My attempt to run came to an abrupt end when my legs gave out and I fell to my knees. I caught myself, avoiding the embarrassment of a face plant, but managed to amuse the other passengers.

Becca was waiting for me inside the terminal. She was laughing as I approached.

"I was going to say how handsome you look in your uniform, but Charlie, you don't look so good, what did they do to you up there?" she said.

"It's gravity," I said. When we embraced, I leaned into her, exaggerating my struggle. Then she planted a kiss on my lips I'll never forget. She spoke volumes with her kiss. It closed the gap created by a year of separation and reminded me she had felt the pain of it as much as I had. I heard someone behind us say, "Get a room, you two." It was cliché, but still made us laugh.

"It's good to see you, Becca, thanks for meeting me."

"Of course, Charlie. Welcome home," she said, then pointed at my name-tag, "or should I call you Bimmy now?"

"Dealer's choice," I replied, "as long as you call me."

She laughed and shook her head, "I'll have to think about it. Let's get you off your feet before you fall over."

"Good idea."

She took my duffle and we took our time walking to her parents' auto-car.

"My legs feel like they each weigh a ton," I said. "I tried to run across the tarmac. I made it all of four steps."

"You exaggerate. From where I was standing, I think you made it two."

"I stand corrected."

We got in the car and held hands while Becca told me about her school and her classes. I was glad to hear how much she was enjoying it. We left the sprawling port and drove into the forest surrounding Arcadia. The trees were a welcome sight after the endless black of space, the dappled light filtering through them was easier on my eyes than the bare sun over the space port, and reminded me of the day I arrived in Arcadia.

The street in front of my house was filled with auto-cars. Katie was waiting on the front porch, alone.

"What are you up to, Becca?"

"You're big news around here, Lieutenant Bimmy," Becca replied, "can you blame people for wanting to welcome you home?"

"To heck with the people, I want to see my dog." I opened the door and stepped onto the sidewalk. I threw out my arms, walked onto the lawn and shouted, "Katie! Come see!"

When she saw me, she bolted off the porch. I knelt on the grass and she threw herself into my arms, which didn't go quite the way I had envisioned. A hundred pounds of fur and muscle slamming into a freshly de-orbited human resulted in me flat on my back and her sprawled out on top of me. She rolled over me, rubbed against me, licked my face, then repeated the process. My uniform was trashed, and I didn't care. The coolness of the grass against my back, the sky glittering in the leaves above me, my dog's joy, Becca standing over me laughing...I had dreamed of joining Space Force as an escape. I had never hoped to find a life filled with joy, security, and love. It was beyond my comprehension before, and yet the dream I never dared have had become my reality. I was in no hurry to get up from the lawn, until I heard the front door open.

I raised my hand into the air and said, "A little help."

Becca took my hand and helped me stand. Katie ran back to the house and passed between my parents, standing side by side on the front porch, smiling. Katie went inside and waited for me in the foyer.

Becca and I walked arm in arm toward my parents. Before I took the one step up onto the porch, I realized I was eye to eye with my father.

"My goodness," my mother said, "did they stretch you? Look how tall you are!"

She wrapped her arms around me and kissed my cheek. It was then I truly felt I was home. Then my father hugged me and surprised me with a kiss on my other cheek.

"My son," he whispered in my ear, "we are so proud of you. Welcome home."

"It's good to be home," I said.

"Mom," I asked, "why are you crying? What's happened?"

"You've come home, Charlie. Tears of joy. Come inside, there's a yard full of people out back who can't wait to see you."

I felt overcome by the moment. I had never experienced such a thing as 'tears of joy.'

Becca placed her hand on my waist and looked up at me. "Now you know how I feel," she said. "What say we get this party started?"

"I say yes, as long as I can have a comfortable chair."

My parents led us to the back yard where a couple dozen people were waiting. There were tables spread around the yard laden with food and drinks, and other tables surrounded by chairs where people sat eating. Everything stopped when Becca and I stepped onto the back porch. Someone started clapping. Before long everyone was clapping, and I heard a familiar voice shout "Welcome home Charlie!"

I looked for the voice in the crowd and found Alan Post, Arcadia's Security Commander, waving at me. I waved back at him, remembering our first meeting. Since my parents had no military experience, Alan had become a mentor during my last year in Arcadia, teaching me the traditions, customs, and unwritten rules of military life. I walked through the clapping crowd, some people slapping me on my back. When I reached Alan, I hugged him. I didn't plan it, but it felt right. He returned the hug with more energy than I expected. When he released me, I waved my hands, asking the crowd to quiet down. When they did, I looked at Alan and pointed at the insignia on my shoulder. "This," I said, "this is because of you. Thank you."

He hugged me again and said, "No, Lieutenant Bimmy, you earned it. But your uniform is a mess…"

"I better go see if I have anything that fits. I feel like I grew a meter while I was in space."

"Maybe half a meter," Alan said.

I looked at the people around me, most of them familiar to me, some of them I knew in passing. "Thank you all for coming. As Commander Post pointed out, I'm a mess. I'm going to change but I'll be right back. I'm looking forward to catching up with you all."

"We'll be here Charlie, at least until the food runs out," I heard Becca's father say. Katie followed me into the house, seeking my attention. I was happy to oblige. We went into my room, a space both familiar and foreign at once. Everything was as I had left it. My baseball caps still hung on the rack, my trusty e-bike against the wall, my sneakers tucked under the foot of the bed, pictures of my family and Becca scrolling in the digi-frame next to my tablet. It was a time capsule of my life, and it hit me as I reconnected with my past that the new chapter of my life hadn't really begun until then, the day I came home from training.

I wasn't a child anymore, and all the things of my childhood, arrayed there before me, were things I would put aside forever. My old clothes wouldn't fit me, so I took off my grass-stained tunic and spent some time sitting on the floor talking to Katie. A few minutes later my father came to the door. He remained at the threshold without speaking, holding a bundle of clothes in front of him.

"Everything okay?" I asked.

"I may never see you this way again," he said, "I'd like to enjoy it while it lasts."

I didn't know how to respond, so I pointed at the bundle, "What do you have there?"

"Clothes for you," he said, "these belonged to Marcus. I'm sure they'll fit you now."

***

My leave flew by faster than I thought time could move. Becca had a week before she had to go back to school. We spent every day together, and most of those were at the beach with Katie. It was the warmest Autumn on record, and the ocean welcomed me home much as my friends and family had.

On her last day in Arcadia, Becca and I sat on the sand, watching the waves roll in, the sun setting behind us. We watched our shadows grow to the water's edge, holding hands as the light splayed out, splashing gold and amber across the sand and sea and sky. Katie curled up on the blanket behind us and fell into a deep sleep. Despite knowing Becca and I would be apart again, this time for longer, I felt it would be all right. Separation would never last between us.

"I can hear those gears grinding away in there," Becca said, "what's on your mind?"

"You, us, the future, the past, everything up to this moment, everything after it."

"And here I was wondering what we were having for dinner," she said. "You're so somber sometimes, Bimmy, I worry about you."

"Not somber, not today. Today I'm...content."

"But you're not happy."

"How could I be? We don't know when we'll be together again. Content is the right word. I do know we'll see each other again, we will have a future together. It's a matter of time."

"And space," she said.

"And space," I replied.

"Do you worry about war?" she asked. "It's all anyone talks about these days, the colonies, the stations, everyone's choosing sides."

"Not the Venusians, those cloud hoppers are broadcasting their neutrality across the entire system. But to answer your question, yes, I worry about it. We spent most of our training planning for it. If the colonies declare their independence, what does it mean for Earth? If we go to war to stop them, what comes after? We can't start killing each other then go back to business as usual once the shooting stops. If we have to use force to hold the Alliance together, it's not much of an alliance, is it?"

"Are you afraid?"

"No, you?"

"I'm afraid of what war might do to you. If you have to kill…"

"You remember the story I told you, about the old man in the wasteland who tried to trap me, the one who wanted to eat Katie?"

"I remember."

"I never told you the full story."

"I always thought there was more."

"I killed him. It was him, or me and Katie. I chose us, and I killed him. If you're wondering what will happen to me if I have to kill again, then you already know. I hate it. I hate it happened, I can still hear him scream, I can still see the blood on my hands. Sometimes I hate myself for doing it…"

"You had no choice, you said it, it was him or you. It was self-defense, you had one option, survival."

"I carry the memory with me everywhere. I can still see his face. I can see his blood pooling in the dust. And the girl, I wish I knew what happened to her. If you want to know how I feel about killing, hate is the best way I can describe it. I hate the idea of it as much as the act. If we do go to war, I'll do what has to be done because I love you, I love my family. But when it's over, I'll carry those lives with me, like the old man's."

"Then I hope for your sake it doesn't come to that," she said, "and if it does, I hope the people in charge are more like you than the dead man in the desert."

We fell silent until the sun was gone and darkness closed in around us. We lay on the blanket, staring up at the night sky, gazing at the moon. I could see the faint lights of Artemis Station, twinkling from within Earth's shadow, and thought of my friends who would be stationed there. I wondered when I would get my orders, where I would be assigned. The wait was wearing away my confidence.

I drifted off to sleep until I felt Becca shaking my shoulder. I looked up at her, the moon burning brightly overhead. She kissed me and I wondered if I was dreaming. I heard Katie snoring nearby. I knew our time together had come to an end. I held Becca in my arms again, until she rolled onto the sand, stood up and reached her hand down to me.

"It's time," she said, "my parents will be worried."

I took her hand and said, "Okay gorgeous, let's get a move on."

"Charles Bimmy, do not call me gorgeous. It objectifies me and I don't appreciate it. I am not gorgeous, or precious, or pretty. I'm a scientist. You should respect me for my mind."

"But you are gorgeous, it's the word I hear inside my head every time I look at you, it's especially true in this moment. And for the record, you have a beautiful mind, too."

"You get a pass tonight, Lieutenant, but next time you call me gorgeous you'll have a fight on your hands."

"Katie," I said, "what do you think? Is she gorgeous or what?"

Katie raised her head and looked at me then at Becca. She made a 'harumph' and dropped her weary head back onto the blanket.

"See," Becca said, "she's with me on this one."

"That response could go either way."

We collected our things, climbed into the auto-car and headed for Becca's house. Long before we entered the city, we could tell something was wrong.

"Why are all the lights out? Have they done this before?" I asked.

"No," Becca said, "this is not normal. Power outage?"

"The car would fall back on batteries if the grid was down, but it's still connected, running on external power."

We arrived at Becca's and hurried up the walk. The front door swung open and her father stepped into the moonlight. He looked at his daughter, then at me and asked, "Where have you been, we've been worried sick. Where's your comm link? I take it you don't know what's happened."

"I'm sorry, Mr. Kiel. We fell asleep on the beach, I...know what?"

"War, Lieutenant Bimmy," he said, "we are at war. I suggest you go directly home. I imagine you have orders waiting for you. Becca, come inside."

"Daddy, we fell asleep, it's our last night...."

"I accept your explanation Becca, but it doesn't make it less irresponsible. Come inside, we have an early departure tomorrow. Goodnight Charlie, and good luck."

Becca glared at him, then turned and kissed me, an act I'm sure didn't go over well with her angry father. I was fine with it. If the war had started, it might be our last kiss. I enjoyed the moment, regardless of how it made her father feel. He'd have to get used to it sooner or later.

Becca looked into my eyes again, then went inside without another word.

"Go," her father said, "and don't forget to send my car back."

Before he closed the door, he looked back at me and said, "I don't want her to get hurt, Charlie, least of all by you."

"Yes, sir, understood."

When I got home my parents were seated in the study, heavy curtains drawn tight over the windows. The news was on a small vid screen on the wall over the fireplace. They hugged me and didn't ask about my late night with Becca.

"Have you heard?" my father asked.

"Mr. Kiel said we were at war, nothing more. What happened?"

"The colonies on Europa and Enceladus have broken from the Alliance, they've formed a Federation. Their first official act was to target Jupiter Station. An hour later Ganymede and Callisto joined them."

"Jupiter Station? There must be a dozen Alliance ships there…"

"The colonists have them now," my father said, "they came in on freighters, they had control of the station before anyone knew what hit them. Some of the ships got away. The rest are in the hands of the colonists. They've got their own fleet now."

"They're gonna need it to hold the station. The Alliance won't let this stand."

"They aren't planning to hold the station," my mother said. "The station is gone, they evacuated everyone who survived the assault then blew it up. They took out the primary comm relay with it, the fools. They broadcast the destruction with their demands after they destroyed the relay. It's taken hours for the signal to get to Earth."

"Does the Council think we'll be attacked? That's nuts, there's no way they can project power this far. They'll hardly be able to keep their ships running without fuel from Titan."

"They're playing chess, Charlie, not checkers," my father said. "Titan is part of this. They're not joining the Federation, not directly. They've declared independence and signed a mutual defense treaty with the ice miners. This was a well-planned set of moves. The useless nature of a blackout aside, one can't blame the Council for being frightened."

"Without Jupiter Station, the outer shipping lanes are defenseless, the pirates will have an easy time of it. It'll take twice as many Alliance ships to protect the freighters. What about the Venusians?"

"Staying neutral, the cowards," my mother said with more sarcasm than usual, "they benefit from Earth for years, then first sign of trouble they tuck tail and run."

"I'm not sure it's that simple, but time will tell," I said. I became aware of a soft beeping barely audible over the vid screen. I went to my room and picked up my comm link, its green light pulsing in time with the sound. I put it on my wrist and swiped. It was a message from Captain Wilson, though she wasn't a captain anymore. The gold and black epaulets and twin silver stars told me she'd been promoted to Rear Admiral.

"Lieutenant Bimmy, your leave is cancelled. There's a shuttle out of Arcadia at oh-nine-hundred. You're on it. You've been assigned to the *Arcturus*. Transport from the dock has been arranged. Your formal orders will be waiting for you when you get there." She paused, looked down at something, then back into her comm screen, as if directly at me. "Lieutenant Bimmy...Charlie...I can't tell you everything, but I can say this, you're being thrown directly into the fight. This was never the plan. It was an honor to serve with you on the *Helios*. Good luck. Wilson out."

The *Arcturus* was the Fleet Admiral's flagship. Some officers spent years trying to get assigned to the ship and never got close. It was the largest starship ever built. It traveled with a collection of battle cruisers, fighters, supply ships, you name it, wherever it went, it went surrounded by an armada. Admiral Wilson said I was being thrown into the fight. It meant a counter offensive was in the works, and the *Arcturus* was at the heart of it.

I went back to my father's study and sat with my parents through the remainder of the night, watching the news and talking about what it all meant. When I told them about my assignment, they expressed relief I would be on a ship far away from the fighting. Flagships were never on the front lines, they reasoned.

I didn't tell them they were wrong. I did what I always did when I had something I didn't want to share. I told them the truth, but not all of it.

# 8

# Among the Lucky

The *Arcturus* was an incredible feat of engineering and space-based construction. Large, heavily armed, faster than any vessel of similar mass, the ship could maneuver with the nimbleness of much smaller spacecraft. When fully staffed it carried over 300 crew. To say I was in awe of the ship would be an understatement.

I got a good look at it on our approach to the orbital dock. The ship, too large to dock, had twelve internal crew decks and four external thruster pods, each pod larger than the shuttle I was on. The forward section of the ship sloped down from the central command deck, curving into flat space where, unlike the rest of the ship, no light shone. The light from the ship's windows formed thin lines from forward to midship, terminating at two sets of cargo bay doors, one atop the other, both open and receiving cargo and personnel. The need for a view diminished where the crewed part of the ship ended and the engineering and cargo sections began, only the occasional flicker of light revealing a porthole or hatch. When the ship was not bathed in the light of the sun, it appeared half its actual size. I could see into the command deck through its sweeping curve of glass, but couldn't make out details within.

The smooth surface behind the command deck was interrupted by the secondary array, a bristling collection of weapons and sensors. The bulk of the weapons were located below the ship's long central axis, dozens of plasma cannons and missile batteries, as well as launch bays for drones, fighters and shuttles. Despite my apprehension about my first assignment, I was excited for the day to have arrived.

"She's beautiful, isn't she, Lieutenant?"

I turned to face the man sitting across the aisle from me. He hadn't spoken more than a few words during the flight. He couldn't miss the fact I'd been staring out the window since we began our approach. He wore civilian clothes, but his bearing was military. He looked older than me by a few decades, with close-cropped hair, tinged grey along the sides.

"She?"

"Some of us are stuck in our ways, every ship is a she to me," he said with a grin, "and she is a thing of beauty."

"Beautiful, yes sir, and dangerous by the looks of it."

"You don't know the half of it. She's full of surprises."

"You know the *Arcturus*? Have you served on…"

"I better know her, she's my ship. Admiral David Porter," he said, extending his hand.

"Sir, Admiral, I'm sorry…I didn't realize…" I could feel the blood rush to my face. I'd imagined what my first meeting with the Fleet Admiral would be like, none of the scenarios involved looking like a fool. I'd blown my first impression before I ever got on the ship. I shook the admiral's hand. "Lieutenant Charles Bimmy, sir, it's an honor to meet you."

He pointed at the name sewn into my uniform above my left pocket and said, "I see. Relax, Lieutenant, there'll be plenty of time for formality once we're onboard. Unlike you, I'm not famous, it's no surprise you didn't recognize me."

"Sir, I'm not famous, and to be honest, I did look you up. But your picture…"

"Is old, like I've become since it was taken. But it's a nice image, I see no reason to change it. Mister Bimmy, I've seen your dossier. One could rightfully say your reputation precedes you. Has anyone told you how you came to be assigned to me, to the *Arcturus*?"

"No sir, Captain…I mean Admiral, Wilson, from the *Helios*, ordered me to the *Arcturus* but I haven't seen my official orders yet. The whole process is a mystery to me."

"I know her well. She was a member of my staff until she gained her own command. I imagine she's disappointed."

"Sir?"

"She's leading a flotilla to Deimos, to protect the shipyards, and remind the people there, and on Mars, where their allegiance lies. She wanted you on her crew, but rank has its privileges. I wanted you on the *Arcturus*, ergo, you're on the *Arcturus*."

"Thank you, Admiral, it's an honor. I never imagined I would serve on such a ship."

"Thank me when the war is over, when we know how this misadventure ends."

"Yes sir, will do."

"Wilson was right about you, you're a serious young man. We need officers like you."

"Thank you, sir. Can I ask you a question?"

"Lieutenant, you can always ask, I make no promise to answer."

"Fair enough, sir. Please don't take this the wrong way, but shouldn't an officer of your rank and experience direct the war from Earth?"

The admiral laughed, "Do you think I'm too old for the job?"

"No, sir," I said, "that would be the wrong way to take it. What I mean is…we're spread thin. The loss of Jupiter Station, and the ships, all the crews, we can't afford to lose more experienced officers, especially if Grace Cheng decides to make trouble."

"You're familiar with the infamous Grace Cheng?"

"Yes sir, she's without a doubt one of the fiercest pirates in history. She's got the numbers, some say 200 ships, maybe more, and the will to make this war a lot uglier than it has to be. I've studied her tactics, read all I could about her, then I looked up her family. I wanted to get the measure of her as best I could."

"Most of my officers are focused on the leaders of the rebellion, not a space pirate hiding in the moons of Jupiter. Her frigates are no match for an Alliance corsair, much less a battle cruiser."

"I've done my homework on the colonists, but I believe Grace Cheng poses an immediate threat. Without Jupiter Station, she can disrupt our supply lines, harass civilian shipping, wreak havoc on us while the colonists sit back and watch. If she leaves them alone or, worse, if they've struck a deal, and that would be smart, she becomes a force multiplier. The colonies get all the benefit of her ships and crew with none of the risk, and we end up fighting two wars at the same time."

"An interesting observation, Lieutenant Bimmy. But not all of her ships are combat-capable, she…"

Before the admiral could say more, the docking clamps engaged, sending a rumble through the shuttle. The overhead lights grew brighter and my seat harness unlocked, releasing me to the microgravity of low-Earth-orbit. It was good to feel weightless again, and to be free from the restraints.

"We'll discuss this further over dinner. Officer's mess is at seventeen-hundred hours. You'll have down time until then. I suggest you take a tour of the ship, then get some rest. There's a member of the crew waiting for you, they'll be assigned to you for a few days, until you get your bearings. I'm not heading to the *Arcturus* directly. Any more questions before we disembark?"

"Yes, sir, I've got a bunch of them, but none need asking today."

"Good answer, Lieutenant. I'll see you onboard."

We shook hands again, and the admiral left the shuttle. I felt relieved. In spite of a bumpy start, I'd made a decent first impression after all.

***

Once all the passengers had disembarked, I went to the rear of the compartment and made myself horizontal, head facing forward, lined up in the central aisle. I gripped the seats on each side of the aisle, pushed back, then pulled forward, propelling myself toward the forward hatch. A young woman in uniform rounded the corner directly in front of me. I threw my arms out, grabbing at anything to stop my forward momentum, which I managed to do, in turn sending my body flipping backwards. My head hit the deck with a resounding thud. I hooked an arm around the back of the nearest seat, jerking to a halt with my legs aiming up, my feet centimeters away from the woman's face. She backed up, and I struggled to get myself upright and standing. When I was more or less vertical, the woman came to attention and saluted. I returned her salute but felt like an idiot. One for two on first impressions, not a great start.

"Lieutenant Bimmy, I'm Ensign Blake," she said. "I'll be your guide for the next few days."

I extended my hand, and she shook it. I could tell she was trying not to laugh.

"It's okay to laugh Ensign Blake, I won't hold it against you."

"No, sir, wouldn't dare. But my advice, you might want to skip the flying, my two cents."

"I guess it's not officer-like, is it?"

"It's not that, sir. Lots of people, myself included, we like micro-G. But sir, you don't seem to be good at it."

"Point taken, Ensign Blake. Maybe we can keep this between us."

"No, sir, not a chance," she said, then she did start laughing, and I laughed with her. I followed Blake from the shuttle onto the dock, then to a smaller shuttle. The shuttle from Earth carried 34 passengers. The one we took to the *Arcturus* accommodated four. None of the seats were occupied. Blake took the pilot's seat and began prepping for departure. The forward bulkhead was transparent. It was like sitting in a bubble. We left the dock and headed toward the *Arcturus* at a brisk speed. The ship grew larger until the hull filled our field of vision. Blake held course until it seemed we were going to ram the ship, then she banked right once, then again, then one more time, rolling the ship through turns in a corkscrew pattern. My body and my head lost sync. If I'd eaten lunch, I'm sure I wouldn't have kept it down. We entered the ship's shuttle bay at speed. I was certain we were about to crash, until Blake spun the shuttle 180 degrees on its vertical axis, opened up the thrusters, and set us down in perfect alignment with the docking clamps embedded in the deck.

She looked over her shoulder and said, "That, sir, is how you fly."

***

Blake gave me a cursory tour of the ship, then showed me to my quarters before heading off to her regular duty assignment. The room was less spartan than my shared quarters on the *Helios*, but still a model of efficiency. Like the rest of the ship, it employed the standard Space Force motif, all white surfaces with black and grey trim. It had the luxury of a portal, framing the orbital dock drifting through space between the ship and Earth below.

I got some rest, then headed to dinner. I arrived early and entered the room to find a single officer seated at the table, the ship's captain. I came to attention and saluted, but he didn't return my salute.

"Lieutenant Bimmy, the admiral's dinners are informal affairs, we come to attention for the old man, but we don't salute. Take a seat and relax, we've got a few minutes before he gets here."

"Yes, Captain."

"In here, you can address me as Davis if you like. It's how the admiral wants it, puts all of his staff on equal footing for a couple of hours. He expects us to speak freely while we're here. It's helped us solve more than a few big problems."

"Good to know, sir, thank you for filling me in."

"It's the least I can do for the newest member of my team. You're assigned to Tactical. I hear you've a keen mind and you're a quick study. You'll need both."

"Are the plans for the counter offensive complete?"

"What do you know about a counter offensive?"

"I know the contingency planning has been underway for a long time. It makes sense. Jupiter Station is gone, we lost most of our deep space fleet on day one, Grace Cheng and the colonists have probably struck a deal. We'll need a win soon. If Mars thinks we're going to lose, they could switch sides and take Deimos and Phobos with them. We can't afford to lose the shipyards of Deimos, or the food supply from Phobos, which is why we've got a flotilla on the way there."

"You've got this all figured out."

"No, sir, but I do like to keep up with what's happening. My father taught me to play chess. I use the same strategic approach to everything."

"Even relationships?"

"No," I said, "I take a more relaxed approach to those."

"Good to know," he said.

The admiral entered the room and we both came to attention.

"It's the three of us tonight, so let's get to it," Admiral Porter said. "Who's hungry? Bimmy, when's the last time you ate?"

"Oh-five-hundred sir, you can count me on the hungry side."

"Good. Davis, have you brought Bimmy up to speed on the rules of our mess?"

"The basics, but he's a fast learner, he'll figure out the rest."

"No doubt," the admiral said. He tapped a panel embedded in the table and a porter entered the room with a tray of drinks. The porter placed a glass in front of each of us and said, "Dinner in ten, Admiral."

"Thank you, Stevens," he replied. He waited until Stevens left the room, then asked, "Has Bimmy shared his thoughts on Madame Cheng?"

"The broad strokes."

"Good, let's dive in. Bimmy thinks the pirates are a major threat, our primary threat. Davis, I know you disagree."

"Yes, sir. I believe we have to engage the rebels, immediately, and on their turf. We have to send a message. History supports my position."

"What history are you referencing?" I asked. "World war two, the

Doolittle Raid on Tokyo?"

"No," Davis said, "but good on you for knowing your military history. I'm thinking more recent, the last war on Earth. When the Atlantic Treaty was broken, our side responded with overwhelming force on the first day. I believe it's the reason we won the war."

"With respect sir, I could not disagree with you more. When the enemy's first tactical nuke went off, it wasn't annihilation on a global scale. But our response, the use of hypersonic missiles to destroy cities, bombardment from space, obliterating entire countries, it was a massive overreaction. The counter offensive was terrifying. The non-aligned nations got in line because they were afraid to get nuked, not because they shared our ideology or cared one bit about our alliance."

"It doesn't matter why they got in line, as long as they got in line. It tipped the balance of the war in our favor."

"I disagree again. The balance of the war was in our favor from the start. Our side was better equipped, better armed, and more ruthless. But look what we did to the planet. Most of Earth is a graveyard, one that gets bigger every year."

"Are you saying," the admiral asked, "we should sit down and talk it out so nobody else gets hurt? We've been talking with these rebels since before they rebelled and it's gotten us nowhere."

"Maybe we should have listened more," I said.

"You're being naive," Davis said. "We can't put the needs of the colonies ahead of Earth. We built those colonies, the stations, the facilities, the machinery, all of it, we built it all to serve the needs of Earth, not the other way around."

"Earth is still dying, no matter how much we squeeze out of the colonies. The fuel, the water, the raw materials, we've used most of it to build and supply more ships and stations, which means more people living in colonies. We won the last war, and lost the planet in the process."

"All right, Bimmy, I'll play along," Davis said. "Let's say you're right. What would you do in response to the destruction of Jupiter Station and the loss of all but two of our ships in the sector?"

"Attack the pirates, take out Cheng and her ships, make them a non-threat. It sends a message to the colonists: we know their strategy and we're ready and able to counter it. It would take out what is essentially their primary offensive capability."

Davis looked at the admiral, who nodded his head. Davis turned back to face me.

"It's an interesting strategy, Bimmy, worth further discussion. But it is naive. When we break Earth orbit, we'll be heading to Europa. The rebellion started there, and it's going to end there. We're going to wipe the slate clean, destroy everything on the surface and start over, like the colony never existed. When the other colonies understand our resolve, they'll come back to the fold and never make the same mistake again."

I was stunned. Europa was the largest colony in the outer reaches of the system, and we were going to kill all of the colonists. It was madness, and my sworn oath made me part of it.

"You're right, sir, they won't make the same mistake twice. But it doesn't mean they won't try again."

"If it doesn't work," Davis said, "at a minimum it gives us one less problem to worry about."

"If it does work," I said, "it gives us a hundred thousand colonists to bury, and an Alliance at the point of a gun."

"Will you have a problem performing your duties on this mission?" Admiral Porter asked.

"One of my instructors at OCS read a quote to me," I replied, "it's centuries old but still relevant. 'A true soldier doesn't fight because he hates what's in front of him, he fights because he loves what's behind him.' I'll do what's necessary to win this war. But it doesn't mean I won't question how we fight it."

"Excellent. You succinctly stated what we expect from our officers on this ship, hasn't he Davis?"

Before Captain Davis could answer, the porter returned with our dinner.

"At last, the food," the admiral said, rubbing his hands together. "We can pick this topic up again tomorrow. I'd rather we talk of less troubling matters while we eat."

***

The ship, like all Alliance ships, ran on Earth time. As the newest member of Captain Davis's staff, I was assigned night watch duties at the tactical station on the bridge. It was a good assignment for me. I didn't mark time the way most members of the crew did. I scheduled my life around my duties, regardless of the clock. For me, night watch was the same as day watch. The difference was the noise. I relished the quiet.

Ten days out from Europa, the noise ratcheted up.

Night watch consisted of three officers: Commander Taggert, the Commander of the Watch; Ensign Philips, the Comms Officer; and me, the Tactical Officer. Four hours into our watch, the boredom was interrupted by a system failure alert.

"Commander, I'm getting a docking clamp malfunction on deck eleven, dock one," Ensign Philips announced.

"That's the admiral's shuttle. Is engineering aware?" the Commander replied.

"There's a team on the way, but the Chief Engineer is not responding to comms."

Commander Taggert's brow furrowed as she considered her options.

"I'm going down there. Get hold of the Chief and tell him to meet me. Bimmy, you have the bridge."

"Yes, Commander," I said, and moved to her console.

When she was gone, Ensign Philips couldn't resist. "Your first command, Lieutenant Bimmy, don't screw it up," he said.

I didn't have a chance for a witty comeback. The comm console burst to life and lit up like a fireworks display.

"What the hell is this? Do you recognize this data? Are we monitoring the CMB?" Philips asked.

I looked over his shoulder and felt the blood drain from my face. "No," I said, "not exactly. I set up a subroutine to monitor for variations at 0.13 percent of the cosmic microwave background. Broaden the scope, I need to know how many hits we're getting."

Philips modified the settings on the array and the screen filled with a dozen points in space, less than a hundred kilometers off the starboard bow, where the first variation had been detected.

"There's nothing there," he said, "it's gotta be an error in the subroutine. I mean, look at the alignment, it's geometric, not random…"

"Give me a 360 sweep, maximum range."

"Lieutenant, there's nothing out there…"

"There is something out there," I said, "run the sweep, pipe the data to the holographic display, make it fast."

"Aye, aye, Captain Bly."

"Now's not the time, Philips."

Philips turned his attention to the controls and ran the sweep.

"For the sake of argument, let's say there is something out there. If there is, what is it? Because all I'm seeing are dozens and dozens of alerts on what looks to me like empty space."

"Pirate frigates," I said. "They coat their ships in an EM-absorbent volatile-compound. It absorbs light and masks their ships' heat signatures. They're almost undetectable, if you don't know what to look for."

"How do you know what to look for?"

"I read, Philips. You should try it sometime."

"We gotta find you some hobbies, Lieutenant."

"Data, projector, quickly."

"Here it comes," he said, "Ta-dah…oh my God."

The holographic projector created a complete view of the ship and its surroundings, up to maximum sensor range, with the ship at the center. It provided a multidimensional view of the ship as it moved through space, commonly referred to as a 'God's eye view.' When Philips sent the data to the projector, it showed the ship surrounded by a cloud of bright orange CMB variation alerts.

"Bimmy, if those are pirate frigates then we're…I mean, they've slipped inside the defensive perimeter without anybody noticing, they've got us wrapped up like a giant burrito. Are you sure about this?"

"They didn't slip by, we flew into their trap, like a fly into a spider web. They're all powering up, it's what triggered the alerts. Wake the admiral, no, get the entire Command staff up here, and get Commander Taggert back, the docking clamp can wait."

"Bimmy, you're taking a huge risk. What if you're wrong? The admiral will not be happy."

"I'm not wrong," I said.

"How can you be sure?"

"Because, Ensign Philips, variations in the CMB do not maneuver in order to follow the Fleet Admiral's flagship, do they?"

I pointed at the hologram. The bubble of glowing alerts around the ship began to compress.

"Forget the comms, sound general quarters, do it!"

Philips sounded general quarters, calling every crew member to their station. It was a familiar sound to me, but this time it was no drill, though I was certain we were all about to be tested.

The blaring alarm was followed by a new alert in the hologram. Unlike the other data points, which presented as orange pyramids, the new alert was a bright red ball.

"Now what?" Philips asked.

"That's Grace Cheng's ship, the variation is different from the rest of the frigates," I said.

"Don't tell me, you know this because you read it someplace. Is there a book of all the pirate secrets anybody can read?"

"Yes, by Mulzac, I'll send you a copy. Her flagship is larger than the rest, like ours. It was built on Deimos and stolen while it was in transit to Titan. Send the coordinates to the forward battery. We have to destroy her ship. If she's gone, the pirates are done."

"Belay that order," Commander Taggert said from behind me. "What the hell are you doing Lieutenant? I leave you on the bridge for ten minutes and you…what in the world…"

Her voice trailed off when she saw the hologram. The captain and the admiral arrived at the bridge, and they wanted answers, too.

When I explained what they were looking at, Captain Davis didn't believe it. Like Philips, he thought it was an error in the subroutine, or spatial anomalies. While we debated the data, the balance of the bridge crew took up their stations.

Then the anomalies opened fire.

The first missile struck us midship, followed by more. We lost the primary cargo bay, followed by our port azimuth thruster. The force of the explosions sent shock waves and fire pulsing into the ship's superstructure.

Every weapon on every ship in the armada was rendered useless. They could see the destruction of the flagship happening before them, but they couldn't see their targets and no captain would risk firing for fear of striking the *Arcturus*.

Captain Davis froze. He stared at the projection, watching missiles come at us from all directions.

"Captain," the admiral shouted, "give your orders, return fire."

The captain didn't break his stare. "We're dead, we're all dead…" he mumbled.

The ship shuddered and keeled as more missiles struck home. Damage reports were coming in from all decks, and still the captain did nothing. The noise on the bridge grew louder as more explosions rocked the *Arcturus*. A section of wall catapulted into the bridge from the rear bulkhead, propelled by an explosion within the hull.

"The captain is relieved. Commander, remove this man from my bridge. Lieutenant Bimmy, get to your station, put some heat on those bastards."

I took my seat at Tactical and dialed up our weapons control system. "Philips," I shouted, "feed the alerts to tactical."

Philips looked at the admiral, waiting for confirmation.

A missile struck the ship forward of the command deck, sending debris into the curved glass, partially obscuring the forward view.

"Follow your orders, Ensign," the admiral shouted over the din.

Philips sent the coordinates to me. I routed them into the ship's weapons system and set all weapons to fire simultaneously, with three plasma cannons aimed at what I felt certain was Cheng's ship. It was a desperate move and would strain our power grid, but I didn't see any other way.

Our missiles were deadly accurate. Once locked on, they wouldn't stop pursuing until the target was destroyed, or fuel was exhausted. The enemy knew this and had no choice. When the *Arcturus* began punching back with a ferocious barrage, the pirates began to flee the battle. One after another, the signals in the hologram blinked out, either destroyed by our weapons, or escaped from the maelstrom, out of sensor range.

Plasma bursts were meant for close quarter fighting, they didn't pursue their target. It was hit or miss. Cheng's ship maneuvered to evade the cannon fire and continued launching armament at the *Arcturus*. I saw an explosion and knew one burst had hit her ship. The red ball flickered, then when out. Whether she lived or died, the Pirate Queen's ship was out of the fight.

But the die was cast, her missiles were launched. One struck the ship aft of the command deck, damaging the secondary array and ripping a gaping hole through the spine of the ship, sending atmosphere and flames streaming into the void. The second missile tore into the flat plane of the bow, obliterating the main sensor array. The hologram went dead, then the damaged rear bulkhead of the bridge exploded. The force of the explosion intensified as it compressed into the reinforced shell of the bridge. I was thrown from my seat and felt a searing pain in my back, a loud ringing in my ears. I tried to stand but couldn't. I started choking on the smoke and heat. I saw Philips crushed against his station, his body run through by a jagged shaft of metal. His uniform was on fire, but he didn't move. The last thing I remember was trying to scream.


I have no cohesive memory of events after the explosion. I knew it killed Philips and several other officers on the bridge, including the captain. I remember someone leaning over me and speaking, shouting to someone else, but I couldn't hear. I remember seeing Philips's body again. I remember the admiral, his face and uniform covered in blood. I was counted among the lucky.

I woke up in a dimly lit room, face down on a soft bed. I was cold, my back hurt, the ringing in my ears was gone, replaced by a soft beeping. There was a whirring and clicking sound coming from somewhere nearby, beyond the opaque white panels positioned around my bed. My throat burned and an attempt to swallow was met with severe pain, like I'd been swallowing molten glass. It hurt to breathe. My face rested on a round cushion, open in the middle so I could look down at a set of small mirrors below. I could see my face, as well as the area on each side of the bed. The face staring back at me was swollen and red, eyes bloodshot. A tube snaked around the edge of the bed, clamped to the cushion before entering my nostril. I tried to lift myself off the bed and found I couldn't raise my head, and my arms had limited range of motion. When I tilted my head to the right, I saw the reflection of someone sitting in a chair in the corner of the room. I couldn't see their face, but my movement got their attention.

"Easy, Charlie, try not to move."

I recognized Admiral Porter's voice. I tried to speak and managed little more than a rasping sound.

"Be still, I'll get you some water," he said. He filled a cup, placed a lid with a straw in it on top, and held it below me so I could drink. It was hard going, but I managed to ease the dryness in my throat enough to speak, but not without pain. He set the cup on a tray and moved my hand to it so I would be able to find it myself.

"Where…"

"Hospital Ship Barton, enroute to Deimos. You need to rest, the graft is healing, but you need to be as still as possible."

"Questions…"

"They can wait, there'll be plenty of time for questions later."

"*Arcturus*?'

"Out of action, but making way under her own power."

"Crew?"

"We lost a lot of friends, Charlie, but you saved most of the crew."

"You?"

"My injuries weren't severe, they had me patched up in no time. I've been stopping by to check on you as much as I can. The doctors tell me your burns are healing nicely, but you need more time. I need you to do as they say, understood? You're no good to me in pieces."

"Family?"

"I contacted your parents myself. They know you're alive and safe, I couldn't tell them more."

The effort to speak set a fire ablaze in my throat. I picked up the cup and tried to drink, but my arm didn't want to follow orders. The admiral supported my hand, and I was able to take a few sips. My hand started to shake. My heartbeat accelerated with my breathing. I was losing control of my emotions. I was confused, groggy, in pain, and scared.

"How long?" I croaked out.

"Charlie, slow it down, catch your breath."

"How long?" I repeated.

"You've been in a medically induced coma for two weeks. They've been bringing you out slowly, little by little."

Two weeks, with no message to Becca, I wondered what she knew, how she was doing.

"Becca…, Rebecca…. Kiel…Arcadia…message, please…"

"Charlie if you don't calm down, they'll sedate you again. If you want to get a message to this person, it will have to wait. You're in no condition…"

"Please…tell her, okay…I'm okay. Please."

He placed his hand on my forearm. "All right Charlie, I'll see what I can do. Rest, no more talking, there's a call button near your left hand. Use it if you need anything. I'll be back to check on you when I'm able."

He left and I stared into my swollen face. I remembered something Becca said to me the first day we met, and decided she was right. Sometimes it's okay to cry. Sometimes it does make you feel better.

Each day after that, my meds were reduced and the fog in my mind started to clear. Several days after I woke up, Admiral Porter came back accompanied by a doctor I didn't recognize.

"Charlie, I've brought someone to meet you. Feel up to talking?"

"Sure," I said. My throat still burned, and my voice was still raspy. Every word hurt.

"I'm glad to hear it. This is Doctor Fitzpatrick. He has experience dealing with your particular injury."

"Back?"

"No, Lieutenant," the doctor said, "burns, more precisely, burns resulting from inhalation. Although, we've found the treatment helps overall healing, speeds it up quite a bit. It will be interesting to watch the progress on your external wounds. A graft this size, even with the latest technology, can take two months to heal. We might be able to knock a few weeks off the timeline. More importantly, we can repair your respiratory system in a matter of days. I have to warn you, it will not be pleasant. Immersion therapy is still new. We haven't yet figured out how to ease the passage from gaseous state to liquid and back…"

"Describe…" I said.

"It's complicated, I'm not certain…"

"Explain the procedure to him, Doctor, he'll understand."

"Of course, Admiral. The patient is immersed in a tank of liquid, it's based on an old technology called oxygenated perfluorocarbon, or P-F-C. We've advanced quite a bit since it was invented, but the important thing is, humans can breathe certain types of liquid, so long as the liquid delivers oxygen and removes carbon dioxide. It's quite pleasant once the patient adapts to the new environment, although some patients report mild hallucinations…"

I didn't need a science lecture, I wanted a process description. "Describe…" I repeated.

"I think what the lieutenant wants is a step-by-step description of the procedure."

"Yes," I said, and gave a thumbs up.

"Well, in a nutshell, we're going to drown you. We'll fill your lungs with a liquid you can breathe, then immerse you in a tank of it. Your body will fight it but if you can control your fear and overcome your body's reaction to the transition, you should see a full recovery of your respiratory system in five to ten days."

"When?"

"When can we start? We can begin prepping you once you sign the release."

"Release?"

"Yes, Lieutenant, we'll need a signed release. Not every patient survives the procedure. Medical Corps requires a patient to sign a release before the treatment is authorized."

"Pen," I said.

The doctor placed a tablet in front of me and pointed at a line at the bottom of a document. "You can sign with your finger, here." I didn't bother to read it. I signed. The doctor pulled the tablet away and added his signature.

"Okay, we're done. We'll have you transferred to my team today, get you prepped, and drop you in the tank tomorrow. Any questions?"

I rolled my eyes, and the admiral saw it in the mirror.

"That's all, Doctor. The lieutenant needs to rest, and I still have a personal matter to discuss with him."

"Very well, Admiral."

"What Fitzpatrick lacks in bedside manner," the admiral said, after the doctor was gone, "he makes up for with exceptional skill."

He removed a vid-card from his pocket and placed it on the tray in front of me. "A message from Miss Kiel. I spoke with her parents, and they connected me with her university. When you're better, I'll expect you to explain why you never mentioned you had such a wonderful girlfriend. I'll leave you to it. Just one more thing, you're being promoted. Try to get some rest Commander, we need you back in the fight."

When he was gone, I tapped the corner of the card and Becca's image appeared, then the video began to play.

"Hi Charlie," she said. "I talked to a nice man named David Porter, he said he was your commanding officer and he wanted me to know you were safe and doing well. All I can say is Mister Porter is a terrible liar. I don't know where you are or what's happening, but I have a feeling you've been hurt. I don't understand why you wouldn't tell me yourself, unless it's bad."

Becca started to cry. I could see the fear and the anger. I cried with her. I was scared and angry, too. I began to regret asking the admiral to contact her.

"I'm sorry I'm crying Charlie, but you know how my mind works. I fill in the blanks with the worst thoughts. At least I know you're alive, and whatever happened to you, whatever you're going through, I know you'll make it, because you made a promise, you promised to come back to me, and one thing I know about Charlie Bimmy, he'll move mountains to keep a promise. You do whatever you have to do, all I want you to do is send me a message. Show me your handsome face, your big smile, I need to see it. And if you think you're not handsome anymore, well, you let me be the judge. I love you, Bimmy. I miss you. I'm waiting."

When the message ended on a still frame of Becca, I picked up the card and kissed her face, then closed my fist around the card and whispered, "I promise."

# 9

# Three Birds, One Stone

I was in a boat on the ocean. I looked into the water and saw something moving below the surface. The world below looked peaceful. I dove into the water. Sea creatures of all kinds swam around me, a small white whale turned its head to look at me as it swam by, moving a flipper, inviting me to follow. I swam after the whale and discovered I could keep pace with it. Then a shadow fell over us and the whale raced deeper, so far down I lost sight of it.

I looked up and saw the hull of a ship passing over, then felt something wrap around me and pull me toward the surface. I passed through the barrier between water and air, caught in a net, lifted from the sea and pulled toward the ship. I couldn't breathe the air. I flipped upside down and tore at the net, then began to vomit. Gallon after gallon of seawater poured from my mouth, my body strained to force it out of me. When most of it was gone, the ocean turned into a smooth white surface, the clouds were replaced by bright lights. I gasped and gulped the air, coughed until my head hurt, then heard a voice say, "And you thought going in was rough."

Doctor Fitzpatrick was standing over me. I was naked, covered in the viscous fluid of the immersion tank, curled up on a wide elevated surface in the therapy room next to the tank. It had been my entire world for five days.

"Did you have to pull me out while I was sleeping?" I asked. My first words since beginning the treatment, the first without pain.

"Didn't they tell you, Commander? Doctors prefer to wake their patients at all hours. It's much more fun for us that way."

"I dreamed I was a fish."

An orderly draped a blanket over me and helped me sit up.

"Did you like being a fish?"

"Yes, until the fishermen came along."

I felt light-headed, and my legs were weak. Otherwise, I felt better than I had since before the battle.

"I think we're going to add you to our win column, Commander. I want to take a look at your graft, then we'll get you cleaned up and let you get some more sleep."

"Sounds good," I said.

The skin graft on my back, printed in a lab from my own healthy cells, began below my neck, spread across my right shoulder, and ran down to my waist. After I dried out, which took the better part of a day, my back looked good as new, only a faint scar outlined the edges of the graft. It was hard to believe how good it looked after having my flesh burned away in the explosion on the bridge. The following day, I was given a clean bill of health and discharged from the hospital ship.

***

During my 27 days as a patient, I'd had no news of the war. I was eager to get to my ship and get caught up. A nurse took me to the shuttle bay and to my surprise and relief, Ensign Blake, now Lieutenant Blake, was waiting for me.

"Blake, it's good to see you again, congratulations on your promotion."

"And you as well, Commander Bimmy. Ready to get off your lazy butt and get back to work?"

"Yes, Lieutenant, I am most definitely ready."

"Then let's do some flyin'."

We boarded the shuttle and launched. It was surreal for me. I'd been in the hospital so long, I felt disconnected from my surroundings. Then Blake did an inverted loop around the hospital ship, and I knew I was back. She banked hard to starboard and flew us directly at the space docks over Deimos, heading for restricted space. At the last second, she pulled the ship into another of her signature corkscrew maneuvers, giving me a dizzying view of Deimos and the Alliance ships spread out around the moon.

"Blake, if you don't mind, I've only recently started walking again,

I'd appreciate less spinning, more straight and level."

"Yes sir, sorry sir."

"Thank you. What's the news? They didn't tell us anything in the hospital."

"The news? The news is you're a hero, what else do you want to know?"

"I'm no hero."

"That's what I keep telling everybody, but nobody listens to me."

"I listen to you, sometimes. Sometimes I even believe what you say, but not this time."

"Seriously, Commander Bimmy, you're a hero. You saved the fleet, the Admiral said so himself. You defended the ship, saved a lot of lives, mine included. If you're not the definition of a hero, I don't know who is."

"We lost the battle, the *Arcturus* is out of commission..."

"Lost? Who have you been talking to? We didn't lose. That's nuts, are you on meds?"

"The first I've heard about us winning."

"They wouldn't have promoted you if we lost. I thought you were supposed to be a genius, I mean..."

"Catch me up, please."

"You want the long version or the short?"

"Which can you finish before we get...where are we going?"

"The *Arcturus*, where do you think? You really are out of it. Okay, short version. After you unleashed hellfire and fury on the Pirate Queen, her frigates tucked tail and ran, which meant the rest of the fleet could blast away without hitting us. The first salvo from us took out a bunch of enemy ships, but the counter attack from our battle cruisers and fighters, it put the hurt on 'em. I mean they lost a third of their attack force in less than an hour. Sixty ships, poof, gone."

"What about Cheng? I know we hit her ship, I saw it happen."

"We've all been wondering how you knew it was her ship. You painted all the ships at the same time when you launched our missiles, made it easy for our side to track 'em down, but her ship was different. We didn't find it until one of our recon ships practically crashed into it."

"Was she alive?"

"No idea, she wasn't on the ship when we found it. But wow, what a wild ship. Like something from a movie, and not a good one. You should check out the images when you get a chance. Commander, what's wrong? Why the sour face? This was a big win for us."

"If Grace Cheng isn't dead or captured, then we'll have to fight her again. I was overconfident, I thought I had her in my sights, I thought it was an easy shot."

"Commander Bimmy, can I give you some advice?"

"Sure."

"Don't snatch defeat from the jaws of victory. We won the battle, we live to fight another day. At least take a victory lap."

"Maybe we'll do it together someday."

"No better time than the present."

Blake jammed the throttle forward and the ship raced toward the surface of Deimos. She pulled up and flew us close over the surface, then we were pulling away again. She rolled the ship, then made an inverted dive.

"There she is, and here we come," she said.

The *Arcturus* was below us, surrounded by space tugs and barges, bathed in light. Blake flew the shuttle into the repair dock, passed over the command deck, then the new secondary array. We flew a complete oval around the ship, then headed for the shuttle bay.

"There you go, Commander, victory lap."

"Thank you, Blake, nice job."

I should have left it at thank you. Another triple corkscrew and we bolted into the bay. With her typical flare, Blake spun the shuttle around and dropped it onto the docking clamps with a gentle thud.

"Blake, I hope you never change. I'll always know to ask for a different pilot."

"Happy to be of service, Commander."

The shuttle dock rolled back and linked with the airlock. When we stepped through, Blake first, followed by me, she startled me with a sudden move, placing her back against the bulkhead, snapping to attention, and saluting.

"Commander Bimmy on deck, ten-shun!"

The corridor was lined with members of the crew. Enlisted, NCO and officer alike came to attention and saluted. Admiral Porter was at the far end of the line in his dress uniform, Admiral Wilson by his side.

I snapped to attention and saluted my colleagues. I thought I would come back to my ship and life would go on as usual, but the admiral had other ideas.

I dropped my salute and walked down the corridor. My crew mates clapped their hands in sync with my footsteps, until I reached the admiral and he returned my salute.

"Welcome home, Commander Bimmy," he said. "It's good to see you looking well again."

"Thank you, sir, it's good to be back. Admiral Wilson, this is a nice surprise. I assumed you'd be on Mars."

"I wouldn't miss this for the world."

"Commander Charles Bimmy, you are out of uniform," Admiral Porter said. "Admiral Wilson will rectify the situation."

"Indeed," she said. She tapped her comm link and said, "Bring it."

I heard someone approaching from behind me, but didn't turn to look. My crew mates again clapped in time with the footsteps until none other than Eric Breuger, my bunkmate from the *Helios*, now a lieutenant, stepped around me and next to Admiral Wilson. When I saw the blue box he handed to her, I knew what was happening. The uniform I was given on the hospital ship was a spare, it had no rank or insignia.

Admiral Wilson reached up and pinned a silver oak leaf to each collar, then installed epaulets with three gold stripes and a gold star to my shoulders. For the second time in my young career, I'd jumped rank. While she snapped the last insignia in place she said, "This is becoming a habit, Mister Bimmy, well done. Salute me, make it sharp."

I gave her my best, and she returned it. Then Admiral Porter shouted, "You are dismissed." My crew mates shook my hand and slapped me on the back, which hurt, and congratulated me on my promotion. One by one they left and went back to work, leaving me alone with the two admirals, and my old friend, Breuger.

"Commander Bimmy," Admiral Porter said after the corridor was clear, "briefing at 1600, my ready room. I know you're tired, but there's no time for rest. Lieutenant Breuger will show you to your quarters."

I looked at Breuger, then at Wilson, then back at Admiral Porter.

"We'll explain everything at 1600," he said, "until then, settle in and send a message or two. I'm sure there's more than a few people who are anxious to hear from you."

After Admirals Porter and Wilson left the corridor, Breuger looked at me with his typical 'I'm crazy and you like it' grin, spread his arms and said, "Come on Commander Bimmy, bring it in."

Hugging your subordinates was against protocol, but in the moment, I wasn't concerned about customs and courtesies. It was good to see a familiar face, one so quick to smile.

"Easy, Eric, I'm not a hundred percent yet," I said.

"Sorry, Bimmy. I'm happy to see you."

"Likewise, it feels like a long time. Let's catch up before Officer's Mess, I need to get to my quarters and take care of a few things."

"Great, follow me, Commander Bimmy, right this way."

"Breuger, I can manage, give me the number and I'll find it myself."

"No can do, Commander, I was ordered to take you to your quarters and I always follow orders. Besides, official designations on this ship went out the window when the insides got rearranged. You'll never find it without me. All kinds of alternate arrangements have been made, and you, sir, get a special accommodation. But don't get too comfy, I hear it's temporary."

"What else do you hear?"

"Not much, but I expect that'll change during our briefing."

We arrived at a hatch with 'COQ 190M' stenciled on the wall beside it. Breuger was right, I would never have found the place. He opened the hatch, and I followed him inside. It was a large space, dark and drab, with none of the refinement of my previous quarters. There were two cots, one on each side of the room, with shelving down the middle to create two distinct spaces. There were no portals in any of the walls. I couldn't tell which walls were external, if any.

"Home sweet home, Commander Bimmy, hope you like it."

"I thought you said it was special. This is not what I'd call…is this ordnance storage?"

"It used to be, it's special because you have the privilege of bunking with me again. Like I said, don't get comfortable, I have it on good authority you'll be transferred off this ship in a couple of days."

"Whose authority?"

"Not at liberty to say, but I do believe our briefing will be a lively affair. See you at 1600 hours."

Once Breuger left, I composed a message to my parents and sent it, then tried to do the same for Becca. I considered foregoing the vid-comm system and sending text since it would get to her faster, but a text-only message would cause more worry than relief. It took a few tries, but I eventually found the words.

***

Our briefing turned out to be as Breuger had predicted. There were familiar faces, including another of my fellow OCS grads, Lieutenant Commander Rachel Jones, in addition to Breuger and the two admirals. There was a new face, too, Lieutenant Soji, a tactical officer under Admiral Porter's command.

We were taking our seats when the door opened and a statuesque man in a red and gold tunic entered the room. He had dark skin, close-cropped greying hair, and exuded the quiet confidence of someone accustomed to being in charge.

"Ladies and gentleman, our guest of honor," Admiral Porter said, "Peter Jay, President of Deimos, welcome to the *Arcturus*."

As was custom, we came to attention and waited for the Admiral to continue, but the president preempted the normal routine.

"Please, everyone, be seated. I'm the president of the smallest colony in the Alliance, there's no need for such formality."

"At ease, everyone, take your seats and let's get started," the admiral said. "President Jay has information to share regarding our upcoming mission. We're going to engage and destroy what's left of Grace Cheng's fleet. Mister Bimmy once told me the pirates were our primary threat. I didn't listen then, but we all know he was correct. Speak freely, one of you may hold the key to the success of this mission, don't let fear or formality keep you from sharing it. President Jay, you have the floor."

"Thank you, Admiral," the President said. "How many of you know the history of Deimos? How we came to be a colony?"

"Your great grandfather, Alexander, purchased the rights to Deimos," Jones said, "and your family has been in charge ever since. Two years ago, the Alliance changed your designation from Deimos Corporation to Deimos Colony."

"A concise history, anyone else?"

The President was amused, which irritated me. This was supposed to be a briefing, not a history lecture. I was about to protest when Soji spoke up.

"You have a small, but well-trained fighting force, ten cruisers, six high speed frigates, the largest collection of freighters of any colony, and in the last fifty years you've built more ships than Earth has built in the last hundred. It's an impressive operation."

"Our people are our success. We work as one for our common goal. Anyone else?"

Again, I tried to speak, but Breuger cut me off. I felt like my colleagues were trying to impress a man they should be questioning, not answering.

"You mined over three hundred cubic kilometers of material out of the core of the moon and moved your entire colony to the interior. You slapped some thrusters on the exterior and spun the rock fast enough to give your colony a gravitational force equal to Earth. You turned the moon into a giant space station."

"I wouldn't describe them as slapped on, but otherwise I'd say you're correct. What about you, Commander Bimmy? You seem eager to join this conversation. What do you know about our little home inside the moon?"

I gritted my teeth, then relaxed my jaw and took a deep breath. So what if he was the President of Deimos? I didn't work for him, I worked for Space Force.

"I mean no disrespect to my colleagues when I say all of this is basic information, Deimos one-oh-one. For me, there are three things to know about Deimos. First, your shipyards can already outbuild Earth's. That makes Deimos the birthplace of starships and vital to the war effort. Second, while you claim to be a representational democracy, your people have chosen to keep your family in power for generations. That seems at odds with democracy. Finally, most importantly, you conduct business with the outer colonies, people many of my colleagues refer to as rebels, via intermediaries on Europa. You trade technical expertise, materials, even personnel, for resources you should be getting from the Alliance. Which leads me to my question for you, Mister President. What are we doing here?"

I expected the President to be angry, to shout me down, to demand an apology, anything but what he did. The President of the most important colony in the Alliance turned to Admiral Wilson and said, "Not afraid to speak truth to power, I see why you like this one."

Then he turned to Admiral Porter and said, "David, I'm inclined to agree with your assessment, I think Commander Bimmy is the right person for the job."

"Agreed," Admiral Porter said.

"Commander Bimmy," the President said, "if this mission is a success, you and I might become good friends."

"You can never have too many friends during wartime, Mister President."

"True, but you need those same friends to keep the peace when the war is over, don't you?"

"It depends on the nature of the peace."

"Commander Bimmy, I am determined you and I are going to be friends. It may be a long journey, but above all else, I am a patient man."

"The journey of a thousand miles begins with a single step," Soji said.

"Confucius?" asked the President.

"Lao Tzu, but it's a common mistake. It's from the *Tao Te Ching*."

"Well, whoever said it, I think it fits. Shall we take our first step together?"

"Yes," Admiral Porter said, "time is short, we have a launch window approaching."

"Commander Bimmy," the President said, "you are correct, I can't dispute anything you've said. We do business with the colonies through intermediaries on Europa. What you don't know is our operation has the blessing of Alliance Central Command."

"Operation?"

"Yes, Commander, the intermediaries are two of my sons. They represent the interests of Deimos, but also protect the interests of the Alliance."

"Your sons are double agents?"

"They were double agents. They managed our trade with the colonies, as I said, with the blessing of Alliance Central Command. Their presence on Europa gave them access to information, the coming and going of ships, the mood among the colonists, the location of various people deemed important by Central Command."

"They've been exposed," I said.

"Yes, they're being held by the colonial authorities."

"Do you think the rebels will harm them," Jones asked.

"No, my concern is the colonists will deliver them to Grace Cheng before I can arrange their safe return to Deimos."

"How do you know they haven't already?" Breuger asked.

"My sons are not the only spies on Europa."

"You want us to go and get them, a rescue mission, what's it got to do with engaging Cheng's forces?"

"Not exactly, Commander…"

"Commander Bimmy," Admiral Porter interrupted, "your mission is to draw out Cheng's fleet. You will take command of the *Ajax*, Lieutenant Commander Jones will be your second in command, Lieutenant Soji will be your Tactical and Comms Officer. Breuger will handle navigation, he'll be your pilot. You will depart for Europa at the next window, in twelve hours. Your route must appear to be surreptitious; we've mapped a route through the asteroid belt that should provide you ample cover."

"Excuse me, Admiral," Breuger said, "you're giving us the fastest ship in the fleet, and you want us to fly it through the asteroid belt on a trajectory that slows us down. Why not take a Mainzer Transit?"

"I said surreptitious, you must appear to be hiding. A Mainzer Transit is too obvious, but the planetary alignment favors us. After you pass through the belt, you'll come into range of Cheng's ships on your approach to Europa."

"She won't be able to resist the temptation," I said, "but there's a conflict here. If we're supposed to be hiding, how do we know she'll find us? I don't know the *Ajax*, but if the ship is fast, and we need a crew of four, it must be a small ship."

"That's correct," Admiral Wilson said, "you'll be a speck in the cosmos, she would need dumb luck to spot you, or you'd have to give your position away, neither of which works for the broader plan."

"Then…"

"Deimos has a spy problem of its own," President Jay said, "hence our current situation."

"Three birds, one stone," Breuger said, "clever."

"Yes," Admiral Porter said, "your mission is to be the stone. You'll draw Cheng's forces out of their hiding place around Jupiter and the fleet will be in position to engage them over Europa. Our ships are taking up positions as we speak. The insurgents on Deimos will be exposed, and when the colonial forces come out to join the fight, we'll drop a team to the surface and retrieve the President's family members from Europa, with some help from friendlies who'll be waiting for us."

I wondered what the odds of success were for such a complicated plan, if they could be calculated in the first place.

"I recognize that face, Bimmy," Breuger said. "What are you thinking?"

"Eric, you're a skilled navigator and an expert on comms, but you're no pilot. I'm thinking we need Lieutenant Blake on this mission."

***

Becca's work had suffered since the call from Charlie's commanding officer. She struggled to keep her worries at bay. When she received word from her roommate, Naomi, about a new message, she dropped everything and ran to her dorm. University policy prohibited personal messages on school systems, as well as personal communication devices in classrooms and laboratories. She thought it was a silly prohibition, but complied all the same.

Winter had come late but had finally set in. Becca left her coat at her desk and relied on the run to her dorm to keep her warm. When she arrived sweating and breathless, her roommate and some friends were waiting for her.

"You didn't watch it, did you?"

"No, of course not, who do you think I am?" Naomi said. "But I did check the origin header. I didn't want to bother you if…"

"Is it from him?"

"You'll have to watch it to be sure, but it has the same beacon identifier as the last one he sent…"

"That was months ago, would it use the same…"

"Becca, watch the message." Naomi said with finality. "We'll be outside when you're finished."

"You don't have to wait around, I'll be okay."

"No way, we have cried too many tears with you over this man. We've earned the right to be here when you dance."

Becca thought about Charlie and how he would respond.

"Fair enough," she said, then shut the door, leaving Naomi and the others to wait in the hall.

Becca touched the blinking light on her comm link, then a still frame of Charlie's face appeared. He was clean shaven, with a fresh haircut, but he looked tired. More than tired. New lines around his eyes and across his forehead, his smile had lost some of its joy. He'd been in space, at war, for a year. She could see it had aged him. But his eyes still held the light she'd always seen in them.

She touched the screen to begin playback of the message and immediately paused it when Charlie said, "Hello gorgeous."

She reset the message and listened again, "Hello gorgeous." He knew she didn't like it when he called her gorgeous, but this time she wanted to hear him say it over and over again. It meant whatever had happened, no matter how it had changed him, he was still Charlie, he was still hers. When she'd heard it enough, she let the message play through from the start.

"Hello gorgeous. I know you don't like the word, and technically I can't see you, but I see you in my memories every day. You are gorgeous, no matter what you say. I know it's been a long time since my last message. I am sorry. If I could have contacted you sooner, believe me, I would have. You assume correctly, I was injured. I can't tell you anything about how or when, but you can see for yourself I'm okay. Other than missing you, I feel good, fully recovered. But there's more work to do here, the pace is quickening. I don't know when I'll be able to contact you again, it might be text-only for a while whenever I have the chance. I've heard my current assignment is temporary, it's all I know, it's all I can say. What I can tell you for certain is I love you, I miss you, and yes, I made a promise, and I'll move more than mountains to keep it. Stay safe. I love you. Bimmy out." Before the video message ended, Charlie touched two fingers to his lips, then touched the lens, then the image froze.

Becca touched her fingers to the image, then to her own lips. She played the message again, this time she noticed his uniform had changed, but she didn't know what rank it signified. She shut off her comm link and turned on her audio player, tuning it to her favorite stream. She opened the door and faced her friends waiting expectantly in the hall.

"Well?" Naomi asked.

Becca turned up the volume on the music and said, "Let's dance."

# 10

# Confrontations

The asteroid belt isn't as crowded a place to fly as one might think. The millions of rocks, held in the belt by the competing gravitational forces of the Sun and Jupiter, tended to keep their distance from one another.

The larger chunks were mapped, and the dwarf planets, like Ceres, had at least a token human presence. But the smaller asteroids had never been mapped and when collisions happened, ship-sized slabs of rock and metal went hurtling in all directions.

Our trip through the asteroid belt might have been exciting with Blake at the helm, but our mission called for a boring ride, with occasional stops to avoid other ships, and Blake delivered. Still, dodging the smaller, unmapped asteroids was not for the faint of heart. The sensors on the *Ajax* could pick up boulders with ease, but maneuvering out of harm's way took a sharp eye, and a quick hand. It was good to see Blake take her job seriously. The moment we made it through without so much as scratch on the ship, after 29 days, I expected to hear a lot of bragging and self-congratulation from her.

"Breuger," Blake said when we left the donut-shaped region behind us, "you have the con, I'm going to bed." That was it. She went to bed, like it was no big deal. I must admit, I was disappointed.

The *Ajax* had a new experimental drive, in addition to the normal thrusters and rocket engines. The G-drive rode on gravitational waves, like a sail catches the wind, enabling it to travel faster than any ship ever built. The force it harnessed was strong but slow to build, it took time to reach maximum speed. Once at top speed, the ship sacrificed maneuverability to maintain velocity. Conversely, it was easy to slow the ship down on approach to a moon or planet.

Twelve hours after departing the asteroid belt, the ship was traveling six times faster than our previous top speed, cutting our travel time to Europa down to four days.

The distance over which the war was being fought, and the dynamic nature of objects in space, resulted in long periods of inaction punctuated by terrifying confrontations. You never knew what you were going to find when you got where you were going, or on your way there.

The rule held fast on our approach to Europa.

"We've got company," Breuger said, "two enemy ships, looks like they haven't caught on to your variance trick, or they haven't figured out how to mask their signature yet."

"Time to intercept?" I asked.

"At our current speed, we'll blow right by them in ten minutes," Blake replied.

"How did they get so close?" Jones asked.

"Either Cheng's pirates spend a lot of time waiting for ships to come along," I said, "or the President was right, Cheng has friends of her own on Deimos. Are they holding position?"

"Yes," Breuger answered, "wait, I've got two more ships powering up. We're going to pass within weapons range. We may have to fight our way through."

"We can't maneuver at this speed," I said. "Blake, how long before we drop speed?"

"Once we hit Europa's magnetic field, twenty minutes, give or take. They'll be shooting at us long before that."

"Bimmy, I'm getting some crazy readings off one of these ships, huge spike in radiation from, I don't know what, Soji, take a look at this. I've never seen anything…"

The darkness of space erupted in a blueish-white explosion, forming a vast expanding sphere of electromagnet energy directly in our path. When the energy hit the ship, we lost power as well as all of our forward momentum. Soji had left his station and was standing next to Breuger, looking over the sensor data, when the ship was struck. He flew forward and slammed into the bulkhead below the main viewer.

The energy wave hit us, passed over us, and was gone. We were adrift, powerless, and our tactical officer was down. I unclipped my harness and drifted forward to check on Soji.

He was dead, his neck was broken and one side of his skull was crushed. His blood floated around me in red bubbles, some of which collided with me, splattering on my face.

"Soji's dead, Jones you're on tactical. Blake, status, can you get us powered up?"

"Yes, Commander, but power cycling takes hours, not minutes. They'll be on us before…"

"Prioritize," I said, "sensors, weapons, engines, in that order, understood?"

"Yes, Commander," Blake said.

"Jones, you have the bridge," I said.

"Where are you going?" Jones asked. "You can't leave the bridge…"

"Do you know how to launch missiles from an airlock?"

"No, Commander, but…"

"Neither do I, but if someone's gonna try it, it should be me. Whatever hit us didn't damage the missiles, otherwise we'd all be dead. Blake, get power to the sensor array, we'll paint the targets and remote the missiles using the sensor data."

"Commander, are you insane?" Breuger said, "You'll blow yourself up and take the ship with you."

"I like this idea," Blake said.

The loss of artificial gravity made it easy to move through the ship. I was inside the armory within minutes of leaving the bridge. It took longer to maneuver the missiles into the air lock and arm them. Without power, everything was operated using levers and valves. Once the missiles were in the air lock and the inner hatch closed, I dropped the pressure in the lock. I ran halfway through the cycle, which was all I needed. I jettisoned the outer door using the emergency override, which fired explosive bolts and sent the hatch hurtling into space. The missiles went tumbling after it, carried by the escaping atmosphere. I was pleasantly surprised when the missiles didn't explode as they left the airlock.

By the time I was back on the bridge, sensors were back online and the pirate frigates were closing in.

"Missiles are away, Breuger you…"

"I've got 'em, here we go…"

The missiles lit up Breuger's display when their rockets fired. Their movement was erratic at first but within seconds they self-corrected and sped off toward their targets.

Two of the ships were struck and destroyed, the remaining two fled, leaving us alone and drifting through space.

"Look sharp, everyone. They'll be back and you can bet they'll bring more ships with them."

"What the hell did they hit us with?" Jones asked.

"Some kind of nuke," Breuger said, "but not like any I've seen before. According to what little data we captured, neutrons from the blast were ten times higher than a standard nuke."

"Worry about it later. Blake, Jones, get us powered up. Breuger, help me get Soji off the bridge."

***

We moved Soji's body to his bunk and strapped it in place.

"I'm going back to the bridge," Breuger said.

I didn't reply. I was lost in my thoughts.

"Commander," Breuger said, "it's not your fault. You couldn't see it coming."

"It doesn't matter, a member of my crew is dead. I'm responsible, no matter how it happened."

"The enemy killed him, not you. If you ask me, you did your job, you kept the rest of us alive. I'll mourn Soji's death when the time comes, but you said it yourself, they'll be back to finish us off. We need to prioritize the living."

I covered Soji's body with a blanket, then tucked it in as best I could.

"All right," I said, "let's get back to work."

The emergency lights blinked off and the primary lighting flickered to life.

"Progress," Breuger said.

"Weapons," I said, "we may not be able to fly, but at least we can fight."

I went to my quarters to clean Soji's blood off my face. When I returned to the bridge, Blake announced, "We'll have full power in five minutes, Commander."

"I thought it would take hours."

"If you do it by the book," Jones said. "If you ignore protocol and throw out all the safety procedures, it doesn't take long at all."

"You sure it's a good idea?" I asked.

"Says the man who blew up an airlock full of missiles," Blake said.

"Point taken," I said. "Don't light the candle yet. Get us underway but keep our energy signature low. We'll have surprise on our side this time."

"Looks like we poked the hornets' nest," Breuger said. "I've got twenty-six ships inbound, all with the same signature."

"Twenty-six ships, that's a bit much," Blake said.

"It's about to get more crowded. Four ships pulling away from the transfer dock over Europa, one of them is one of ours, or used to be," Breuger said.

"Any sign of the fleet?" Jones asked.

"No, not so much as a shuttle. We're nowhere near the rendezvous point. If they're out there, this would be a good time to make an appearance."

"They're out there," I said. "Blake, put us on a course to Io."

"Altering course…why Io?"

"When the admiral said the alignment was fortuitous, I didn't understand, so I did some research. Io orbits Jupiter twice for every Europa orbit, four times for Ganymede. The sulfur mines on Io are fully automated, including the freighters hauling the stuff out. That's where I would hide the fleet, in all that traffic. They could blend right in, add a ship to the mix every few days until the forces are gathered. If I'm right, and the fleet is there, we can lead the enemy to them."

"What if you're wrong?" Jones asked.

"Then we'll use Io's gravity to slingshot toward Ganymede. The enemy ships won't go too far from home, they'll leave it up to their friends on Ganymede to deal with us. We'll buy ourselves a week to figure out our next move."

"We're being hailed," Breuger said, "one of the pirate ships."

"Maybe they want to surrender," Blake said.

"On screen, and lock onto the signal, I want to know which ship it's coming from."

When the image of a woman appeared on the main viewer, I knew it was Grace Cheng. She was dressed in a shimmering green jumpsuit, her long black hair draped over her left shoulder, cascading down to her waist and wrapped in a thin twisted ribbon of gold. She was festooned in jewelry, necklaces, bangles, rings on every finger. I wondered how she could function with so much metal on her body.

"Alliance vessel," she said, "you are outnumbered and your ship is damaged, you cannot escape. Stand down your weapons and prepare to be boarded. Surrender, and I will show you mercy. Continue to fight, and you will know my wrath."

"This is Commander Charles Bimmy, Earth Alliance. The answer,

Miss Cheng, is no."

"Have it your way, Comm…"

"End transmission. Jones, you have a lock?"

"Locked and loaded Commander."

"Fire at will. Blake, light the candle, full power to main engines. It's time to fly."

"Roger that, Commander."

"We don't have enough missiles to shoot all of them," Breuger said.

"I'm aware. All we need to do is keep the enemy focused on us until our ships make their appearance."

"Now would be an excellent time for them to show up."

"I agree. Jones, status."

"Missiles away, still tracking. They're not running away this time…"

"Multiple explosions," Breuger said, "I count six detonations so far, but…it doesn't look right. Some of the explosions, they're too small to be ships, it's like the missiles are detonating without hitting anything."

"Countermeasures?"

"More like decoys. I think we're shooting at ghosts."

"What about the colonial ships?"

"Hanging back, looks like…standby…I'm reading multiple Alliance ships powering up, heading two-four-zero, multiple inclinations, dead ahead. I count twenty, a full squadron of fighters."

"Fighters," Blake said, "Out here? How'd they get here?"

"Doesn't matter, as long as they're ours," I said.

"Look," Breuger said. He transferred the output of his console to the main viewer and we watched the fighters engage the pirate frigates. The enemy had fallen for their own trick, they'd flown into an ambush. The Alliance fighters were small and nimble. They carried a limited supply of missiles, but put them to good use. The pirate fleet was being torn apart. When the missiles ran out, the fighters moved in closer and opened fire with plasma weapons.

"Blake, come about, get us in the fight," I ordered.

"The fight's gonna be over…"

"Not the pirates," I said, "the colonial ships. We're gonna chase 'em all the way back to Europa."

"Too late," Breuger said, "they're done for."

Two Earth Alliance cruisers had opened fire on the ships from Europa, destroying three and disabling the fourth. More Alliance ships began to appear, filling the view screen. The largest of the cruisers moved into orbit over Europa and began bombarding the colony.

"What are they doing?" Breuger asked, "The colony is defenseless, it's not a threat! Why are they…"

"Scorched earth," I said, "they're making an example of them."

"What about President Jay's family?" Jones asked, "We're supposed to rescue them, not kill them."

"Hail the ship," I ordered.

"They're not responding."

"They'll kill everyone…it's criminal…it's genocide," Jones said.

I thought about the people on the surface of Europa, remembered the screams of Mrs. Carter, recalled the blood of the man I killed in the wastelands, remembered the body of my crew mate. I could not let this stand, the death of so many people, my soul would not survive it.

"Not on my watch. Breuger, I know they can hear us. Keep transmitting. Blake, put us in front of the cruiser."

"What if they fire on us? We can't stand up to a battle cruiser…"

"We can't stand by and watch this happen. We have to try to stop them."

"He's right. Lieutenant, follow your orders," Jones said.

Blake brought the ship into Europa orbit and maneuvered toward the Alliance cruiser still bombarding the surface. The *Drache* was raining missiles and plasma bursts onto the colony's surface installations, destroying many of them in the first salvo. The mines below would offer protection for the colonists, until they collapsed, burying any survivors alive.

"Jones, target their missiles, that ought to get their captain talking," I said.

"Yes sir, with pleasure," Jones replied.

When the next salvo of six missiles launched, Jones opened fire with our plasma cannons. Half the missiles were hit, but the remaining three struck their targets on the surface. A fireball erupted below and continued to burn.

"They hit the atmospheric generator," Breuger said, "they don't have much time left down there."

"Line us up, Blake. Jones, keep firing…"

"Incoming transmission, it's the Captain of the *Drache*, Captain Rudnev, and he does not sound happy," Breuger said.

"Good, put him on screen."

"What's the meaning of this Commander? Remove your ship from my field of fire or I swear to you I will destroy it."

"Bombarding a defenseless civilian population, destroying an entire colony, it's criminal, I aim to stop you."

"Have you lost your mind? I have my orders! This is war! There's no crime…"

"Whoever issued those orders can stand trial with you."

"Tactical, destroy that ship," the captain shouted.

Someone offscreen replied, "Captain, it's one of ours…" before the screen went blank.

Seconds later, another salvo of missiles fired toward the surface. This time, Jones intercepted five of the six.

"Look," Jones said, "the second cruiser is taking up position. Commander, we can't stop them both…"

"It's the *Saratoga*," I said, "it's not supposed to be here."

"What do you mean?"

"Admiral Wilson's ship, I saw it in a dock over Deimos. I don't know how they could be here…"

"She's here, and she's hailing us."

"You know what to do."

The admiral appeared on our screen and said, "Commander Bimmy, stand down, that's an order. I'm sending a boarding party to the *Drache*. I'm ordering all ships to render aid to the colony. Your ship will dock with the *Saratoga* immediately."

"Understood Admiral. Our airlock is out of commission…"

"That's what happens when you use it as a missile launcher."

"You saw…"

"We all did. Bring your ship alongside and we'll extend a pressure duct until we can repair your lock. Wilson out."

Once we were docked a medical team came aboard and collected Soji's body. We followed them to the *Saratoga's* morgue to pay our last respects. I felt the weight of my responsibility hit home, thinking about the message I would compose to his family.

In keeping with Space Force tradition, Jones recited "The Song of Distant Home." When she finished, Blake remained next to Soji's body.

"Commander," she said, "if you don't mind, I'd like to stay for a while."

***

The admiral tapped her fingers on the conference table in her ready room and stared at me, then glanced at the remaining members of my crew. "You've created quite the situation here, Commander. News of

110

this will spread like a virus."

"Admiral," Blake asked, "who gave the order to destroy the colony?"

"That's none of your concern, Lieutenant, but you can be certain they'll be dealt with. The question I have to deal with is what to do about Commander Bimmy."

"You should promote him, give him a medal at least" Jones said. "Commander Bimmy is right, there's no point winning the war if we're going to lose the peace."

"I was thinking more along the lines of a discharge in lieu of a court martial," Admiral Wilson replied.

The door to the ready room opened and an Ensign stepped in. He leaned down and spoke to the admiral, but I couldn't hear what he said.

"Bimmy, you stay put. The rest of you are dismissed. Return to your ship and await further orders."

After my crew was gone the admiral opened a cabinet and poured us each a drink.

"Commander Bimmy," she began, "Jones is right, I think a promotion is in order."

"A minute ago, you wanted me gone. To be honest, I'd be fine with it. If this is how we're going to conduct the war…"

"Oh, get off your horse already, Bimmy. I swear, sometimes…listen, what you did was impressive, and between you and me, I'm glad you did it. Rudnev is a tyrant. But we have to stick together. If Alliance ships start shooting at each other, we'll do the rebels' work for them. I need you to understand my position."

"I do," I said, "but Admiral, would you have let him obliterate the colony if we hadn't intervened?"

"No, but there are some complicating factors."

"Care to enlighten me?"

"We can't use our comms while the ships are cloaked."

"That explains a lot. When did we get cloaking capabilities?"

"We've had the tech for years. It was invented in your home town, Arcadia. Top secret stuff, hard to implement but works great when you get it right."

"I assume it's on a need-to-know basis."

"You assume correctly. There are spies everywhere, maybe on your ship, who knows?"

"You think a member of my crew…"

"It's within the realm of possibility."

"What aren't you telling me?"

"We've managed to scale up the G-drive. The *Saratoga* is the first cruiser to get one. We're upgrading ships as fast as we can. Your people back in Arcadia are an inventive bunch, but they don't put much thought into the practical implementation of their inventions. It's one thing to build a prototype in a lab, another entirely to build a new system at scale with the resources we have. We've been recycling everything we can, stripping obsolete stations and ships for what we need, even some not so obsolete ones. The war is becoming a stalemate. We needed this win to get momentum back on our side, as much as we need cloaked ships, and faster ships."

She drained her glass, then stared at me long enough for it to become uncomfortable.

"I have a new mission for you," she said. "The third bird is on its way. Thomas and Michael Jay have been rescued, they're coming here. You will take them back to Deimos, then rendezvous with the *Arcturus*."

"I don't have room for two passengers."

"Lieutenant Commander Jones is staying with me. You've got a return launch window in two days. We'll get your ship repaired and resupplied."

The Admiral poured each of us another drink. I had never been one for alcohol, but on the first sip from the second glass of whiskey, I had a moment of inspiration.

"Admiral Wilson, is anyone talking about peace? Is anyone trying to find a way to stop the killing?"

"Alliance Central Command has kept the channels open to the colonies, but they haven't been in a talking mood. They seem to think a stalemate is a win for them."

"Maybe it's time we changed the nature of the conversation. Maybe it's time we made them an offer they'd be fools to reject."

"What sort of offer?"

"What's the oldest alliance in the history of Earth?"

"Skip the rhetorical questions, what's your point?"

"The Silk Road, it lasted two millennia and spanned most of the known world, thousands of kilometers, hundreds of cities, nation-states, fiefdoms, all united around a single purpose: profitable trade."

"The Silk Road wasn't an alliance, it was a trade route, nothing more."

"I disagree, it was more than a route on a map, it was people abiding by a mutual agreement, everyone benefited from its existence. A merchant could trust the stability of the Silk Road because everyone needed stability."

"I don't see it, Bimmy, a trade agreement doesn't solve anything, not in the long term."

"It does if everyone benefits in the gain and everyone shares in the pain. We need a realignment of the power structure in the solar system. We need a Federation of our own, one the colonies will want to join, one based on equity for all the members. If we finish off Cheng's forces, the colonies won't have a chance against us. Who will build ships for them? Deimos? Not happening, not after we deliver the president's sons back to their family alive and well."

She swirled the whiskey in her glass, then set down her drink. "You might be onto something here, let me think about it. I might run it up the chain, see if there's any appetite for the idea. Until then, take good care of the Jays. Run silent until you get to Deimos. If your idea plays out, their family will be more important than ever."

# 11

## You Run, Or You Die

Becca awoke to blaring sirens echoing through her dorm and across the campus outside. Naomi was getting dressed, in no hurry to leave their room. The clock on the nightstand displayed 4:17 AM. Becca knew, this time, it wasn't a drill.

"We have to go," she said, "grab a blanket and let's get out of here."

"You go ahead and run to the basement half dressed, not me, no way, not again."

"It's not a drill, look at the time. Drills happen on the hour, never at some random time. We have to hurry," Becca said. She wrapped a blanket around herself and tugged on Naomi's arm, trying to get her to move faster.

"Stop it Becca! I can't buckle my belt with you yanking on me. If you think I'm…"

An explosion rocked the building, sending Naomi and Becca to the floor. A second blast shattered the windows, showering the room with glass.

"Okay, not a drill, let's go, let's go!" Naomi shouted. She scrambled to her feet, pulling Becca up with her, then opened the door. A third explosion tore a hole in the side of the building and sent them tumbling into the hallway, already crowded with students trying to make their way to the stairwell and down to the basement. Someone screamed, others were crying. Panic was setting in.

"So much for all the drills, this is a mess. Come on," Becca said, "we have to get out of this building."

Becca turned into the flow of people and began pushing into the oncoming wave.

"What are you doing?" Naomi shouted over the noise, "Bomb shelter is the other way," she said, pointing over her shoulder.

"Fire escape is this way!" Becca shouted back.

Naomi pushed her way around and in front of her friend and began bulldozing through the mass of students pushing against them. "Stay close," she shouted over her shoulder.

Becca grabbed Naomi's belt and said a silent thank you to her for taking the time to get dressed. They made it out of the press of bodies and turned the corner at the end of the hallway. They ran to the end of the corridor and lifted the large window overlooking the fire escape. Other students saw them and followed them through the window. They scrambled down the three flights of steps and reached the ground seconds before another explosion struck a nearby building, reducing it to rubble.

"Where to?" Naomi asked.

Becca began running. "The gym, there's a shelter there."

Some of students who came down the fire escape with Becca and Naomi stayed with them as they ran, a few stayed behind to look for friends. They were in the middle of the quad when their dorm erupted in a ball of fire, destroyed by another explosion. The bombardment was quickening its pace, leveling buildings across the campus.

Naomi stopped and looked back at their dorm, fully engulfed in flames. When Becca realized Naomi had stopped running, she turned back and grabbed her by her belt again.

"Snap out of it, Naomi, you run or you die," Becca screamed.

Naomi still didn't move. "All our friends…," she said.

"What?" Becca couldn't hear what Naomi said, but it made no difference in the moment. Becca pulled on Naomi's belt, but she wasn't strong enough to move her. Naomi continued to stare into the conflagration. "I'm sorry," she shouted at Naomi, then raised her hand. Naomi grabbed Becca's hand before she could slap her. Becca pleaded with her, "Please Nay-Nay, we have to move."

Naomi looked around, then back at Becca, "Okay…okay, let's go," she said.

They ran across the open quad as their campus, the last international technical university on Earth, was torn apart and set ablaze. When they arrived at the gym, the multistory glass facade had been reduced to a pile of shards glittering in the firelight. Becca had lost her slippers while they ran and cut her foot on the broken glass.

"Piggy-back," Naomi said, and turned her back to Becca.

"I'll slow you down, keep moving," Becca replied.

"You weigh less than a dry noodle, get on."

Becca climbed onto Naomi's back and felt her friend's muscles strain to lift her. Naomi picked her way through the debris. Once inside she set Becca down on the tiled floor. They paused long enough to pull a shard of glass out of Becca's foot, then moved further into the interior of the building.

"Which way?" Naomi asked.

"Stairwell, around the corner next to the elevator, there's a marker next to the door."

They hurried to the stairwell, Becca's injured foot leaving bloody prints across the tile. The door was ajar, held open by a book.

"Why is it…"

"It's a fire door, whoever got here first did us a favor, leave it there," Becca said.

Emergency lights cast a red glow as they descended the stairs. After four flights, the light began to brighten. They heard a voice below, shouting up at them.

"Hurry," the voice shouted, "we're closing the inner door!"

The last landing was bathed in light from the interior of the shelter. Two students who had fled the dorm with them, Ellie and Jiao, were struggling to close the heavy steel door. Becca ran into the shelter, then slipped and fell to the floor. Naomi grabbed the edge of the door and helped pull it shut. Another explosion rocked the building above them, sending debris down the stairwell. When the door was closed, they threw the latch, locking themselves inside.

Becca scanned the interior and looked up at Naomi.

"Where is everybody? This place was built to hold a hundred people. "

"I don't know," Naomi said.

"Wherever they are," Jiao said, "there's nothing we can do for them."

# 12

# **Mulzac**

While the name was singular, the term Mainzer Transit referred to any number of points in the asteroid belt where ships could enter the belt and follow a specific trajectory to an exit point. Since everything in space was moving all the time, traveling in a straight line was the exception, not the rule, and the Mainzer Transit one chose was relative to the starting point on either side of the asteroid belt, and a ship's location on the elliptic.

The important aspect of this concept for me was that we could plot our course along a 'Mainzer curve' and travel at a much higher speed using the gravity drive.

Like a sailboat, the gravity drive required the *Ajax* to travel at an angle to the direction of the gravitational forces the drive captured to achieve maximum speed. A Mainzer curve through the asteroid belt happened to be ideal for this purpose. We arrived at Deimos 18 days after departing Europa.

Thomas and Michael Jay took up shifts to fill in for our missing crew. While Thomas was trained as a medic and his brother a soldier, they were born in space and joked they were piloting ships before they could walk. Breuger, Blake, and I, found the brothers to be excellent shipmates, especially after they fleeced us at poker, then gave us our credits back.

After weeks cooped up in a small spaceship, I was looking forward to the relative open space of the Deimos Colony, and my return to the *Arcturus*.

On final approach to the colony, Michael Jay took over as pilot while his brother kept up a running monologue about their home and their family.

"You're gonna like our brother," Thomas said. "You two have a lot in common. He's adopted, like you, but you'll know it when you see him, not much family resemblance. He also hates pirates, so I'm sure he'll want to hear all about how you defeated Cheng not once, but twice."

"I don't hate the pirates, or Grace Cheng," I said, "it's my job to fight them, that's all."

"Yeah, well, pirates didn't murder your entire family. Our father, before he became president, was on long-range patrol when he found one of our freighters adrift. Everyone on board was dead, Reggie's whole family. They'd left Reggie behind on Deimos because he was sick. Our families were close, my dad wanted him to know he'd always have a home with us. We adopted him and he's been our big brother ever since."

I began to connect the dots as Thomas spoke, and realized who he was talking about.

"Your brother, Reggie, did he keep his family name?"

"Yeah, it confuses people, but he wanted to honor his family, keep the name alive, so he still goes by..."

"Mulzac," I said, "your big brother is Major Reginald Mulzac."

"The one and only," Thomas said, "you know about him?"

"Of course," I said, "I read his book. I've read everything I can about his tactics, how he led the fight to clear the pirates from the belt, drove them all the way to Jupiter. He pioneered the battle strategies we studied. He was way ahead of his time."

"Don't get all starry-eyed when you meet him, he'll never speak to you again, he's touchy about it."

"I'm surprised he hasn't retired," I said.

"Retired? How old do you think he is?"

"I don't know, forty..."

"You're over by more than a decade. What did you read?" he said with a laugh. "It's another thing he has in common with you, he got an early start. He was sixteen when he joined the Colonial Marines. That man is driven, and nothing motivates him more than..."

"Something's wrong," Michael interrupted, "the dock is closed."

The open interior of Deimos contained both the colony and its docks for shuttles and other small craft, like the *Ajax*. In expectation of the war, the colonists had constructed a massive gate, like the shutter of a moon-sized camera, made of overlapping layers of metal that slid together to close off the interior.

"Breuger, how many ships are in Deimos orbit?" I asked.

"I count three Alliance ships, two in repair docks, everything else is colonial, and most of those are tenders, tugs, freighters. I don't see any cruisers. Something is most definitely wrong."

"Are we in comm range of the *Arcturus*?"

"I sent a ping, no response," Breuger said.

"Commander," Michael said, "there's no reason to run silent anymore. I suggest we hail the colony. I give you my word, no matter what's happened, you and your ship will have safe passage."

"Do it."

"Deimos Control, this is the *Ajax*," Michael said, "do not fire on our ship, we are not your enemy. Request permission to dock. I repeat, Deimos Control, this is the *Ajax*, do not fire on our ship, we are not your enemy."

"*Ajax*, this is Deimos Control, cease your approach. Transmit your identifier on frequency two-seven-one for verification."

"Commander…"

"Go ahead Michael, send it."

"Yes sir, sending the ping."

"Commander, I've got two ships on approach, coming up fast. No idea where they came from, Alliance frigates, weapons hot."

"Deimos Control, this is Michael Jay, do not fire on our ship, we are not your enemy," Michael shouted.

"Easy, Michael," I said, "never let them hear your emotions. Whatever is happening, no one's fired on us yet."

"I don't like it. First, they try to blow us up on Europa, now they want to do it on our own doorstep. Not the welcome I was expecting."

"We've been off comms for a couple weeks, there's no telling what's happened. Let's stay calm and see how it plays out."

"Yes sir, staying calm."

"*Ajax*, this is Deimos Control, you are cleared for entry, dock nineteen. We're opening the door. Welcome home, Lieutenant Jay."

"I guess anger might be a good strategy after all," I said.

"I think it's more about the name," Breuger chimed in.

The giant iris opened at a snail's pace, gradually revealing the bright interior of Deimos. After thirty minutes of watching and waiting, we received final clearance to enter, escorted to the door by the two

Alliance frigates.

"Would you look at that," Thomas said, "damn near every dock is taken, no wonder we're at nineteen."

"Busy place," I said, "what's the procedure?"

"We dock, then we wait for instructions."

***

The docking infrastructure at the center of Deimos was unlike anything else in existence. At the center sat a circular platform, the hub, with artificial gravity and a set of tubes leading toward and away from it. Dozens of tubes and locks led to the hub and could connect to the docks, all of which were fixed in position. It resembled a giant glittering flower made of crystalline panels, tubes, and a reflective metal framework. It enabled a gradual transition between the zero-G dock and the one-G inner surface of Deimos, where the colony's inhabitants lived.

Unlike the docks, the hub turned with the rotation of the moon, giving occupants a steady, non-spinning view of the surface, albeit from a perspective perpendicular to the surface. The entire assembly floated in the center of a spherical void roughly six kilometers in diameter.

"*Ajax*, Deimos Control, you are cleared to disembark on gangway Delta Nine. Commander Bimmy, President Jay sends his regards."

We floated weightless through the airlock out to the gangway, through a second airlock, then transitioned to a short stairway. One more airlock, and we stepped directly onto the transfer hub. Each successive transit of an airlock brought the corresponding structure up to both the gravity and the rotational speed of the platform. The hub platform never touched any of the stairways leading to it, instead turning a few centimeters below the bottom step. The hub itself was encased in a pressurized chamber, with redundant air locks at strategic points along the perimeter. Once on the hub, the gravity simulated Earth's.

Two lift tubes were attached to the center of the hub at ninety-degree angles to the plane of the platform. If the hub was the flower, the lift tubes were its stalk. Because it was aligned with the central axis of the station, gravity was minimal within the lifts. A passenger stepped into one of the openings and let the airflow carry them up or down, depending on the direction of flow.

"I'm surprised your parents aren't here to greet you," I said to the Jay brothers.

"Whatever happened," Michael replied, "it has my people on the defensive."

We dropped through the lift tube and arrived in a pressurized bowl-shaped structure, with corridors curving up and away from the landing point, connecting to the inner cylinder of the colony. We moved through one of the corridors into the main terminal. I looked up through the glass roof and saw the transfer hub hanging in the central space directly above us. The dizzying change in orientation left me with a mild case of vertigo.

Major Mulzac and President Jay were waiting for us when we arrived at the terminal.

"Commander Bimmy, Major Reginald Mulzac, Colonial Marines" he said and shook my hand, "you've met my father, President Jay."

"Commander Bimmy, welcome back. I apologize for the lack of hospitality. There have been developments during your transit. Michael, Thomas, welcome home. The family is eager to see you. You're to report directly to the bunker for debriefing."

"The bunker," Thomas said, "what's the threat?"

"You'll find out when you get there," the President said, "Commander Bimmy, we've arranged accommodations for you and your crew…"

"Mister President, with respect, I need to know what's happening, then I'll decide if my crew and I need accommodations."

The President glanced at Major Mulzac and raised an eyebrow. I swear I saw the beginning of a smirk before he said, "Follow me. Mike, Tommy, we'll catch up with you at the bunker."

My crew and I were led through a series of corridors, then down a stairwell into the shell of the colony. We entered a room carved from the bedrock of the moon. Down another corridor we arrived at a sealed hatch, guarded by a single soldier. He snapped to attention and saluted, then opened the hatch. We passed into a darkened room resembling the bridge of a battle cruiser, with officers and crew at their stations, and large view screens curving along the walls.

"Welcome to Deimos Control," the major said, walking ahead of us, "please don't touch anything."

President Jay slipped his arm across my shoulders and leaned down, "Please forgive my eldest, Commander Bimmy, he means no offense."

"None taken," I said.

"We are grateful for the safe return of my sons, and for the risks you took on behalf of everyone at Europa, on both sides of the line."

We followed the major into a conference room, and he motioned for us to be seated. "History-altering events have occurred while you were running silent through the belt," he began. "Commander Bimmy, you made a proposal initially viewed as absurd and naive, but it's become all the rage. We'll get to it in a minute. The catalyst for change is what's most important and placed us in our current defensive posture."

"Earth," I said, "there's been an attack on Earth."

"No way," Blake said, "how could they…"

"The commander is correct. Details are still sketchy. They used four of the Alliance ships captured at Jupiter Station, breached Earth's security perimeter, and attacked key targets on Earth and Luna. There are more Alliance ships unaccounted for, hence our current posture."

"How?" Blake asked. "Every ship has an identifier, they should have been spotted…"

"Human error, modified codes, disabled transponders, the 'how' of it is still unknown," the major said, "but we do know the 'why' of it. And we damn sure know the net result."

"Targets, Major, what did they hit? How many casualties?" I asked.

"We don't have complete information, but if early reports are accurate, I'd say they bloodied us damn good before we took out their ships. Most recent casualty count is in the five-figure range, and climbing."

"Us…you're sticking with the Alliance?" Breuger asked.

"It's an appropriate question, and the answer is…not exactly," the president replied, "Deimos, Phobos, Mars, most of the colonies, possibly Venus, we're all joining the Sol Federation."

"What the heck is the Sol Federation?" Blake asked.

"Ask your commander, it was his idea. Delegates are gathering at Phobos for talks as we speak, thanks in no small part to Mister Bimmy and the rest of you."

My crew stared at me and waited for me to speak. I looked at the president and said, "I think we'll need those accommodations."

# 13

## Alive and Well

It was hard for me to trust that people at war for over two years had declared a ceasefire and assembled to talk. That was the net result, as Major Mulzac called it, of the attack on Earth. Humans still couldn't travel at the speed of light, but news could, at least in space. While we traversed the asteroid belt, news of the battle at Europa, and our intervention, had reached every human settlement in the solar system.

Two days after the battle for Europa, in a horrific coincidence of timing, a splinter group of rebels, ardent separatists, arrived in Earth orbit and assaulted the planet. The brutality of what amounted to a suicide mission left the entire Sol system in shock, and pushed the colonists to seek peace.

The rebels feared retribution of the sort my crew and I had prevented at Europa, and rightly so. They realized they could never win, and a stalemate, for them, was now worse than losing. By the time we arrived at Deimos, the warring parties had agreed to talk. Admiral Wilson presented, for the second time, the Sol Proposal, based on our conversation in her ready room. This time, both sides were ready to listen. The first agreement was to hold those responsible for the atrocities against Earth and Europa accountable for their deeds.

We remained at Deimos for four Earth days waiting for our orders, with little news of Earth. On the fifth day, detailed reports of the attack began to arrive. For the first time since the war started, I felt real terror, not for myself, but for Becca.

She was listed as missing, presumed dead. It wasn't clear why the

University had been attacked, but the theory was simple. The enemy could see it on their targeting scans, so they destroyed it. Unlike Arcadia, the University had not implemented comprehensive blackout procedures.

The longer I went without definitive news of Becca, the more difficult it became for me to focus. I started working through old messages from her. A trove of them, both text and video, were waiting for me when we broke our comm silence over Deimos. I thought of what I would say to her, if she survived, and what I might say to her parents, if she hadn't. I considered taking the *Ajax* back to Earth to find her. Duty compelled me to stay and await my orders, but love and fear, and a growing sense of desperation, were clouding my judgement.

In her last message she was thrilled to tell me the Hoffman Institute had determined how she had ended up in the middle of the street after passing through an artificial wormhole. "It's about time," I thought. It had to do with a soliton wave experiment, something I knew nothing about. It reminded me of the day we met, and I lost myself in the memory of her, the touch of her hand, the sound of her voice, the way her face lit up when she said my name.

My comm link snapped me back to reality with an incoming call from Admiral Wilson. The first thing I noticed was her new rank, then her exhaustion.

"Commander Bimmy, it's good to see you again. I would have contacted you sooner, but I'm sure you understand, given the circumstances."

"Of course, Admiral, congratulations on your promotion."

She glanced at her shoulder and said, "It didn't come to me the way I'd hoped. I'd like to discuss it with you. I need you on Phobos, as soon as possible."

"Admiral, what about Earth, Rebecca Kiel, I need…"

"Commander Bimmy, I read your request. We're dealing with issues impacting the entire human race. I empathize with you, but I can't spare you, the future hangs in the balance…"

"With all due respect, Admiral, I see no future for me without Becca. I need to know what happened to her, one way or another. The not knowing, it's…"

"Commander Bimmy," she said, exasperated, "haven't you been tracking the daily reports? I put a flag on her name, her status changed today, this morning, Earth time…"

My hands were shaking, I tapped away at the console in front of me, but the biometric scan failed. I couldn't get my credentials correct and became frustrated.

"Charlie," she said, "take it easy, look at me."

"Yes, Admiral, my apologies, I've been reading the reports every day, my credentials aren't working…"

"Miss Kiel is alive and well, she made it to a shelter, she has minor injuries, and I'm sure being stuck underground for several days took its toll. I've been holding off ordering you to Phobos until we had definitive word. We have it, and I need you here. I assumed your request for transfer was triggered by her status change, but your reunion will have to wait."

My emotions were a jumbled mess. I was relieved Becca was okay, but the thought of her buried alive pained me. I wanted more than ever to see her again, to hold her in my arms. Two years was a lifetime to me, but knowing she would be there when I got back to Earth allowed me to focus.

"Yes, Admiral, my crew and I will be underway within the hour."

"I said as soon as possible Commander, not right this minute. There's a matter you'll need to attend to on Deimos first. The President and his family, which is most of the people on Deimos, want to show their appreciation. I'm sorry I won't be there, Major Mulzac will be my stand-in."

"I don't understand…"

"I'm promoting you. How does it feel to be the youngest captain in the history of Space Force?"

My head was spinning. "I'm not sure…thank you, Admiral, it feels good, damn good."

"Congratulations, Bimmy. Wrap up your business and get to Phobos quick as you can. You'll need a dress uniform. Send your bio scan to the quartermaster on the *Arcturus*, they'll get it sorted out by the time you arrive."

"The *Arcturus*? Has Admiral Porter's flagship been…"

"Not his ship anymore, I'll explain when you get here, Wilson out."

***

The sendoff by the people of Deimos was subdued. No one was in the mood for celebration. I appreciated the brevity of the president's speech, but didn't care for the labels he placed on me, words like 'hero' and 'harbinger of peace' and worst of all, 'Father of the Sol Federation.'

Never in my life had I felt like a hero, and I knew the body count of my battles well enough. As for the Sol Federation, having an idea was one thing, putting it into practice another.

President Jay pinned the silver eagles to my collar. "Congratulations, Captain Bimmy," he said. "I fear we'll never be able to repay the debt we owe you and your crew."

"You owe me nothing, sir. I followed my orders."

"I will decide what I owe, and to whom I owe it," he said.

He walked away as I saluted, leaving me holding my salute, unsure what to do next. Laughter rippled through the crowd, until Major Mulzac took his place and returned my salute.

"My father is not one for military customs," the Major said.

Major Mulzac attached my new epaulets to my shoulders, each with four gold stripes and a single gold star. "Youngest captain, you beat me by less than a month," he said.

"Sorry, Major."

He slapped my shoulder. "Come on, let's get this done."

I tried not to smile, and failed, then saluted. He returned the salute, then shook my hand. Blake and Breuger congratulated me, then Lieutenant Michael Jay marched forward and delivered a salute. "Congratulations Captain Bimmy, I'm looking forward to joining you on the *Ajax*."

I couldn't hide my surprise. "Welcome aboard, Lieutenant," I said and returned his salute.

When the ceremony was over, I was introduced to the president's wife, Letitia Jay. Tall, slender, deep-brown skin and thick braided hair, eyes of amber and a smile to melt iron. When she shook my hand and said, "Congratulations Captain," I blushed, which amused her. I could see then where Thomas got his looks, while Michael favored his father. "Thank you, ma'am," was my terrible reply.

"She had the same effect on me when we first met," President Jay said later, when he escorted me and my crew back to the dock. We said our farewells and boarded the *Ajax*. With Blake at the helm, we set off for Phobos, and the uncertain future of the Sol Federation.

Where Deimos was an industrial powerhouse, Phobos was the opposite, an agrarian masterwork. The closer of the two moons, it zipped around Mars three times every Martian day. Phobos was twice the size of Deimos but orbited the planet at a third of the distance from the surface, about 6100 kilometers.

The people of Phobos had built domed greenhouses to shelter their farms, without the greater gravity of Earth or the inconvenient pull of Mars. They lived on the surface, protected from radiation by vast solar installations drifting several stories above their settlement, farming energy as they farmed the soil. The soil was from Earth and Mars, enriched with other essential components from across the solar system. The moon was also an excellent launching point for the massive ice chunks tossed down onto Mars. Freighters delivered their frozen cargo to Phobos, the colony took its cut, then tossed the bulk of the ice down to the surface. It was the most inefficient, and cheapest, method of terraforming humans had yet devised.

Phobos was a wealthy colony, rich in food, energy, and the water to make life sustainable.

This 'New Eden,' as some called it, was where leaders from across the system convened to decide the future of the solar system.

We landed at a private terminal in the residential sector. All the primary sites were taken. The location would give us an opportunity to see how the people of Phobos lived.

A gangway extended from the terminal to our ship. We entered the tube and were carried along by air, pushed into the tube at one end and pulled back toward the terminal by the same system.

The colony was, in a word, astonishing. By the time we reached the commercial terminal, I had a new appreciation for the dissatisfaction of the outer colonies. Through the windows lining the airbridge, we could see the city laid out in a circular pattern intersected by transparent pressurized breezeways radiating from a central hub. The community rested beneath solar arrays fifty meters overhead, which were tethered to the surface rather than supported by beams. Some of the breezeways were larger in diameter than our ship, and all of them were lit from within by panels embedded in the floor. The gravity on the surface of Phobos was so low a person could jump off the planet with little effort. People inside moved through the air from one place to another, never touching the base beneath them. Where multiple breezeways connected, domes were built with masses of green vegetation, 10 meters high, growing at the center of each dome. There was so much greenery, I could see how they earned their nickname.

Commander Jones and a young ensign met us at the terminal.

"Captain, welcome to Phobos. Breuger, you look rather squeamish, please try not to vomit until you get to your quarters."

"Good to see you too, Jones."

"Commander Jones, thanks for meeting us," I said, "I didn't see the

*Saratoga,* are you on the *Arcturus?*"

"Things are moving fast. Admiral Wilson is waiting for you, she'll bring you up to speed. I'll be your attaché during your stay here. Follow me, we can walk and talk. Ensign Wright will show your crew to their quarters,"

"At-tat-shay," Blake mispronounced, "fancy."

"Lieutenant Blake," Jones said, "watch yourself, no one here is in the mood for your brand of humor."

"Apologies, Commander," Blake said.

We walked without talking, the tapping of our boots echoing against the gravity plates, until Ensign Wright peeled away, followed by my crew. Jones and I continued on together.

"All right, Jones, what's on your mind? I thought you and Blake were friends."

"Friendship ends where rank begins," she said.

"Is that true for us?"

She stopped and faced me. It seemed she wanted to tell me something but couldn't find the words, or was duty-bound to keep silent.

"Speak freely, Commander, it stays between us."

"After you left Europa, and Earth was attacked, the *Saratoga* was tasked with gathering the peace delegation and bringing them to Phobos."

"I'm aware."

"Truth and reconciliation," Jones said, "everyone wants peace, but the price is accountability, for the attack on Earth, and for the destruction of Europa."

"There can't be peace without justice," I said.

"Then you'll understand. Admiral Porter has been arrested. I know he was your mentor. I'm not supposed to discuss it."

At first, I was stunned, but when I considered the conversations with Admiral Porter, I saw the bigger picture. "It makes sense," I said, "the reason he gave me the *Ajax,* why Rudnev got the order to destroy Europa. He wanted me out of the way. He knew how I felt."

"In my view, he wanted you dead. He was willing to sacrifice all of us. Admiral Wilson arranged to have me on your ship. Something didn't seem right to her. Her instincts were spot on."

"That's how the pirates got the jump on us. But Wilson laid a trap for everyone, including Porter."

Jones had made up her mind. "You need to hear the rest from

Admiral Wilson. Follow me."

I met the admiral in a room near the administrative center of the colony. She was seated at a round table with a rectangular plastic box in front of her. She was speaking to someone on her comm link when I entered. She continued her conversation and motioned for me to sit. She slid the box across the table to me, waved her hand at it, and continued her call.

"I don't care what the delegate from Viridian Station wants," the Admiral said, "tell her we're all in the same boat and they'll have to make do. Wilson, out."

"Sorry, Captain Bimmy," she said with an emphasis on 'Captain.'

"Not a problem, Admiral, I know you're busy."

The box contained my new dress uniform, neatly folded inside. It was an impractical color for a uniform, bright white with light grey piping.

"I hope it fits, you'll need to wear it in a few hours."

"Is this why you wanted to see me?"

"Not entirely, there's more we need to discuss, starting with Admiral Porter. I'm sorry to tell you he's been arrested."

"For Europa," I said, "I should have seen it coming."

"He discussed his plans with you?"

"My first day on the *Arcturus*, dinner with the him and Captain Davis. Davis told me about the plan to wipe out the entire colony. When I objected, Admiral Porter asked if I'd have a problem following orders."

"I take it you said no."

"I said I would do what had to be done to win the war, but not without questioning the way we fought it. He may have taken it as a no. Neither of them objected to the answer. After Captain Davis was killed…"

"Porter went to great lengths to place his people in key positions across the fleet. Europa was his first target, but he had others in mind. After you stopped Captain Rudnev, the plan started to unravel. I had my suspicions, but it took a few good officers, like you, to bring the full truth to light."

"Did Admiral Porter set us up to get killed? Did he even care about the Jay brothers?"

"I don't know. He told me you were meant to be a distraction, a decoy for Alliance and enemy ships alike. He also insisted he had nothing to do with the nuke. Cheng's forces hit you with an Alliance-made neutron weapon, designed to disable a ship without destroying it. Whatever Porter's intent, I doubt Grace Cheng would keep a captured Alliance crew alive. Your stunt with the airlock took everyone by surprise. For the record, Captain, don't ever do it again, at least not while I'm watching."

"I'll do my best," I said. "How did the pirates know where we would be? They weren't expected to engage until we gave away our position. It's a one in a billion shot to meet us like they did."

"That's the more difficult aspect of this conversation," she replied. "Your crew was compromised from the start. Soji was Porter's man."

"Soji gave us away…"

"Yes, afraid so. There's more. Blake and Soji were in a relationship. It ended weeks before your mission, on bad terms. Bad luck you chose her for the mission."

"Was she involved in the plot?"

"There's no evidence, but I'm reassigning her all the same. I need shuttle pilots, and I think you know she's one of the best."

"Depends on how you define best," I said.

"Indeed. Let's talk about more urgent matters. You need to look sharp and be on your toes. I've assigned you to the Venusian delegation for the opening ceremonies tonight. This is a diplomatic mission. They need some persuading to join the Sol Federation, and you're the person for the job."

"Why me?"

"Because I told them this was your idea."

"I'm no diplomat…"

"You're a natural. Be yourself, you'll do fine. They didn't come all this way to go home empty-handed. Find out what they want and get them to come around."

"Then what," I asked, "it's been a long time since I saw home."

"I'm sorry Bimmy, no, I've got another mission for you and the *Ajax*. When you're finished, I'll authorize three months leave, it's the best I can do. The war might be over, if the talks go well. If it is, then we start the next phase, winning the peace."

I thought about what I would do with three months on Earth, how I could spend the time, if I survived long enough to spend it.

"What's the mission?"

"Two of our stolen battle cruisers from Jupiter Station are still out there. The delegation from Europa assures me the mastermind of the attack on Earth is on one of those ships. You're to hunt them down and destroy them, capture the crews if you can, but your priority is to eliminate the threat. As long as those ships are out there, we're still at war."

"That's a tall order for one ship. They could be anywhere."

"Not anywhere. Jupiter, hiding with Cheng's fleet, plotting who knows what. I'll send you all the intel we have so far."

My odds of seeing Becca again were worsening by the second. "Admiral, I'm an optimist but even I think this is suicide. One ship, against a fleet, I don't see how it can be done."

"We're upgrading the *Ajax*," she said, "stripping the cloaking mechanism from one of my ships and installing it in yours. You'll be invisible, they'll never see you coming. Get in, destroy the ships, get out, then you're homeward bound."

I hadn't considered the option of upgrading the *Ajax*.

"A cloak will be useful. Anything else you can spare?"

"Don't push it, Captain, you've already got the best attack ship in the fleet."

After my meeting with Admiral Wilson, Jones showed me to my quarters and left me to rest until the evening's events. I watched a message from Becca and was sad to hear about the deteriorating conditions in Arcadia. My parents' messages never mentioned the changes there, probably to spare me the worry. Before I left Deimos, I'd sent Becca a message of my own, with questions about soliton waves and their connection to her errant trip through a wormhole. Her response included a paper published by the scientists who'd made the discovery, which I decided to read at some later date.

Moving around Phobos took some getting used to, given the limited use of gravity plates. Few walked, and those who did were usually weighed down by equipment. You drifted from place to place, using a bounce-float technique. If you put too much into the effort you'd tumble, or flip, or crash into the ceiling. Many of the corridors employed the same air movement technology used in the airbridge, simplifying the process. Once I got the hang of it, I decided it was a fine way to get around, even if I did bump into things along the way.

I met Jones outside a theater converted into a conference hall for the peace talks. When I came to a stop a few paces away, she grinned and said, "Not bad, Captain, it takes most people days to acclimate to Phobos. You look like an old hand at this."

"Can it with the flattery Commander, I know I look ridiculous. Please, tell me they've got gravity plates inside."

"Once you're inside, it's wall-to-wall Earth G."

"Great, let's get in there before I hit the ceiling again."

The theater was another domed structure with a round stage at the center. A screen bisected the room. On our side, tables had been arranged in concentric semi-circles around the stage. Other delegates, officials, military personnel and the like all flowed into the room with us, seeking their tables, stopping to speak with attendees they knew, or wanted to meet. It was a noisy affair while the tables were filling up.

I was expecting a dozen delegates from Venus, not the single individual who greeted Jones and I when we approached their table. I looked at Jones who shrugged and proceeded with the introduction.

"Ambassador Arthur Gorman, this is Captain Charles Bimmy. I'm Commander Rachel Jones."

"It's an honor to meet you, Captain Bimmy," the Ambassador said and extended his hand.

"The honor is mine, Ambassador."

"Please, call me Arthur. Have a seat."

"As you wish, Arthur. My friends call me Bimmy," I said.

The Ambassador pulled out a chair for Rachel and waved his hand over it.

"That would make me Rachel," Jones said, taking her seat, "thank you, Arthur."

We were all seated on the same side of the table, the Ambassador between Jones and me, facing the stage. A lectern stood on the stage, flanked by the proposed new flag of the Sol Federation. It was a simple design, an iridescent sunburst on a field of black, signifying our commonality as citizens of the solar system.

"Are you enjoying your visit to Phobos?" the Ambassador asked.

"Yes, it's an interesting place, and you?"

"It is, as you say, interesting. The gardens are quite nice, but I miss the warmth of the sun, the beauty of the clouds, and if I'm being honest, the gravity. Have you ever visited Venusia?"

"No, but I've read about it. I'm especially interested in the ballast technology you use to maintain your floating structures..."

"And what about you Rachel, have you ever been to Venusia?"

"Yes, I have, many times. My mother was stationed on Mercury. We spent our holidays in Venusia, and a few days on Venus once."

"Wonderful," the Ambassador said, "it is rare to meet someone like you, we get so few visitors to our world. Captain, you must come for a visit, you will be my guest. I'll see to it you have an engineering tour. I know nothing of how our cities stay afloat on the atmosphere. I'm of no use for such things."

"Thank you, Arthur. If I ever have the chance, I'll be sure to pay you a visit."

"Excellent, I will count the days," he replied.

"Arthur," Jones said, "I thought there were more Venusians in your party. I'm surprised to see you alone."

"Oh no," he said, "it's me and the crew of my ship. They have no interest in affairs such as this. They're getting a tour of their own, inspecting the solar array."

We waited for the Ambassador to keep the conversation flowing. When he didn't, I tested the waters with a more relevant question.

"Ambassador Gorman…," I began.

"Arthur…" he replied.

"Arthur," I said, "Venusia has a history of neutrality, which I respect. I question why your colony sent you, unless there's been a change in your leadership's position."

"We're getting right to it, are we?"

"I think Captain Bimmy is trying to keep the conversation lively," Jones said.

"I'd like to discuss it before they start serving food and making speeches. I apologize if I've offended you. I'm not a diplomat. I think Venusian membership in the Federation is critical. In the interest of transparency, my job is to figure out what Venusia wants and how we can make it happen."

"Captain Bimmy, we Venusians respect directness in negotiations. I will be direct with you. Venusia's needs are simple: we want Mercury. Secure the charter and we'll join the Sol Federation, deny us the charter, and we will remain independent."

"You can't be serious," Rachel said.

"Is Mercury so precious?" the Ambassador asked.

"What the Commander means is there's nothing there but a shuttered military outpost and the remnants of a failed mining operation. It's hard to imagine why you'd want it. It's where dreams go to die, if you ask me."

"What a fantastic turn of phrase, Captain Bimmy. Our purpose has nothing to do with dreams. My people have devised a novel way to exploit Mercury. We would start by blanketing it with solar arrays, much like the array above us."

"Then why not go ahead and do it?" Jones asked.

"The simple answer is we're risk averse. We don't want to make an investment without a charter. More importantly, Mercury has a problem we cannot solve. Our membership in the Sol Federation is predicated on control of Mercury, but we can't occupy the planet by force. Since the Second Marauder war, we've had no military of our own."

"I told you there's nothing there. The base was abandoned a year after the mining colony failed, there's no military presence…"

"But there is, I have seen the images myself. Two Earth Alliance ships, and quite a few civilian ones, have taken up residence there. They're repairing the base. Either your government is keeping secrets from you, or the right hand has lost track of the left."

I looked at Jones, then back at the Ambassador, "Ambassador Gorman, you'll get your charter, you have my word."

I stood and shook hands with the Ambassador. "I apologize, I have to leave, Commander Jones will take it from here," I said, then left before Jones could protest.

If the admiral's intelligence reports placed the stolen ships near Jupiter while they were in fact on the other side of the system, setting up a base on Mercury, someone was feeding her false information and Earth was still in grave danger.

Like she'd said, until the ships were captured or destroyed, we were still at war.

# 14

# A Generous Gift

"You overstepped on this one, Bimmy," the admiral said, "giving away a planet falls a bit outside the authority of a ship's captain."

"Stones and birds," I said, "we take out the ships, the Venusians believe we did it for them, the Sol Federation gets its newest member."

"Do you honestly think they don't know those ships are rebel controlled? Think about it..."

"Not the point. He handed us those ships despite Venusia's neutrality. You can send a battle group and..."

She started entering commands in a screen embedded in the wall. "No can do, Captain, this is still your mission. Consider the alignment. The *Ajax* can get there before any ships we send from the Earth. Look," she said, as a course plotted out on the screen, "we're here, Earth is moving away, Mercury is doing its regular zippy run around the sun, if you leave in the next...nine hours, you'll be in Mercury orbit a full three weeks before a ship from Earth can get there. You've got the fastest ship in the fleet and the shortest trajectory to Mercury."

"There are bound to be some of Cheng's ships there, too. We need more than the *Ajax* to take them on..."

"You want me to pull a few battle cruisers away from the most important peace conference in human history on one man's word? I won't do it. Your mission is to hunt down those ships, wherever they are. I'll gamble this time, but if the ships aren't there..."

"If the ships aren't there, we have bigger problems. If Gorman is lying to us, then there's more at play here."

"If he's telling the truth, we have a spy in the intelligence network, or a fool," she said. "Either way, you're going to Mercury."

"Any chance I can get a couple of those neutrino weapons?"

"Absolutely not, the last thing we need is more nukes moving around the system."

I stared at the course plot glowing on the screen behind the admiral. "Where are those weapons stored?"

"Luna," she said.

"And how did one end up in the hands of a pirate?"

"We're still working it out."

"The nukes would have had to get to Cheng before we left Deimos. If we start from there and work back…" I started tapping commands into the screen. "This is the alignment when the *Ajax* left for Europa. Let's assume the weapons were on a ship in the armada. If we step back in time, they'd have to be dropped off along the way, then picked up after our ships moved on. Can you overlay the ship movements…"

"I see where you're going," she said. She entered time parameters and the course of the armada prior to the first attack by Cheng's forces.

"Nothing," I said, "not a single ship dropped out of formation, no ships joined. It's a dead end."

"Don't be so quick, let's try going forward to the attack. The *Arcturus* tracked every ship in the armada right up until the bridge was destroyed."

The display lit up as the attack played out. "Got it, right there, that's our bandit." She pointed at a ship identifier moving away from the battle. "The *Emerson*, it's a recycler, glorified garbage can," she said, "perfect place to hide a few bombs."

On screen, the *Emerson* reversed course and headed back toward the armada as an unmarked ship approached and came to a stop at the same coordinates. It held position for several minutes, then sped away when the *Arcturus* unleashed its firestorm of missiles and plasma.

"How many are we dealing with?"

"Inventory check says a total of three went missing." She opened the *Emerson's* personnel dossier. "I'll be damned, the captain is Eliza Franklin. She's a civilian contractor, married to Kendall Franklin. Mister Franklin happens to be the intel officer who thinks we should be heading to Jupiter."

"We've got more than one conspiracy on our hands," I said. "How can we exploit this?"

"I like the way you think. First order of business, we leak news of your mission to Jupiter, standard disinformation campaign, then we get you on your way to Mercury. You start prepping for your mission, leave the rest to me."

"Will do, Admiral. Where's the *Emerson* now?"

She tapped at the screen and the ship's location appeared.

"They've left the armada, let's see what course…"

"It may say Earth," I said when the ship's flight plan was displayed, "but the course they're on won't take them anywhere near Earth. It looks like they're heading to…"

"Mercury," the Admiral said. "Gorman speaks the truth. They'll have nukes, two Alliance ships, and a planet all to themselves.

"This is gonna get messy," I said. "I'm short a crew member, who can you spare?"

"This new data changes the situation. Gorman and Mercury, it's more than a rumor. You'll need more ships, not more crew."

"I disagree," I said. "This makes it easier."

"Explain."

"We know where they are. We commandeer the *Emerson*, and the nukes, then remote pilot the freighter into orbit and nuke Mercury, problem solved."

"What about the ships?"

"I need to think about it, but my hunch is most of the crew will be on the planet, not on the ships. Colonists tend to prefer terra firma."

"Bimmy, if you pull this off there'll be a medal in it for you, probably another promotion."

"I'm not in it for those," I said. "I want to end this and go home to my family. But I'd like to promote Breuger. It's overdue."

"I'll start the process today, anything else?"

"Crew," I said, "I need one more. Who can you spare?"

"I'll find someone, what else?"

"I'd like to raid your ship's armory, if you don't mind."

"Your ship is being re-armed, you'll be fully loaded by the time you leave."

"It's not the ship I want to arm, it's the crew."

***

The last thing I wanted was to pull Commander Jones from her assignment on the Fleet Admiral's staff, but when she reported to the

*Ajax* with a crate of firearms in tow, I was pleased on both counts. I needed crew members I could trust, and ships like ours didn't carry much by way of assault weapons. Weapons we would need if we hoped to take the *Emerson*.

"Welcome back, Commander Jones," Breuger said. "Did you miss us?"

"No," she said, "but I missed this ship. I've always dreamed of spending my career on a tiny little attack boat."

"For the record," I said, "when I said I needed more crew I did not name names, but I'm glad the admiral chose you. Welcome aboard."

Jones leaned in and whispered, "Don't tell Breuger, I volunteered."

"My lips are sealed," I replied.

"I come bearing gifts," she said aloud. "Where do you want these?"

"Lieutenant Jay, if you please," I said.

"Yes, sir," the lieutenant said. "Nice to see you again, Commander." He took the crate from Jones and headed aft.

"Likewise," Jones replied. She watched him leave the bridge then asked, "How much do you trust him?"

"Enough to keep him on my crew."

"Good enough for me."

A few hours later, we were underway to a refueling stop at Deimos to build our cover story. Major Mulzac was waiting for us at the orbital fuel depot. He boarded the ship while our propellant was topped off and presented me with a package. He carried a duffle bag with him.

"A gift from my parents," he said. "They heard you played."

I opened the case and was impressed by the quality of the chess set. The board was metal, the pieces were stone, with magnets embedded in the base of each piece. After countless matches against the ship's computer, I enjoyed the feel of the pieces, to have a board in front of me again. "This is a generous gift, please thank your parents for me."

"They would be grateful if you could win a few matches against my brother. He's got it in his head he's a grand master."

"I'll see what I can do."

"I've never been on one of these ships, can you point me in the direction of my quarters?"

"Quarters...?"

"I know your mission, you need me."

"What do you know?"

"Admiral Wilson briefed me after you left Phobos. You have no experience in boarding ships. The mission you've taken on requires more specialized skills. When it comes time to board the freighter, with your permission, I'll take the lead."

"We risked life and limb to get two Jay sons out of harm's way and we're taking two back into the fight. How do your parents feel about this?"

"I'm too old to worry about it, but if you don't mind me being direct, my father feels a lot better about this mission with me on it than without. I'd prefer to have more marines, but I've managed this with two soldiers before."

"All right, Major, I have a condition. Once we're underway you'll train the rest of us. We'll take the freighter together or we won't take it at all, agreed?"

"Agreed. Quarters?"

I pointed at three stripes running horizontally along the port side of the corridor. "Red will take you to engineering and the armory, gold will take you to the bridge, and green will get you to the staterooms. Last hatch on starboard is all yours. Welcome aboard, Major."

The major paused before heading into the main deck of the ship and said, "Captain Bimmy, I think it would be better for both of us if you called me Reggie, or Mulzac if you like, for the duration of the mission. The crew needs to know you're in charge."

"The crew knows who runs the ship, but I'll think on it and let you know where I land."

The major grinned and shook his head, "My father was right about you, you've got layers," he said.

We departed Deimos using a standard vector toward a Mainzer Transit. Once out of visual range, we engaged our new cloak. It distorted the visuals on our main viewer and killed our comms and sensors, a simple way to know it was working.

"Let me get this straight," Breuger said. "We are invisible, but we are also blind and mute."

"It would seem so."

"I don't like it," he said.

"You'll get used to it," Jones said, "adjust the refresh rate on the view screen, it will clear up the distortion." Breuger made the adjustment and the screen stabilized.

"I'm sending you a course change, Mister Jay," I said, and tapped my comm link to send him the new data. When he plotted the coordinates and the route appeared on his screen he pushed away from his console and turned around to face me.

"Captain," he said, "it's the wrong direction and ends at nowhere. Do you mind explaining?"

"It's some good news, and some bad. The good news, we know the location of our targets. They're at Mercury. The bad news, they've got a contingent of Cheng's forces with them. We're setting an intercept course for a freighter. It has two nukes in its hold, and we mean to take the ship, intact if possible. If not, we destroy it then move on to Mercury. Our primary mission is to destroy the captured alliance ships, and anyone who tries to stop us. The nukes should make quick work of it."

"We're deploying nukes? On Mercury?" Lieutenant Jay asked. "Reggie, did you know about this?"

The major looked at me before he responded. I nodded my approval and he replied to his brother. "I've been briefed. We will take the freighter and deploy the neutrino weapons as planned, preferably in space, but planet-side if necessary. I've spent my career driving pirates out of the inner system, I'm not about to let them gain a new foothold. Those rebels are refitting the station on Mercury, they're planning to stay, and they're acquiring nuclear weapons. Our mission is to stop them, by whatever means are necessary. The captain has asked me to train all of you in close-quarter combat. We begin at oh-eight-hundred."

"Any more questions?" I asked. When no one spoke up, I continued, "Lieutenant, lock in the course. We've got a narrow window to catch our quarry, and without comms we won't know until we get there if they stayed their course. Until we get where we're going, we run silent, we run dark, understood? Jones, you have the con."

I left the bridge and went to my quarters. I was desperate for some down time. First, I read a message from my parents, and finally one from Becca. Becca's message made me laugh, so perfect in its directness.

> *Charlie,*
> *Did you review the research?*
> *Still waiting for your thoughts on soliton waves.*
> *Love, Becca*

# 15

# No Accounting for Luck

"All stop! Bimmy, you're dead, mission fail."

By our fifth day of combat training, I'd been killed twice. I sensed the major was getting tired of me dying so frequently.

"You stepped into Breuger's line of fire," he said. "When we move forward, if you hear 'advance' it means stay in your lane of approach. If you have to cross the corridor to get to cover on your left, the command is 'Moving left, cover' and you keep your butt in place until you hear the response, 'covering.' Got it?"

"Yes, got it, sorry Major."

"Don't be sorry, Bimmy, be alive. Okay, let's reset. Defenders, you are attackers, switch positions and do it again."

I wasn't alone in getting killed. We'd all had weapons training, but never practiced commandeering a ship. Sometimes you don't know what you need until you need it.

Lieutenant Jay and I began playing chess in the ship's wardroom at the end of our shift. We had the wardroom to ourselves most of the time. Breuger joined us once and watched our chess match until he left the room mumbling about watching paint dry.

Michael was talkative at first, but after losing our first three matches he became laser focused. It was interesting to see how a person's ego could cloud their judgement. I thought about how others viewed me, and if I was any different from the lieutenant when you got down to it. I was tempted to let him win our fourth match but decided a cheap win was worse than a fair loss. It was the right choice. By the time we played our thirteenth match, we were at six wins each. On its surface, chess appears quiet and introspective; in reality, there's a war seething below.

When he attempted the gambit I had used against my father years earlier, I tried to give him a second chance. "You sure you want to do that?" I asked.

"No psych games, Bimmy, not gonna fall for it. Your move."

"As you wish," I said, then moved my knight, capturing his pawn.

"You're going down, Captain," he said with complete confidence.

He made the move I expected. I sent my bishop into the fray and said, "Checkmate."

His reaction was similar to what mine had been. The mistake was easy to see after it happened, but hard to see coming.

"What the hell happened?" he said. "I had you."

"You play chess the way I train for combat, reckless," I said, laughing. "But don't let this one get you down. I made the same mistake once and got the same result. It's the twin oblique angles, the mind has a hard time visualizing the move."

"Yeah," he said, still perplexed. "You'd think I'd never played before. When you took my pawn, I didn't notice the lane you made for your bishop, I was so focused on your queen."

"Exactly what happened to me," I said. "Same time tomorrow?"

"I think my parents gave this to you to torture me."

He was laughing, but I was hardly listening anymore. A thought was tickling the back of my mind, scratching for attention. My brain latched onto something and wouldn't let it go.

"Bimmy, are you okay? Was it something I said?"

"I'm fine…Michael, what do you know about wormholes?"

"Wormholes? That's easy, you ever see one, stay away from it. Done. But they don't exist, so why worry about it?"

"That's up for debate, but they can be created. My girlfriend went through one when we were kids. They're called Einstein–Rosen Bridges, but I like wormhole better. Her parents invented a machine able to connect two places…"

"I've heard of it, but you're talking about E–R bridges after you beat me at chess, what's the connection?"

"Becca went through a wormhole, thinking she would end up at the location of the receiving device. But she didn't, she ended up in the center of town, in the middle of the street. They spent years trying to figure out how it happened, and how to reproduce it. They finally got the first part sorted out, a soliton wave experiment near the receiving device, but they never tried to reproduce the accident."

"If memory serves, those things have extreme resource demands, the materials, the energy, they can barely move one person. It's interesting tech, but it doesn't scale."

"Your information is out of date. It does scale, but they've been looking at it all wrong. Becca sent me the research and she's been after me to discuss it. I finally got around to reading it. I might have an idea how to open a wormhole, send a ship through it, and end up wherever you want to go. It's been right in front of me all this time."

"I'm not seeing it."

"It's like the oblique angles, the knight and bishop's moves, you open a door and propel yourself through it. It's not obvious until it's obvious."

"What are you going to with this inspiration?"

"Nothing. I mean, I'm going to read all I can about soliton waves and gravity drives and wormholes. Becca is constantly sending me material to study. She keeps me on my toes. But this is a side show. Whether I'm right about this idea or wrong, I've got to stay focused on the mission. But if we get through this, I'm going to dig into this idea, soon as I can."

"Not if, Captain Bimmy, when."

"You're right, *when* we get through this."

***

We arrived at our intercept point, de-cloaked long enough to establish a comm link with a relay satellite and send a data burst, then went dark again. Eight hours later, our target came into view, right on time. In relative terms, it was a close call. I didn't like the short window, but if anyone had been listening when we broadcast, it would have looked like a transient radio burst, something most freighter captains would ignore. True to form, the freighter continued on its route.

Our cloaking mechanism prevented us from using our sensor array, which meant I had no way of knowing if the nukes were on the *Emerson*. My gut told me they were there, and I would have to risk the lives of my crew to get them.

"Major Mulzac, contact in ten minutes. Breuger, line us up with their trajectory and start bringing us in. Jones, Jay, get ready."

Our plan was as simple as we could make it. Move in close, take out their electrical systems with an EMP strike, hook the freighter with our grapples, and board the ship. Once hooked, the cables would go rigid and keep the ships at a fixed distance. It wasn't much different from taking a ship on the high seas of ancient Earth, except space ships tended to explode when they collided. If the EMP did its job, the enemy's ship would go into an emergency shutdown and lock down the engines. They'd be fish in a barrel.

Mulzac, Jones, and Jay were suited up and stationed in the cargo bay airlock. Breuger maneuvered the *Ajax* and had us running a parallel course. He matched the speed of the *Emerson* and started closing the gap between the ships. I moved to the tactical station and prepared to fire on the freighter.

The pulse weapon took ten seconds to charge. "Firing in three, two, one, firing, firing, firing," I said, and sent the weapon on its way. It struck the freighter, and the running lights of the ship went out. Its engines continued to burn for a few seconds, then shut down as expected.

"Firing grapple." Four harpoons shot out from our ship and sunk their teeth into the freighter's spine.

"Go, go, go," I heard Mulzac shouting over the radio in his helmet.

"Breuger, kill the cloak, I need sensors," I said.

The cloak dropped and Breuger adjusted the main view screen. The assault team was halfway across the cables, moving toward the target. I punched up the sensor array and swept the freighter, scanning for the neutrino signature. Until then, I feared we wouldn't find the weapons. Instead, I was horrified to discover the ship had not two, but twenty nuclear weapons in its hold.

"They can't go blasting away in there," Breuger said.

"There's no turning back," I replied. "Mulzac, do you read? The birds are in the nest, and they've got lots of company."

"How much company?" he replied.

"Twenty, repeat, twenty birds in the nest."

"How many crew?" Mulzac asked.

"I'm reading four life signs...."

"Do we abort or go forward," Jones asked.

Before I could reply Major Mulzac spoke up.

"We keep going."

"Captain?" Jones asked.

"He's right, keep going."

"We're being hailed," Breuger said, "they want to talk."

"How? We took out their systems, comms shouldn't be working…"

"It's shortwave, I think I can clean up the audio…"

"Give me thermal imaging first, I want to see what's happening over there."

Thermal imaging lacked fine detail, but it enabled me to watch the movement of everyone on the ship. Once I had a view into the freighter, I was ready to talk.

"Do it, open the comm."

Initially there was only static, then I heard a woman's voice pleading with us, "…of the *Emerson*, we are unarmed, I repeat, this is Captain Eliza Franklin of the *Emerson*, we are an unarmed civilian ship, hold your fire."

"Captain Franklin, this is Captain Charles Bimmy, stand down and prepare to be boarded. If your crew resists, we will open fire."

"We will not resist," she said. "Captain Bimmy, you've no doubt scanned our ship, you know our cargo. If you open fire, you'll kill us all. You have my word, we will not resist."

I made a motion for Breuger to silence the comm with the freighter.

"Major?"

"Yeah, I heard her. I don't believe it for a second. Have her open airlock three, then watch the crew. If they don't move, we might be okay. If they gather at the airlock, they're getting ready for a fight."

"Standby," I said, and nodded at Breuger to reopen the channel.

"Captain Franklin, open your airlock number three, let my team in, then we'll talk about your cargo."

"Opening airlock three, it'll take time without power…"

"You have five minutes to comply or we'll cut our way in."

"Understood."

I monitored the freighter's occupants and saw one crew member working to open the airlock. Two more moved aft from the bridge to join the one already in place.

"Mulzac, looks like a greeting party at the airlock, three crew, one still on the bridge."

"They want to fight, we're about to breach the outer door."

"Breaching the door…we're inside the lock…Mikey, secure the outer door, Jones, help me with this thing…breaching inner door…"

The freighter crew held their position at the airlock. Mulzac's gambit was paying off. He and the team entered the ship through a lock adjacent to the aft cargo deck. The assault team was inside the freighter and taking up position in the cargo bay before the crew was aware their ship had been boarded.

Our team ditched their pressure suits and made their way forward, passing through the hold containing the twenty nukes. The *Emerson's* crew still hadn't caught on. Once Mulzac got his team far enough forward, the bombs would be shielded from the fight.

"Breuger, get Franklin back, let's keep her distracted," I said.

"Comm is up."

"Captain Franklin..."

"Where is your boarding party, the lock is open," she said.

"It's slow going, they're on their way. Captain Franklin, I have to ask, what are you doing with a ship full of nukes? It doesn't seem wise..."

"What would you have me do, drop 'em off at Luna?"

"Yes, I'd prefer they go back where they came from, not to some..."

Before I could finish, the freighter's crew moved aft from their position at the airlock and opened fire. One of our team fell back while the others moved forward, then stalled. The crew of the *Emerson* wasn't backing down.

"You bastard," Franklin scream, "you hurt my family and I'll take us all out!"

"Tell your people to stand down, no one needs to get hurt."

"We've got you outnumbered and out gunned. You want those nukes, come over and get 'em yourself."

"She's gone, comm is out," Breuger said.

"She's joining the fight," I said, "I need to get over there. If we don't come back, put some space between you and their ship, then destroy it. Those weapons cannot..."

"Understood, destroy the ship, yes sir."

I hurried to the airlock and donned my suit. I grabbed a plasma rifle, strapped it into place, then exited the lock.

"Breuger, status," I said.

"The team is falling back, enemy closing, I think Jones is down. They're moving aft, toward..."

"Where's the crew now?"

"Ten meters aft of the lock and moving. Our team has taken up position inside the cargo bay..."

"How many?"

"I count four, their entire crew, the bridge is empty."

I made my way across a cable and grabbed onto the freighter's hull. I pulled myself into the open outer door of airlock three and when the chamber was pressurized, I opened the inner door. I drifted into dim light, broken by flashes of weapons fire.

The *Emerson's* crew had no idea I was behind them. I had a clear shot at two of them, a woman and a young man. I took aim at her and fired, then fired as many blasts at the other crew as I could before pulling myself back into the airlock. I crouched in the lock and waited, then leaned out when the shooting stopped.

The major looked at me from the end of the corridor, his face grim. "What did I tell you about fighting in your suit Bimmy?"

I opened my visor, "Don't do it, there's no way to hide in these things."

"There's no accounting for luck," he said, "come see what we've done."

I floated the length of the corridor and looked down at the bodies crumpled on the deck. One of my shots had struck the young man in the back, leaving a bloody smoldering hole through his body. My first shot at Captain Franklin struck her in the head, burning much of her skull away. I felt bile rising in my throat and turned away. I began to vomit through the open visor of my suit, with enough force to splatter the deck and the interior of my suit with bile, and the remnants of my last meal, some of which remained suspended in air, drifting away from me.

"Another reason not to fight in a suit," Mulzac said.

When I stopped retching, I avoided looking at the other bodies. "Where's Jones?"

"Cargo hold, wounded, Michael is looking after her," he replied, "come with me, we've got more work to do."

***

On the bridge of the *Emerson*, we began restarting the ship's systems while Breuger docked the *Ajax* to the freighter. Lieutenant Jay helped Commander Jones back to our ship. Breuger then joined us on the bridge of the freighter.

"This is a fine ship," he said, "I didn't know freighters did so well."

"They don't do this good," Mulzac said, "makes you wonder if they're true believers or everyday profiteers."

"They chose a side," I said. "They chose themselves, their family, if their hearts weren't with the rebels, who cares? Whatever their reason, they didn't choose our side. They would have killed us if we didn't kill them. It's all I need to know."

We worked in silence until the ship started coming back to life.

"Breuger," the major said, "come with me, there's some unfinished business…"

"No," I said, "remote access is our priority. Breuger stays here, I'll go with you."

We returned to the scene of the battle and checked the cargo of neutrino weapons for damage. When we finished, finding none of the bombs had been hit during the battle, I found myself standing over the bodies of the captain and the young man I shot. The major helped me move them next to the other dead crew. We wrapped them in tarps, then placed them in a storage compartment. It served no purpose. The bodies would be destroyed with the ship when we got to Mercury, but I wanted to afford their remains some degree of dignity. I also didn't want to look at them anymore, to be reminded of what I'd done. It was gruesome work, but I didn't get sick again.

"How you holdin' up, Bimmy?" the major asked.

"I'm fine," I said, "I don't know what happened to me before…"

"It's normal," he said, "happens to most the first time."

"It's not my first time."

Mulzac stopped working, waiting for me to continue.

"I was thirteen," I said, "I was attacked, I defended myself. I didn't wait around to watch him die, but there's no doubt I killed him."

The major didn't respond.

"Don't judge me for what the world made me do," I said

He looked at me for moment, then took in a deep breath. "Charlie," he replied, "I'm sorry it happened to you. No kid should have to fight for their life. Anyone who judges you for defending yourself, they're wrong, plain and simple."

I turned away from him and said, "Reggie…I'm sick of it all, the killing, the loss, the fear, I've had enough to last me two lifetimes. I want to be done with this war. All I ever wanted was a life that meant something, had more to it than fighting to survive. Every time I think I've found one, the universe lines up against me."

I felt his hand grip my shoulder, and I didn't pull away.

"It's all right, Charlie. You have every right to feel this way. It's easy for people to forget how young you are, how much has been asked of you. I've been exactly where you are, more often than I want to admit. I've been at this nasty business for a long time. I look at you, and I see a kind and decent human being, I see a young man who has risen to every challenge he's ever faced. It's an honor to serve with you."

The steady pressure of his hand at my shoulder calmed me. "Thank you, Reggie, it means…"

Before I could finish, Breuger's voice boomed out over the ship's comm system, "Captain to the bridge, we've got two ships inbound, no transponders, but they've got Alliance signatures."

Major Mulzac dropped his hand from my shoulder and I turned around. There was nothing more to say, but the moment changed our relationship. I felt like I had gained a brother. I acknowledged his support with a nod of my head, then we went to the bridge.

"How long?" I asked Breuger when we arrived at the freighter's command deck.

"Ninety minutes. I was working on the remote, I didn't look at the long-range scanner. I'm sorry, I…"

"No apologies, Breuger, what's our status?"

"Remote access is ready on this side, I've got work to do on the *Ajax*, I need ten minutes."

"We could ditch the freighter and move the weapons…"

"Not enough time, we can't transfer all the weapons to the *Ajax*," Reggie said, "we'll have to destroy the ship, let the enemy get close and set off the entire load of nukes."

"Light up twenty neutrino bombs all at once, we'd never survive," I said. "There's no way this day is going be our last, there's got to be…"

"Domino effect," Breuger said. "We turn tail and run, but we drop a nuke every few thousand meters. When we get to the last one in the hold, we leave it and get back to the Ajax. We blow up the ship and it sets off a chain reaction while we head in the opposite direction. The worst we get is no worse than we've already had, but the other guys, they get the full…"

"It's space, Breuger, the shockwaves are omnidirectional. But you're right, they'll be in the middle of the mess, and we'll have a chance to make a getaway."

"I do not like this plan," I said, "but I like it better than the alternative. I'll stay here, offload the cargo, while you remote pilot from the *Ajax*. Once the job is done, I'll go EV and you can scoop me up."

"This is my side of the mission. I'll stay back and offload the bombs," Reggie replied.

"Are you pulling rank on me, Major?"

"Have you ever used a loader-skin, in a pressure suit?"

"What's a loader-skin?"

"If you don't know, I don't need to pull rank."

"Point taken. Breuger, get back to the *Ajax* and get to work. Reggie, I'll help you get suited up."

Twenty minutes later, I was back on the *Ajax*. I went to the infirmary to check on Jones. I slid the door open and found Breuger kneeling beside her, one hand touching her face, the other holding her hand. She looked at me, and I could see she had been crying. Breuger lurched to his feet and began stammering, "Captain, uh, sir, I, we…"

"As you were Lieutenant, I should have knocked."

I slid the door shut and went to the bridge. I didn't care about the nature of their relationship, it was none of my business. Jones was too injured to report for duty, they might as well have a moment before we started setting off nuclear explosions in space. I took my seat on the bridge, and Breuger soon followed.

"Breuger, retract the dock. Reggie, comm check," I said.

"Comms good," he replied.

"We're ready over here," I said.

"Roger that, I'm all set, let's go."

"Dock is in," Breuger said.

"Put the freighter on heading one-eight-seven, match our plane, maximum speed."

"Firing maneuvering thrusters, bring the freighter around to one-eight-seven."

"Lieutenant Jay, steady course and speed, as soon as the major is back onboard, cloak the ship."

"Yes, Captain."

"Look sharp boys, here we go."

***

Our speed made it difficult for Reggie to eject the bombs from the hold at regular intervals. We had to slow down. Then the unexpected happened. The enemy ships arrived at the first bomb drifting in our wake and stopped to pick it up.

"Lieutenant Jay, what's our count?" I asked

"Number seventeen is up next."

"Last one Reggie, drop it and get off the ship."

"I can make it," he said.

The strain in his voice and his heavy breathing told me the task was wearing him down.

"Your side of the mission is over, Major. We won't have time to pick you up if we keep at this, drop seventeen and get out of there."

"I was thinkin," he said through ragged breaths, "we should keep one of these, you know, in case…"

"Check your oxygen, I think you might be getting low."

"They're not big, I can carry it with me."

I silenced the comm and looked at the Major's younger brother.

"Is he okay?" I asked.

"He gets like this when things get hairy. Says humor eases the stress."

"He's being funny, he's not serious?"

"It's a fine line with him, you should probably ask."

I reopened the comm and said, "If you seriously want to bring one of those with you, you should plan to bunk with it. I don't want in my cargo hold."

"I've slept with worse," he said.

"I didn't need to hear that," I said.

"Seventeen is away, I'm leaving the ship, don't forget to catch me."

"Get him on screen, Breuger. Lieutenant Jay, deploy the grip."

Reggie burst forth from the open cargo bay of the freighter, tumbling head over heels through space. He was still in the loader-skin, he must have run across the gravity plates of the cargo deck and shut down the suit as he reached the opening. His timing was perfect, but his motion wasn't. A jet of white propellant spewed out from the suit, reducing his rapid tumble to a manageable slow roll.

The grip was like a tiny spaceship, it could be remotely 'flown' to its target, then clamp down on it. It was tethered to the ship by a long cable, which, in turn, coiled inside the cargo bay. Once we had a hold on the Major, the coil reversed and he was pulled into the ship.

"I'm in," he said, "cargo door closing, why aren't we moving?"

"Engaging cloak."

"You heard the man, let's get moving, maximum speed," I said. "Jay, standby on weapons. Breuger, give me a count, every ten thousand meters."

When we were fifty-thousand meters from the freighter, I gave the order to fire. The missile sped away and we continued to put distance between our ship and the target.

"I need status on the enemy ships."

"They're alternating, leap frogging each other to pick up the nukes," Breuger said, "about to grab numbers five and six."

"Perfect," Reggie said. He took a seat at the comms console. His uniform was soaked with sweat. "They're in for one hell of a surprise."

"Five seconds to impact," Lieutenant Jay said.

The missile struck the freighter dead center, ripping it apart. The neutrino bomb exploded as planned and the domino effect began, each successive explosion building on the previous. The enemy ships couldn't escape. Where we had been struck by a single bomb, they were being hit by a torrent of energy waves. Alliance battle cruisers were stout ships, but these were no match for the forces they encountered.

"How's our distance, Breuger?" I asked.

"It's gonna be close," he said.

"How close?"

"Brace for impact!"

Unlike our previous experience, the explosive force was not moving counter to our direction of travel. We didn't slam to a halt, we were picked up and carried forward, then flipped over and rolled like a shell in a wave pushed up a sandy shore. We lost power the moment the wave enveloped us. The main capacitors were drained of their energy and the primary force at work on the inside of our ship was centrifugal, generated by the uncontrolled roll. Anything not bolted or strapped into place was thrown around the inside the ship until it slammed into a bulkhead and stayed there. I could feel the pulsing of our emergency thrusters trying to get the ship back on a level plane. The ship was responding, the movement becoming less erratic with each passing second. Once the energy wave from the blast passed over us, the ship settled into a steady trajectory. Emergency lights blinked on, but the ship was silent, all systems shut down, we were again adrift in space. This time we couldn't count on a fleet of ships waiting in the darkness.

"Breuger," I said, "check on Jones. If she's able, have her walk you through the restart sequence she and Blake used last time we got scorched."

"Yes, sir, be right back."

Breuger unstrapped, pushed off his seat and drifted toward the rear hatch.

"Bimmy," Reggie said, "I have a confession to make."

"Don't tell me," I said, "you're sleeping with a nuke tonight."

"More like two, but I was hoping you weren't serious."

"I didn't think you were serious…"

"Brother, tell me you didn't," Lieutenant Jay said, "how are we still alive?"

"Not sure, the cloak, dumb luck, why does it matter? We made it."

Breuger reappeared and said, "Michael, you're needed in the infirmary. Commander Jones has a head injury, looks bad."

"You got it."

"How serious?" I asked.

"She was thrown from the bunk, smacked her head on the bulkhead. She needs to be in a hospital, not a glorified closet. The sooner we get moving, the better."

"Then let's get started. What do you need?"

"Your permission to ignore all safety protocols, throw caution to the wind, you know, business as usual."

"We earned that," the major said.

"Wait, what did I miss?"

"Major Mulzac brought some friends back with him from the Emerson."

Breuger looked at the major, then at me, then back at the console in front of him. He shook his head and said, "Captain Bimmy, if we survive this mission, do not be surprised when I request a transfer."

# 16

# I Don't Want to Die for You

Under Breuger's steady hand, the ship gradually returned to life. When main systems were up and running, I went aft to see Commander Jones. Lieutenant Jay had not returned to the bridge. I was worried we had a more serious medical emergency on our hands.

I was right to be worried.

Jones was pale, confused, and angry. Lieutenant Jay was doing what he could for her, but his skills and our equipment were limited. Despite its recent history, the *Ajax* wasn't designed for lengthy deep space missions.

"Where's the admiral?" Jones was saying. "I need to get to work, I can't…who are you?"

"Lieutenant, a word," I said.

Michael joined me in the corridor and the look on his face made it clear he was concerned.

"She's not good. She doesn't know where she is, what's happening, can't respond to basic instructions or questions, can't remember how she was hurt. This is serious, she needs a properly equipped hospital, or she's not going to make it."

"How much time do we have?"

"No way to tell. Head injuries are tricky, hard to manage. If she's got ongoing bleeding, she might have hours, or she could have days, there's no way for me to know. I know this much, she will not improve on her own."

"All right, stay with her, do what you can, we'll figure something out."

I left the infirmary to return to the bridge, stopping to check on the ship's subsystems as I went, deep in thought and more worried than ever. Aside from being a member of my crew, Jones had been my friend since OCS. I couldn't lose her.

By the time I reached the bridge, I'd made up my mind. "Breuger, send out a distress signal, all ships in the vicinity…"

"Not everyone out there is friendly," Reggie replied, "no one knows we're here. We should complete our mission."

"The mission is on hold. Breuger, send the distress call."

Ten minutes later, we weren't alone anymore.

"We've got multiple ships inbound," Breuger said, "on multiple vectors."

"Friendlies?"

"We've got ships with Alliance identifiers, a Venusian luxury liner, a couple freighters, and we've got some pirate frigates inbound from Mercury to top it all off."

"That's a heck of a response to a distress call. Is anyone hailing us?"

"No, sir. I don't think they're all responding to the call," Breuger said, "I think they're coming to see what exploded out here in the middle of nowhere, so close to Mercury. We lit one heck of a candle."

"Who's nearest, the liner or the Alliance ships?"

"The Venusians are practically on our doorstep."

"Hail them," I said.

"Yes sir," Breuger said, "hailing the cruise ship."

"What's your plan, Bimmy?" Reggie asked.

"The best medical facilities will be on the Venusian liner," I said. "These others aren't much better equipped than us."

"What about the pirates?"

"One problem at a time. Michael, set an intercept course, best possible speed."

The Captain of the Venusian ship appeared on the view screen.

"This is Captain George Fryatt of the Olympus, with whom do I speak?"

"Captain Charles Bimmy, of the *Ajax*, we are in need of medical assistance, we have an injured crew…"

"Captain, we cannot respond to your distress call. There are multiple armed vessels converging on this sector. This is a luxury vessel, unarmed and defenseless, we cannot get into a battle, you'll have to…"

"Excuse me, Captain, but I'm certain you're familiar with the code of the Interplanetary Spacing Guild, and the relevant obligations you face. Would you like me to quote it to you?"

"I'll not be spoken to in such a manner by the captain of a broken-down…"

"A master of a ship actively traveling in space," I began, "which is in a position to provide assistance, on receiving a signal from any source stating persons are in distress during space flight, is bound by legal and moral mandate to proceed with all speed to their assistance. That is the law as it is written, if you do not render assistance, I will be obliged by my oath to board and commandeer your ship, and place you under arrest. If you doubt my resolve in this, I suggest you contact Ambassador Arthur Gorman. We are in this sector at his request."

Captain Fryatt's expression changed at the mention of the Ambassador's name. He hesitated, then said, "Standby."

The screen went blank, but the channel was still open. Seconds ticked by, then minutes. We continued to close the gap between our ship and the Venusian's. They weren't changing course, which I took as a good sign.

Captain Fryatt reappeared, with an adjusted attitude.

"Captain Bimmy, you have my apologies. Chairman Gorman has instructed me to assist you. We are transferring docking instructions. We will have a medical team waiting for you. Please make haste, I will not wait long. This ship and all onboard are my responsibility. We're tracking four non-aligned vessels approaching at high speed, my navigation team estimates they will be in weapons range in three hours."

"Understood," I said, "thank you, Captain. We'll be docked in thirty minutes, you'll have time to leave the sector, we'll cover your withdrawal. Bimmy out."

"He called Gorman 'Chairman Gorman,' I thought he was an ambassador," Reggie said, "what's he Chairman of and why don't we know about it?"

"Whatever he is, I'm glad I got to meet him. Fly us in. Breuger, head aft and help Lieutenant Jay prep Jones for transfer. It's gonna be a quick turnaround, we won't have time for a social call. Once she's safely aboard the *Olympus*, we're getting underway."

"Where to?"

"Mercury," I said, "we're gonna finish what we started."

"What about those other ships? Those are pirate frigates, no matter what the Venusians call them."

"We're gonna finish them, too. I'm tired of these people always showing up to spoil the party."

The gangway was extended when we came alongside the *Olympus*. Breuger and Michael transferred Jones when docking was secure. Breuger stayed back and returned to the ship a few minutes behind the Lieutenant. He took his position on the bridge, and stared at his console.

"Eric," I said, "this is the best we can do for her. She's got a fighting chance."

"I know. But I keep wondering what drives your decisions. How many more of us are going to get hurt or killed because you don't know when to run from a fight."

Breuger's words stung, but I needed to let them sink in and give careful consideration to my response. Anger would only escalate the situation.

"Eric, I'm sure there's a long list of transgressions I'm guilty of committing, but needlessly risking the well-being of my crew is not one of them. Rachel could die, and if you think it doesn't weigh on me, then either you've forgotten who I am, or you're not thinking straight. We all knew the risks when we took the oath. We all have our moments of doubt, of fear, of justified anger. But our mission is bigger than any one person. If I never get to see my family again, but I know my family is alive, and well, and protected from harm, that's a trade I'm ready to make."

Breuger turned in his seat and glared at me.

"I don't want to die for you."

"I'm not asking you to."

"Four enemy ships, or more, and you want to charge right at them. Unless I'm wrong, it looks like suicide."

"I have too much to live for, as do we all."

"Then what's your plan?"

"Stealth mode, intercept course, de-cloak and fire on the ships, make haste to Mercury. If they survive and chase us, we drop another nuke and keep going. We get to Mercury, we drop the last nuke on the surface and call it a day."

Breuger looked at the Major and then Lieutenant Jay.

"It's a good plan," the lieutenant said.

"I'm in," Reggie added.

"It's a good plan," Breuger said after a pause, "but I'm officially requesting transfer off this ship when this mission is over."

"Fair enough, you'll have your transfer. Until then, we've got unfinished business, let's get moving."

"Yes sir," he said, and turned back to his console.

"Major, run a weapons system check, make sure nothing got damaged. I don't want to be out there shooting blanks. Lieutenant Jay, send a data burst to the *Arcturus*, include the ship's log."

As we moved away from the *Olympus*, I took time to appreciate the beauty of its curves and sweeping lines, the multicolored surface, the epic grandeur of it. I hoped I'd get the chance to take Gorman up on his invitation to visit Venusia. With ships like the *Olympus*, I could image what their cities were like. The ship's observation decks were crowded with passengers and crew, watching our departure. We passed the ship's bridge and the crew came to attention at the broad window and saluted.

***

We ran full-out once we were away from the cruise ship. Burning fuel on top of the g-drive was a risky gamble. We arrived at our intercept location and all I could do was hope our heat would dissipate before we showed up on enemy scanners.

With the cloak engaged, we had to rely on visual. We waited in silence for the frigates to change course. When they maintained their heading toward our previous location, the ambush was set, the hunt was on.

"Lieutenant Jay, you'll have seconds to get a lock once we de-cloak."

"Roger that."

"Reggie, get ready, I want full tracking on our missiles. Breuger, we're faster than them, keep a healthy distance. I don't want to mix it up with any survivors. We fire and we run."

"Yes sir."

"Ready when you are, Captain."

"Drop the cloak and fire at will," I said.

"Dropping cloak, acquiring targets, firing one."

"Tracking one," Reggie said.

"Second target locked, firing two."

"Tracking two...the enemy ships are altering course."

"Heading, be specific Breuger," I said.

"They're running sir, heading two-six-five, declination four-one relative to our operating plane."

I knew we had them. Never run from an ambush.

"Pursuit course, keep your angle at three-eight degrees."

"Locked on targets three and four, missiles away."

"Impact on one, tracking three and four."

A bright flash lit up the view screen, followed by another.

"Impact on two, one ship destroyed, one disabled. Incoming, incoming, tracking three missiles inbound, deploying countermeasures."

"Evasive, Breuger. You break my ship, I'll expect you to fix it."

"Missiles locked, firing five, firing six."

"Tracking…"

An explosion off our starboard bow shook the ship, causing minor damage. A second explosion was closer, but the *Ajax* remained intact. The third missile was closer still, the explosion sent vibrations through the hull and a loud scraping sound echoed through the ship.

Another bright flash lit up our screen.

"Hit on three, target destroyed, enemy is deploying countermeasures, four is a miss…five is a miss."

"Hold fire, standby on weapons," I said, "give six a chance to do its job."

"Tracking six…it's inside the countermeasure, closing, closing…"

One last explosion, and the battle was over.

"Target destroyed," Reggie announced.

"Nice work, lay in a course for Mercury. Let's go burn that rock and go home."

"What about the disabled ship, shouldn't we finish them off?" Lieutenant Jay asked.

"I say let 'em rot out here with the rest of the bodies," Reggie replied.

"We leave them," I said.

"Captain, with respect, we shouldn't give them a chance, you always say finish what you start…"

"Lieutenant Jay, I appreciate your enthusiasm but they're worth more to us alive. Last report had seven pirate frigates at Mercury. I'm counting on the remaining ships coming to rescue their comrades."

"You're laying a big bet on a bunch of outlaws."

I had seen what my crew had missed, a spot of brilliant green on the disabled ship's flank, bisected by a black line. Only one pirate frigate would have such a marking.

"No, I'm not," I said. "Not when it's their queen who needs rescuing."

***

Grace Cheng knew many pleasures in life, and the greatest of these was revenge. She loved to ruin her enemies, to destroy all who defied her, to extract her pound of flesh from any she deemed owed her one. By her accounting, Captain Charles Bimmy owed her many more than one.

In her rage at her crew's failure, she executed her tactical officer, then threatened to do the same to her engineer if he did not repair her ship.

"Madame Cheng," the engineer said in reply to her threat, "I cannot repair an engine which is no longer there. Perhaps you would like me to get out and push?"

"If I thought it would work, you would already be out there," she raged.

Grace Cheng had known success in battle for so many years, she refused to accept yet another defeat. She would live to fight another day, as she had on the day she became a pirate, when she was forced to join those who attacked and overran her family's charter to Ganymede. She had turned fifteen on the journey. It had taken years to rise through the pirate ranks. She would do whatever it took to maintain her position.

She slapped her engineer, then turned her anger toward her communications officer.

"Why don't I have comms," she demanded.

"The main array is damaged, we're working as fast…"

"Work faster!"

More threats followed. An hour later, when the array was repaired, Grace Cheng was reassured her methods were always correct. Fear was an excellent motivator, fear of death the greatest of all.

"Contact our forces, have everyone rally here, we're going home."

"Everyone," her comms officer asked, "even the…"

"What part of everyone do you not understand? Do as you are told!"

The order was sent and the remaining pirates on Mercury and in orbit above the planet began to leave, alarming the leader of the rebels working to restore Mercury Station to operational status.

"Madame Cheng," the comms officer announced, "Chancellor Ellis would like to speak with you."

"Sure," she said, "let's hear what she has to say, this could be fun. Put her on the main viewer."

"Madame Cheng," Ellis said, "why are your ships breaking orbit? We have…"

"You have nothing," Cheng replied, "your battle cruisers are destroyed, you have no offensive capability without me, and I have spent too much blood and treasure on your foolish dream. You have a rock with a hole it in, nothing more. Why should I waste more of my time on you?"

"We have a deal…"

"No, we had a deal. You broke it when you lost your ships. Good luck to you, Chancellor of Nothing, Ruler of Nowhere. You will need it."

Cheng slashed her hand through the air in front of her throat and the comms officer cut the link to Mercury.

"How long before our ships arrive?" she asked of no one in particular.

When no one replied she shouted, "How long!"

"Six hours, Madame Cheng, the first ship will arrive in six hours."

"Good," she said, "I will be in my stateroom having a nap. Wake me when they get here."

# 17

## **Surrender**

"What do you mean, no ships?"

"No ships of any kind in orbit over Mercury," Reggie said, "not so much as a derelict freighter."

"What about the surface?"

"Scanning, standby."

"Looks like you were right," Lieutenant Jay said, "they went to save their queen."

"Maybe, but why send every ship? I think this is something else. Breuger, put us in polar orbit over the station, low as you can get us, right down in the shadow."

"Yes, Captain, low and dark."

Mercury was special in a number of ways, including its orbit and the timing of its rotation. Its orbital dynamics and close proximity to the Sun resulted in radical temperature differences across the surface. The best locations for surface installations were at the poles, where the temperature remained a frigid –94° C. The deep craters in the polar regions provided protection from the sun and a ready source of water in the form of millions of kilograms of ice, enough to support a silicate mine and military station for years, until the mine started losing money. After the mine shut down, the Earth Alliance abandoned the planet.

The place was stripped to the bones, but the bones left behind were significant, including a small space port and a pressurized habitat.

It was an inhospitable place to build a colony. I assumed the separatists had chosen it for the available structures, or for its isolation. If they wanted to be separate from the rest of humanity, they'd picked the right place.

"No ships on the surface," Reggie reported. "There are life signs, all clustered together in the main habitat. Hard to get an accurate count, but I'd say at least thirty people are down there."

"Diehards or leftovers?" Lieutenant Jay asked.

"Doesn't make much difference, they don't appear to be a threat," I said. "Keep scanning, Cheng can be clever when she puts her mind to it. No more surprises."

"We came all this way for nothing," Reggie said, "and with two nukes along for the ride."

"We still have to clear the planet," I reminded him, "but it does seem the fireworks are over."

"We're being hailed. Someone on the surface wants to surrender."

"Then let's not keep them waiting," I said.

"Federation vessel, hold your fire. I repeat, hold your fire. We are no threat to you."

"Federation? What he's talking about?"

"We've been out of touch for a while, sounds like the talks at Phobos went well," Breuger replied.

"This is Captain Charles Bimmy, of the *Ajax*, identify yourself."

"Captain Bimmy, my name is Nolan Santos, we surrender, we have arrested Chancellor Ellis. We are prepared to deliver her to your custody. I beg you, do not fire on us, we…"

"Stop," I said, "I accept your surrender. You're safe as long as you don't do anything foolish. I don't know this Chancellor Ellis, explain your situation."

"You don't know…"

"We were sent here to destroy the rebel presence on Mercury. It has not been a pleasant trip, and comms have been spotty. Tell me what I don't know."

"The treaty of Phobos, every station, every planet, everyone, they all signed it. The Sol Federation is the new order, but there were conditions."

"Of course there were."

"The governments of Ganymede, Europa, Earth, they all declared her a war criminal for the attack on Earth. We've got her locked up, like your guy, Admiral somebody, they both have to stand trial…"

"Admiral Porter," I said.

"Yes, him…"

"Mister Santos, what is your status?"

"I don't understand, we surrendered…"

"I'm interested in how many people you have there, your supplies, any medical emergencies…"

"There are 41 of us, 11 children. We have sufficient supplies to share."

"I don't need supplies, I need to know if you can stay put until a ship can get here and collect all of you."

"How long will it take?"

"How long can you hold out?"

"Three weeks, five if we ration…it would help if you took Chancellor Ellis off our hands…"

"What's with the Chancellor title? Chancellor of what?" the Major asked.

"It was her dream," Santos said, "the New Republic, we all bought into it. Then she attacked Earth, we lost our ships, our allies abandoned us, it's turned into a nightmare…"

"From my perspective, you're lucky, as far as I'm concerned, you're all criminals. Keep your Chancellor, ration your food, I'll make sure a ship gets here before you all starve to death."

"No, Captain! You can't leave her here, she's nothing but trouble. She still has supporters…"

"Not my problem, you chose the path, you get to walk it. Bimmy out."

"Captain, I didn't know you had it in you," Lieutenant Jay said.

"What?"

"Cruelty," he said.

"Not cruelty, strategy. How much faster do you think a ship will get here if this Chancellor person is still down there? We take her with us, and a relief ship might never come. There's plenty of people on Earth who would be happy to see everyone down there die a slow death, the children included. I'm not taking any chances. And I'm not about to land this ship. We'd be outnumbered nearly ten to one. You heard the man, she still has supporters, I'm not putting us in that mix."

"We leave them here, then what?"

"I'll make my report to Admiral Wilson. This is a problem for her to solve. Then we're going to Venus; the alignment favors us, it'll be a short hop."

Breuger's eyes lit up and a broad smile crossed his face for the first time since before Jones was injured.

"Captain Bimmy," he said, "this might be your best plan yet."

***

We stayed in orbit two days, then used Mercury's gravity to slingshot toward Venus. The gravity drive did the rest. We were on our way to Venusia, the collection of cities drifting in the dense cloud atmosphere enveloping Venus. Admiral Wilson informed us the Sol Federation was born, and Ambassador Gorman had been elected Chairman of the High Council. Our 'Battle of Mercury' and the surrender of the remaining 'forces' on the planet marked the official end of hostilities. The war was over. I didn't have to fight anymore.

The most important thing for me was the end of the last message from the admiral. "After Venusia," she said, "it's time to turn for home. Enjoy your leave, you've earned it."

Breuger's promotion was approved during our mission, but I had no insignia on hand to hold a ceremony. When I told him, Breuger left the bridge, returning with everything we needed.

"They're Rachel's'," he said, "I don't think she'll mind."

We held the ceremony, Breuger was promoted, and I told him his promotion was retroactive. It meant he had substantial back pay coming his way.

"You must have put in for this before we left Phobos," Breuger surmised.

"A few hours before we left."

"You never thought to mention it to me?"

"What happens if they turn it down? If you didn't know…"

"Turn it down? The famous Captain Bimmy? Who in their right mind would turn down a request from the Father of the Federation?"

"Don't say that, Reggie, please, no."

"The Boy Genius…"

"Definitely not, no way."

"Harbinger of Peace…"

"A lie."

"Defender of Europa."

"Okay, but that title has to be shared."

The transit to Venus gave us an opportunity to put the stress of the war behind us. We sent messages to our loved ones and, for the first time since OCS, I felt comfortable sending my location and itinerary to

Becca and my parents. There were times I thought about those who had not survived to see the peace. Some I would miss, others I would not, but I knew I would never forget any of them.

We arrived at Venusia eight days after departing Mercury. I had no expectations other than picking up Commander Jones and getting the tour I'd been promised, then heading home, with a stop at Luna to be rid of the two nuclear bombs tucked away in our cargo hold.

Instead, we were treated to a hero's welcome and paraded around Venusia Central for all to see.

Commander Jones had scars, like the rest of us, but she had made a strong recovery under the care of the Venusian doctors. Once the festivities ended, she and Breuger disappeared. We didn't see them again until it was time to leave.

The *Olympus* had been a good indicator of what to expect from Venusia. It was a wondrous place, gleaming curved towers rising up from open green spaces, all bathed in sunlight filtered through tinted glass domes and panels. Vast areas were planted with trees and grass, public parks larger and more beautiful than anything left on Earth. Most of the trees were fruit-bearing, as were the shrubs and vines. Vegetable gardens lined and dotted the green spaces. You could take a walk and have a meal and dessert while you took in the sun. Beneath it all, an engineering marvel many times larger than the cities held everything aloft. The beauty of the place explained Venusia's stance on neutrality. They had much to lose.

On the second day, I was invited to breakfast with Chairman Gorman. I was led to his residence, where a young man, about my age, greeted me at the door.

"Welcome, Captain Bimmy," he said, extending his hand for me to shake, "I'm Oscar Douglas, please come in."

"A pleasure to meet you, Oscar," I said.

He led me into the residence and Chairman Gorman entered from an adjoining room. He threw his arms out, "There he is," he shouted, "the hero of our time."

I was not expecting a hug, but what could I do? I hugged him back.

"It's good to see you again, Chairman Gorman," I said.

"Titles are unnecessary between old friends, don't you think?"

"Well, sir, Mister Chairman, I…"

"Charlie, stop it, I told you to call me Arthur. Consider it an order if it makes you more comfortable."

"Actually, yes, it does, thank you, Arthur."

"Come with me, Charlie, breakfast is waiting. Oscar, we're not to be disturbed."

"Yes sir, of course."

I followed Arthur to a glass-enclosed veranda overlooking a park far below. Tufts of clouds drifted by at eye level and beams of light mixed with passing shadows to create a grand moving kaleidoscope of color. We sat at a small table laden with fresh vegetables and fruit, boiled eggs and hearty breads with pots of jam and butter. It had been years since I'd seen such a feast. We ate and made small talk until Arthur called for the table to be cleared. Hot tea was served and the Chairman at last arrived at the point of the meeting.

"Venusia is even more beautiful from here, don't you think?" he asked.

"Yes, it's more than I expected."

"Not many people know our secret, we get so few visitors. I understand Commander Jones is doing well. I'm glad our people were able to help her. She has many friends here."

"I'm grateful for the assistance. Captain Fryatt…"

"You threatened to commandeer his ship."

"I felt it was necessary."

"Would you have done it, board the ship, arrest him, risk the political fallout, all for one person?"

"I will always do what I think is right, no matter the consequences."

"Even if some might think your actions are illegal?"

"What are you getting at?"

"You risked so much to save one person, how much would you risk to save millions?"

"That's a loaded question. You know I prefer directness…"

"Then let me speak plainly. The human race is dying. The population is no longer self-sustaining, not on Earth, not in the colonies, not on Mars. Our numbers, across the solar system, decline with each generation. Earth, the one planet on which we can exist without pressurized structures, where humans can walk in the open and breathe the atmosphere, has been blighted by war, mismanagement, disease. It is dying before our eyes. It is too far gone to be saved in time for humanity to return there in great numbers. I think you know this."

"It seems to me humanity is thriving, look at your colony, Venusia is a paradise…"

"Appearances are deceptive. We achieve our limited success

through strict population control, and a degree of austerity many find burdensome. But those who leave invariably return. They find no place better."

I waved my hand over the table between us, "If that meal is what you call austerity, sign me up."

"Growing food is not the challenge. Growing our population, ensuring the survival of our species, that is our common challenge. We are fortunate, we grow more food than we need. We have a large surplus we are able to export to Earth, but Earth demands less of us each season. Did you know at this moment there are more humans living off Earth than live on it?"

"I didn't, but it seems to go against what you're saying."

"Venusia commissioned a census of the Sol system. I will send you the report, the findings are stark. The number of humans alive today is less than half the number from my father's generation. The number has declined each year since Earth's last war, since the rise of the Alliance as the sole power on the planet."

"You can't blame the Alliance…"

"It was a turning point. The rise of a one-world government had both positive and tragic consequences. But I want to speak of the future. I want to speak of your future, and of a young woman named Rebecca Kiel."

"How do you know her? What's she…?"

"You sent a design concept for a superliminal ship to Miss Kiel. I know this because her parents proposed a reallocation of the resources from their new Gateway project to the construction of a ship based on your concept. I know this because the proposal was rejected by the Council of Arcadia."

"I wasn't aware. The war is over, the Sol Federation…why not build it without Arcadia?"

"There are many reasons, the politics of it for one. Putting politics aside, it is the same reason so much of the technical wonders from Arcadia go unrealized; a lack of resources. They have built two full-scale devices and they were planning two more. But their project will end with installations on Luna and Mars."

"What's the problem?"

"They require one of the rarest elements known to science, Promethium. Less than two thousand grams of it have been collected. Each device, each Einstein–Rosen bridge, requires 350 grams. The entire quantity known to exist has been allocated to the Gateway project."

"This is a good time to get to your point."

"All right then. There are many people who believe the Council of Arcadia is mistaken on this matter, many people in high places who are unable to exert their power to change the collective will of the members, either from fear or a lack of understanding of the stakes, or both. Those of us who feel this way would like you to join us."

"What makes you think I can change…"

"You can't, but there is another way."

"What are you asking me to do?"

"We would like you to reappropriate the devices assigned to Luna and Mars."

"You mean steal them."

"Yes, Captain Bimmy, precisely."

***

"You can't be serious," Reggie said. "Do you trust this person?"

"Yes, I'm serious" I said, "and no, I have no reason to trust him. In fact, I think he's lying to me. I think he wants the Promethium for Venusia so they can control interstellar travel. Now that we've got a ship design, he wants Venusia to own the ships. It's a power play."

"A person you don't trust has asked you to steal two of the rarest devices in the known universe, from your girlfriend's parents no less, and deliver them to him…"

"I didn't say I was going to do it."

"You didn't say you weren't," Michael said.

"I told him I would assess the situation when I got to Earth."

During the conversation in the galley, Jones and Breuger kept silent, but it was becoming obvious Jones had something to say. She kept rolling and unrolling an empty foil bev-pack, as if she could wring another drop of liquid from it. She was putting me on edge.

"Rachel, please, throw it away or speak your mind, the noise is teeth-grinding," I said.

"I've known you long enough to know you're leaving something out of this conversation," she replied.

She had me there. I had no intention of stealing the E–R bridges and handing them over to Gorman. But his proposal had me thinking about a plan of my own.

"You're right," I said, "but before I say more, you should know this could end our careers, all of us, and get us thrown in prison. You should leave the room if…"

"I'm not leaving until I hear what you have to say," Breuger said. "I can't think of anything worth risking prison time for, but you've surprised me before. My career, not a problem, I'm resigning my commission when we get to Artemis Station. Tell us your idea, your secret will be safe whether we like it or not."

I knew Breuger and Jones were planning to resign. They had relatives on Luna and could find work with ease. I was happy for them, and their relocation to Luna could help the plan I was going to lay out.

"Anyone else?"

When no one left the galley, I started talking.

"It's not much of a plan, pretty basic so far. I will take the two devices, if Becca and her parents are on board with it. I'm not stealing from my family. If they say yes, Becca and I will be on the ship with the E–R bridges. I checked the mission plan and they're set to launch the gear on a shuttle during my leave. At the orbital dock, one crate goes to Mars, one goes to Luna. The one to Mars will be empty, the one for Luna will have both devices. We'll follow the Luna crate and when we get to Artemis Station, load it onto a ship and head to Deimos."

"This is where we come in," Michael said, "you'll need to refit the ship."

"Correct, we'll repurpose one device and keep the other in reserve," I said, "I'll send you the plans Becca and her parents drew up."

"How do you propose to get a ship? They don't hand them out like party favors," Jones said.

"And you can't walk around Artemis Station with a crate full of advanced technology. People will notice," Breuger added.

"Your brother works there…"

"No way, not involving him, he's got a family," Breuger said, "he's more likely to turn us in than help."

"I wouldn't ask him to help, but you could ask him for a job."

"Okay, let's say I do, what about the ship?"

"That's where you come in," I said to Jones, "you've got relatives in flight ops and in decommissioning…"

"You want me to talk them into giving you a mothballed ship? What do I to tell them?"

"Not mothballed, but a soon-to-be decommissioned ship would be helpful. The *Mercury* would work for this. It's not scheduled for recycling until long after we need it. You could say your former captain wants to show off for his new bride, spend a couple of days on a sightseeing tour on his honeymoon."

"Becca hasn't said yes," she said. "You haven't even popped the question, and there's no sightseeing in Luna orbit."

"I think it's a metaphor," Breuger said.

"Whatever it is, it's not good enough, keep trying."

"She's right," Reggie said, "it's a terrible plan. I've got a better idea, and it doesn't involve all the subterfuge or a stop on Luna or mothballed ships, too complicated and bound to fail. Before I say more, because I'm not sold on any of it yet, I want to know what you're planning to do with this ship you want our people to retrofit."

"The destination is an exoplanet, Luyten b. Becca thinks it's human-compatible."

"What if she's wrong?"

"That's the beauty of it," I said, "if Luyten b doesn't check out, there are other planets in the system's habitable zone."

"All right, then answer me this, why?" Reggie asked. "Stealing a starship, defying the Council, deceiving…everyone, that's a lot of risk, even for you."

"Because I'm tired of being a pawn in someone else's game. We were pawns over Europa. We were pawns over Mercury. And now Gorman wants to play us for whatever plans he's cooked up. I'm done, I'm not going to be a pawn anymore. It's time to be a player."

<h1 style="text-align:center">18</h1>

# Beyond Tomorrow's Sun

On approach to the orbital dock over Earth, all I could think about was seeing my parents, Becca, my dog Katie. The plan took a temporary back seat to my personal life. Three years was a long time to be away. I wondered if Katie would forgive me for leaving her for so long.

After we docked, my crew left first, each committed to their part of the plan to abscond with the E–R bridges, the Gateways as they had been named. Breuger and Jones escorted the two nukes to Luna, the Major and Michael remained onboard the *Ajax*, then it was my turn to leave after a comm with Admiral Wilson, a final mission debrief. I strapped into my seat aboard the shuttle and dropped through the atmosphere toward the space port along the coast, a short ride from Arcadia. A short ride from home.

I expected to see my parents, Becca, her parents, and hopefully Katie.

The people of Arcadia wouldn't have it.

It looked to me like half the population was there to greet me, so many people crowded the viewing stands and tarmac. A band played, people clapped and cheered, banners waved in the breeze. I found out later the majority of the city's remaining population had turned out for my homecoming.

Katie bolted toward me and threw herself into my arms when I knelt down and braced myself for impact. Becca had to wait to kiss me until after my dog had her say. Once Katie had sufficiently covered me with her fur, she allowed Becca her turn to greet me.

When Becca threw her arms around me and kissed me, I nearly toppled over.

"Hello gorgeous," I said.

"Hello handsome," she replied, causing me to blush.

I hugged my parents, then Becca's parents. It was a nice reunion, but too public for my liking.

Members of the Council of Arcadia made speeches, then, to my horror, I was asked to say a few words. I've always been taught the key to good communication is brevity. I kept it short. I had no way of knowing it would be broadcast across the Sol Federation months later.

"Thank you, everyone, it's good to be home. This is…more than I expected. I guess you never know what the day is gonna bring," I said, as laughter rippled through the crowd.

"Joining Space Force was my dream, but I knew nothing about war. During the worst of it, all I thought about, every day, was 'I hope my family is safe.' It saddens me to think about the families who won't get to welcome their loved ones home again. I wish we could have found our way to peace sooner."

I paused and the crowd fell silent. The city had contributed its share of technology to the war, but it was Becca who had felt the bitter sting of it first-hand, as I had.

"Someone once said, and I'm gonna mess up this quote, but they said something like…yesterday is gone, tomorrow doesn't exist, today is all we have. I think if today is all we have, then we better decide what we want tomorrow to look like, and the day after. The sun's gonna rise, we'll go about our business, then the day will be over again. I hope we can think beyond tomorrow's sun, beyond our own lives, beyond all the things we worry and fight over, and look out at the future and find a way to face it, to shape it, to make things better than they are today. I think we can do it. I think together, we can do it. Thanks for being here today, it means a lot to me and my family."

I looked down at Katie, leaning against my knee, panting away with her tongue hanging out, oblivious to anything but me.

"Now," I said, smiling again, "if you don't mind, I'd like to go home and get some rest. Thanks again, everyone."

I waved at the crowd, and was surprised by the eruption of cheers and applause.

An aero-van waited for us on the tarmac. We climbed aboard and rose into the sky. The flight back to Arcadia was strangely quiet. Halfway home, I broke the silence.

"What's wrong?" I asked.

"Charlie," my mother began, "we're so happy you're home, news can wait. We'll talk later."

"No, Mom, let's talk. Something's wrong, I can tell. I can handle bad news. Seems to me everyone's heard it but me. What is it?"

"We were impressed with the data you sent," Becca's father said. "We sent a proposal to the Council to build a ship."

"They rejected it," I said.

"I'm afraid so. They believed in the concept. But they won't reallocate the resources. There are other, more pressing concerns, than building a new class of starship."

Becca hadn't said a word since we boarded the vehicle, but the look she gave me spoke volumes.

"I made you a promise," I said.

"It's okay," Becca replied, "we'll figure something out."

I stared out the window, watching the landscape shift from rocky coast to the orderly streets of Arcadia. The green lawns were burnt brown and many of the trees were dead or had been cut down. It was a shadow of the city I remembered. It was starting to look like Greenfield.

I reached down and scratched Katie behind her ears.

"What do you think, Katie," I asked, "is now a good time?"

Katie let out a low rumble, a sound I decided to take as her note of approval.

I looked up at my parents, then at Becca's.

"Mr. Kiel, Mrs. Kiel, I'm gonna ask Becca to marry me. How do you feel about that?"

Becca couldn't help herself. She laughed. A loud, side-busting, make-your-eyes-water laugh. My timing, this time, was perfect.

Within a week, we were married in a simple ceremony, with our families and a handful of friends in attendance.

A few days later, Becca, Katie and I took the auto-car and drove through a dusty field and over a hill pockmarked with tufts of weeds, to the place where the road ended at a low barrier. The lush underbrush was gone, the larger trees had fallen or were dying, ready to topple over. The remnant of the road heading west was more visible than when I had traveled it. We didn't speak at first. I walked back to the top of the hill and looked over the city I loved, at the ocean in the distance, its allure still strong. I sat in the road and Katie sat beside me. Becca sat down with Katie between us.

I don't know what Becca expected, but she would indulge me only so much. When the silence grew too heavy, she broke it with her usual blend of directness and kindness.

"Charlie," she said, "I don't know what's going on, but I think there's something you want to tell me. Whatever it is…if you're having second thoughts about us…"

"No, Becca, never would I have doubts about us," I said. "But there is something I need to ask you."

"Then ask me."

"If there was a chance, even a slim chance, we could go to Luyten b, how much would you risk for the opportunity?"

"You and me together?"

"Of course."

"Everything," she said, "I would risk everything."

***

Becca's parents had misgivings about sending her through a wormhole on an untested ship, but they knew their daughter. Once Becca made up her mind, they couldn't stop her. Instead, they agreed to help.

Once they agreed to participate, I had to tell my parents as well. They deserved to know our plans. I had dinner with them the night before we launched and told them everything.

My mother did not take it well.

"You understand how superluminal travel works," she said with a healthy dose of sarcasm.

"Theoretically, yes," I replied, avoiding the reality behind her question.

"Charlie, son," Henry, said, "we'll be long dead by the time you get back, if you even get back. As will Katie. Is it worth it?"

"Five days," I replied, "it's the max we'll stay in orbit."

My mother was becoming frustrated. She slapped her hands down onto the table, "Time in orbit is not the issue," she said, "thirteen light years, there and back, if you survive, it could be eighty, ninety years here on Earth, depending on how fast you travel. A lot will have changed."

"A lot has already changed," I said. "I can't sit around and wait for Earth and everyone on it to waste away. The new Federation buys us some time, but eventually there won't be an Earth to come back to.

What future will it be for me and Becca?"

My father reached across the table and took my hand. "How fast do you think you can travel with this new ship?"

"If it works, and I think it will, then it won't be a matter of how fast we travel. Becca thinks we won't travel at all, technically speaking. She says this is more like teleporting than traveling. We'll use the E–R Bridge to fold space-time, then punch through it with the soliton drive. It's a modified gravity drive. We should be in orbit in a matter of minutes."

"You make it sound so simple," my mother said.

I couldn't fault her for her sarcasm.

"Mom, I know you're skeptical. But if this works, we'll be there and back in days, not decades."

My mother looked between me and my father, choosing her words with care.

"I'm not going to stop you. I'm not going to get in your way. But I think you're making a mistake. I hope it doesn't cost you too dearly. You should spend some time with Katie before you go, she's been miserable for three years, the least you can do is spend tonight with her."

She left the room without another word. I thought I saw tears in her eyes, but couldn't be certain. Her ploy to get me to stay one last night in my childhood home worked. I slept in my old room with Katie curled up next to me on the bed. In the morning, I took her for a long walk, followed by a mostly silent breakfast with my parents before leaving them and making my way to the spaceport, where Becca was waiting.

My heart was heavy, but my mind was clear. I knew we had to try, and I believed we had a fighting chance to succeed. I met Becca in the lounge and we took a table away from the other passengers.

"How'd it go?" she asked.

"As good as you might think. They're not happy. You should have seen the look on Katie's face when I left. I wish I could explain it to her."

"You could still bring her along. There's another launch in a week...."

"A dog, in space, through a wormhole? No way, not even Katie. Adds to much complexity."

"This is going to work. I've checked and re-checked. The calculations are accurate, the design is sound. We'll make the roundtrip in no time. If the planet checks out, we'll bring her along on the next trip. And our parents, if they want to come along. Anyone who wants a new life on a new world, they'll have the chance because of you."

"Because of us," I corrected her.

"Ok," she said, smiling, "because of us."

We were interrupted when a clerk approached our table.

"Captain, Mrs. Bimmy, would you like to board early? It's a full flight…"

Becca was laughing too much to listen to my response. The clerk stepped away, confused.

"Can you imagine," she said, "Becca Bimmy? I could never say it with a straight face."

"I think it has a nice ring to it."

"No," she said, "I might be a captain myself one day. Captain Kiel sounds better to me."

"How about we start you off at commander?"

"Whatever you say, Charlie. Commander Kiel it is. Maybe I'll switch to calling you Bimmy, while we're at it."

We laughed all the way to the transport which would take us to the launch tower. I was still amused by the whole discussion when we arrived at the orbital station several hours later. I got a glimpse of the *Ajax* in space dock as we arrived and started feeling better about Reggie's plan.

My mood turned serious when we ran into Admiral Wilson.

"Bimmy," the admiral called out, "what brings you back to space so soon?"

"Admiral," I replied, "what a surprise. I thought you were on your way to Phobos."

"I was," she said, "but I have business on Luna. We're expanding the research station at the southern pole. The Venusians want a team there, they've asked me to sort out the details. We're still short on trust these days. What takes you to Luna?"

"Our honeymoon," Becca interjected, "and some business of our own. Becca Kiel," she said, extending her hand toward the admiral, "it's a pleasure to meet you, Admiral. I've heard so much about you."

"So, you're the young genius. Apologies for missing your wedding, it takes more notice when you're millions of kilometers away."

"I didn't get much notice either. Will you be staying at Artemis Station long?"

The shuttle to Luna was an hour away from the dock. We had some time on our hands. Becca kept the admiral talking for most of it. I took the opportunity to step away and meet with Major Mulzac.

I found him in the cargo transfer bay. The crates from the Hoffman Institute labeled for Luna and Mars had been moved into position, waiting to continue their journey.

The crate containing the two Gateway devices we were making off with was labeled as my personal belongings. When the cargo boss on Earth didn't object to the weight, I sensed my mother's hand at work.

We stowed the crate on the *Ajax*, and I returned to the lounge to get Becca away from Admiral Wilson. By the time I got back, the shuttle to Luna was fifteen minutes from docking.

"There you are," Becca said, "I was worried you weren't going to make it."

"Me too," I said. "I ran into an old friend. Any chance I can pull you away for a quick hello?"

Becca and I excused ourselves and left. We boarded the *Ajax* and I introduced Becca to Major Mulzac. In a way, I hadn't lied to the Admiral, but the broader deception still nullified the minor truth. It was a habit from my childhood I'd never broken.

"You can call me Reggie, I doubt I'll still be a Major when all of this is said and done."

"And your brother is Michael, Charlie told me a lot about you both."

"Mikey should be here any minute. Bimmy has been mostly tight-lipped about you," Reggie said, "I look forward to getting to know our newest partner in crime."

Michael joined us on the bridge and the introduction was repeated. We'd been a tight-knit crew on a small ship for a long time, yet Becca slipped into the dynamic like she'd been there all along.

When the arrival of the shuttle was announced, Reggie and his brother went to their stations and Becca took a seat at tactical. "What do we do?" she asked.

"It's a little chaotic when shuttle passengers start to disembark. We'll use that to cover our departure," Reggie said, "from there on, it gets boring."

***

Were it not for Admiral Wilson, we would have made it halfway to Deimos before anyone missed us. But the devil is in the details, and we missed more than one.

When we didn't show up for the flight, the admiral used her authority to hold the shuttle, and when we didn't respond to comms, she ordered the dock's crew to look for us.

I had no choice, I lied to the admiral. I contacted her on my personal link and she answered right away.

"You're holding up the shuttle, I can't keep it here forever."

"My apologies Admiral, Becca's ill, space sickness, it's her first time off-world. We'll have to hold up here and wait for the next shuttle, I'm sorry."

"You should have sent word, I'll be late for my appointment on Luna, it's not like you to be so inconsiderate. You may be on leave, but you're still an officer. It's a bad look, Captain."

"Yes, Admiral, understood. Maybe we can meet up when we get to Luna."

"We'll see," she said, "Wilson out."

"She's got a temper," Becca said, "is she always this way?"

"She's got a lot on her plate," I said.

We also failed to shut off the ship's transponder before we left Earth orbit. It was like having a huge spotlight on the ship as we made our way through the darkness of space.

The admiral must have seen the *Ajax* burn its engines. It was logical for her to assume we were on the ship. She hailed us using the shuttle's comm system. The longer we ignored her, the angrier she became. She didn't like being duped, especially by one of her protégées.

We weren't far from Luna when a short-range patrol ship took up an intercept course.

"Twenty minutes to weapons range," Reggie said, "they're burning all they've got. We can outrun them, but we'll use a lot of fuel."

"How long before the gravity drive is at max velocity?"

"An hour," Reggie said, "but we'll be at seventy percent in thirty minutes."

"Five minutes," Becca said, "max burn for five minutes and we'll stay out of their range. They'll never catch us."

The three of us stared at Becca, dumbfounded. Becca had done the calculations on the fly, faster than a human could punch the numbers into a console.

"What?" she asked, "it's math."

"Full burn, Reggie, five minutes," I said.

"Full burn, brace yourselves," he said.

The main engines fired and the force shoved me into the back of my seat. The ship rumbled and shook for a few seconds, then settled into smooth acceleration. At the five-minute mark, Reggie throttled the ship back. The pursuit ship did the math as well, and gave up the chase.

Over the following days, Becca filled us in on the function of a soliton wave drive, and the modifications needed. It was surprisingly uncomplicated, once you got down to the basic concept.

"Why can't we use the g-drive?" Michael asked, "save ourselves the trouble."

"It's true, gravitational and soliton waves can both propel the ship," Becca said. "Gravity waves are more predictable in some ways, and can deliver more consistent power over distance. It's important to understand a soliton wave can be a gravity wave, or a light wave, or even a wave in the ocean. Calling a wave a soliton wave just means it's solitary, it's permanent, and it can be highly localized, but it doesn't have to be."

"That clears it up. Let's say I understand you," Michael said, "I still don't see why we need a soliton wave to enter a wormhole. Why not rocket propulsion if the g-drive won't do the trick?"

"As far as we know, we can't use traditional propulsion inside a wormhole. Once you fold space-time, whatever momentum you carry into the opening, that's it, that's all you have, unless…"

"Let me guess," he said, "unless you are propelled by a soliton wave."

"Correct," Becca said, "a soliton wave is permanent, unless an external force acts on it to disperse it. Think about light passing through a prism, the individual frequencies are dispersed by the prism. With a soliton wave, inside a wormhole, any dispersion effect is canceled by the Kerr effect, which means the wave's shape, its amplitude, frequency, strength, none of it changes. Imagine catching a single wave and riding it versus catching wind in a sail, most of the wind passes over and around the sail, but when you ride a soliton wave you have access to all of its directional energy at once for as long as you ride it."

"I don't see why we can't open the wormhole and use our main engine to push the ship to the event horizon and let the wormhole do the rest," Reggie said.

"Because…," Becca began, then changed her approach, "we should look at the schematic, it's easier to describe it with images."

She entered commands into her tablet then asked, "Can you port this to the main viewer?"

"Absolutely," I said. I was reminded of all the hours Becca had spent helping me catch up on my studies. When it came to teaching, she was a natural.

"Perfect." She walked to the view screen and pointed. "The structure is attached to the front of the ship. The E–R bridge, the Gateway, is redesigned here to sit at the tip of each of these four posts pointing forward. When the wormhole opens, we use a soliton wave to move forward and simultaneously swing the posts back over the ship. We're not so much moving toward the wormhole as we're expanding it and pulling it towards us, like pulling a blanket over your head. This is where the event horizon will grab us and pull us through, the soliton wave will ensure consistent sustained directional momentum, and there you have it, we've gone through a wormhole. The key point is that the object generating the wormhole can't propel towards it because it would continuously push the event horizon away from itself. The soliton wave allows us to maintain forward momentum, even as we're drawing the event horizon closer to us, until we're eventually pulled into the rift. The soliton wave then allows us to continue our movement and maintain course, both while, and after, we transit the wormhole."

Reggie looked at me, shook his head with a grin, and said, "How did you come up with this?"

"I didn't," I said, "not exactly. Becca came up with it. It's how we met."

"You met in school?"

"No," Becca said, "it was the middle of the street, and it wasn't planned. I didn't think it through, but we got lucky, the soliton wave experiment was happening the same time I was entering the wormhole and…"

Reggie was incredulous, "You're telling me you've done this before? You've been through a wormhole?"

"Yes, I thought you knew. It's how Bimmy and I met, hasn't he told you?"

"No," he said, "but it's a story I'd like to hear."

"Maybe another time," I said.

"Can we step back," Michael asked, "because I am either missing something or this plan is not going to work. I've never been surfing, but I've seen video of people surfing, and what they always do is sit in the water and wait for the right wave to come along. Are we going to sit in space and wait for a soliton wave?"

"No," Becca said, "you could if you wanted, but you would wait a long time. What we're going to do is tune the drive to a specific frequency and amplitude, to match the frequency and amplitude of the wave we want. If we stick with the surfing concept, we don't need to ride the wave all the way into shore, in fact, we're not riding it anywhere. All we have to do is make contact with the wave's energy and the soliton drive does the rest."

"That doesn't answer the core question," Reggie said, "how long does it take to encounter one of these waves. How common are they?"

"Oh, I see, I took the analogy too far. We're not waiting for the wave to come along, we're capturing a gravity wave and converting the energy into a soliton wave. The more energy in the wave we convert, the more energy we have in the soliton wave."

"In other words," I said, "we're taking the g-drive concept to the next level, directly converting gravitational force into sustained propulsion."

"Why didn't you say that in the first place?" Michael asked.

****

We were halfway to Mars when the Sol Federation declared us criminals and offered a bounty for our capture. The decree was broadcast across the system, but Admiral Wilson sent a comm directly to the *Ajax* informing us my career, and our freedom, were forfeit. For Becca and me, the situation was binary. If we failed, we wouldn't be around to suffer the consequences. We'd be dead or stranded lightyears away from the Federation. If we succeeded, we'd have a good case for mercy. As for Reggie and Michael, they wouldn't make the trip with us, but would be safe on Deimos until the outcome was known.

Four days later, with our destination in site, one of Grace Cheng's scout ships opened fire on us. When Lieutenant Jay fired a plasma burst across the enemy ship's path, it was sliced open across the bow, and whipped into an uncontrolled spin, its air supply jetting out through its hull.

A distress call went out from the damaged ship. Given the circumstances, I didn't feel obliged to help. Peace or no peace, pirates would always be the enemy, at least until they stopped trying to kill me.

A few hours from our destination, we found ourselves confronted by no less than thirty of Grace Cheng's ships. Her message was pointed. "Charles Bimmy, shut down your engines and prepare to be boarded. Do as I say, or I will fire on your ship. You have five minutes to comply."

"Not so fast, Cheng," said a woman's voice over the comm, "the *Ajax* is under the protection of the Deimos Colonial Authority. Withdraw, or we will open fire. Check your scans, you know you're outgunned. I'll give you the same courtesy, you have five minutes to comply."

"What's happening," Becca asked.

"The distress call," I said, "like moths to a flame, and we lit the candle."

"The transponder," Michael said, "we never shut it off. Every ship in range will know we're here, and we're too low on fuel to use the cloak any longer."

"I count six cruisers out of Deimos, attack formation," Reggie said.

"We outnumber you," Cheng said, "I don't care what weapons you have, I'm ordering you to withdraw or face the same fate as Charles Bimmy."

The pirate ships maneuvered to gain tactical advantage over the battle cruisers. The cruisers were some of the finest ships ever built, large and bristling with weapons. They were also slower and less maneuverable than frigates. It would be a close fight, and from my perspective, the pirates had the advantage.

"Reggie," I asked, "does the ship in quadrant four look familiar?"

"They all look familiar to me…"

"Look at the flank, the green and black marking, it's Cheng's flagship."

"What do you want to do?"

"Light it up, fire at will."

"Targeting…firing one…missile away…"

Before the targeted ship was destroyed, a different ship returned fire. I wondered if Cheng had learned not to ride her marked ship into battle.

"Return fire, evasive…"

"Deploying countermeasures," Michael said.

"Firing two…missile away…"

"We can't stand and fight, there are too many of them. Make for the battle cruisers, get us some cover."

Cheng's smaller vessels pursued us, but weapons fire from the colonial ships provided a moving screen. The first volley from the cruisers damaged several pirate ships; Cheng's response disabled one of the battlecruisers. When one of the Deimosian ships moved to defend the stricken ship, the balance tipped in the pirates' favor.

We watched and maneuvered, firing whenever we had a clear target.

A second battlecruiser took heavy fire and her crew abandoned ship before it exploded, splattering debris across our hull.

"If this keeps up, our side is gonna lose," I said.

"We need to get out of here," Reggie said. "If we run, and they chase us, we might be able draw them closer to the colony and surface batteries could open up."

It was risky. We couldn't be certain the Deimosian ships would continue fighting when we ran. I was about to give the order when the battle took an unexpected turn.

Becca pointed at the view screen and shouted, "What's happening in quadrant two?"

One by one, the pirate frigates began to explode, until the remaining ships fled.

"It's the *Arcturus*, with a Federation battle group, they're lightin' up the pirates," Michael said, his voice rising with his excitement.

Admiral Wilson had arrived. I met the development with mixed emotions. I was relieved the battle would soon be over, but I couldn't help feeling we had jumped from the frying pan directly into the fire.

"I'm not sure we're any better off."

"We're being hailed, it's Captain Roberts, Deimos Ops Commander, on the *Haruto*."

"On screen, Mister Jay."

"Captain Roberts, this is Captain Charles Bimmy of the *Ajax*. We thank you for your assistance."

"I know who you are," she replied. "We've been expecting you, Captain Bimmy. Reggie, Michael, good to see you again. Quite the entrance. Next time, don't bring so many friends home with you. Captain, you're cleared for Deimos station, dock seven. We'll see to it you have enough time to get locked in, Roberts out."

"Aunt Sally looks upset," Michael said.

"Who could blame her, look at this mess," Reggie replied.

I saw the confused look on Becca's face.

"It's a small colony, everybody's family," I said.

We flew through the colonial battlecruisers and the debris field from the battle, doing our best to stay out of the firing line of the Federation ships. We listened in as the admiral hailed the *Haruto* and made her demands.

"Captain Roberts, this is Fleet Admiral Wilson of the Sol Federation High Council. The *Ajax* is the property of Earth, we're here to retrieve it. Stand down your weapons and we'll render assistance to your fleet. Do not interfere with our capture of the *Ajax*."

"Admiral Wilson, we could use your help, but I'm not prepared to surrender the *Ajax*. My orders are to see them safely to Deimos. If you have a problem with my orders, take it up with President Jay."

There was a long pause before the admiral responded.

"Captain Roberts, stand down your weapons and we will assist in rescue and recovery. We will not pursue the *Ajax*. Provide clearance for my shuttle to dock at Deimos and arrange a meeting with President Jay."

"Thank you, Admiral. Standby for further instructions."

Our approach and docking went faster than our previous visit. Since the war was over, the door to the interior was open. Becca asked the same question I'd asked on my first arrival at Deimos.

"What next?"

"We wait for clearance," I said.

"How long does it usually take?"

"It depends, but with two of the president's sons onboard, things could move faster. Either way, all we can do is sit tight and wait."

Before Becca could reply, the comm panel lit up.

"Captain Bimmy, welcome to Deimos. You and your crew are cleared to disembark. Please use gangway Alpha-3. President Jay sends his regards."

# 19

# The Unknown

"Admiral Wilson," Becca said, "I'm sure this looks bad from your perspective. If you let us explain…"

"It looks bad from any perspective," the admiral said. "Theft of a starship, a costly battle, upending the peace…"

"A peace my husband helped win," Becca said.

We were in a lounge in the main terminal, facing off over a round table carved from stone. President Jay and his wife had met us there to discuss our plans before allowing Admiral Wilson to join us.

"Everyone," Letitia said, "please take a deep breath and have a seat. Sniping at each other will get us nowhere."

"I'm all ears," the admiral replied.

Once everyone was seated, Letitia turned to me again.

"Captain," she asked, "why don't you tell the admiral what you were telling me before she arrived?"

The admiral stretched out her arms, palms up, and said, "Whaddaya got for me? What's so important you'd throw away the lives of so many people, including your own?"

I knew the admiral well enough to know she was barely masking her rage.

"If there's one thing I learned from the war," I said, "it's that we're doomed as a species if we don't act."

"Humanity is thriving," the admiral said, "we've spread across half the solar system."

"That's what I used to think but, with respect, you're wrong. The

Venusians figured it out, I've seen the data. The human population has been in decline since before I was born. The drop in our numbers accelerates with each generation. The successful colonies are successful because they limit population growth. The ones struggling have a constant need for more resources. Have you seen the mining station over Titan? It holds three times as many people as it was designed to support. It's no wonder the colonies rebelled. In our lifetime, even the Earth won't be able to sustain what's left of its population."

"What's that got to do with stealing a starship?"

"We need a new home, a place where people can walk around the surface of the planet, like on Earth. A place with abundant resources, a place people will want to live. We don't abandon what we've built, we give ourselves enough time, and the Earth enough time, to turn things around. I want a future with Becca, a meaningful, peaceful life. For us, and anyone else who wants it."

"No such place exists," the admiral said, shaking her head. "I don't see where you're going with this…"

"You're wrong again," Becca interjected. "There is a place, a planet like Earth. We have a way to get there. Or a way to try, which is better than nothing."

"I've seen the schematics," the admiral said, shaking her head, "you want to bolt an untested device to a starship and ram it through the fabric of space-time. If that's not crazy, what is?"

"It's not crazy," President Jay said, "it's genius. I'll admit, there's a fine line between the two, but this lands firmly on the side of the latter. We're going to modify Charlie's ship, and we're going to help these two test it."

"It's not Charlie's ship," growled the admiral, "it's stolen property."

Letitia, First Lady of Deimos, smiled politely, "You're making a habit of being wrong today, Admiral."

"Enlighten me."

"The *Ajax* was cleared for launch by Artemis Station. They may not have been transparent about their intent, but they had permission to launch. No one bothered to ask for a flight plan so, technically speaking, they never violated one. You see, if you look at it from this perspective, the notion of Charlie as thief, it doesn't, how would you say…pass muster."

The admiral flushed red with anger. She was about to speak, then her anger dissipated. She was looking at Becca, eyes focused like lasers, until her expression softened further.

She let out a long sigh, then sat back in her chair.

"You would risk your freedom, your future, your lives for this, both of you?"

"I'd say we already have," Becca replied.

"And you," the admiral said to the president, "you would risk your membership in the Sol Federation, based on this sketch of a plan?"

"You heard her," he said, "we already have, we don't intend to stop."

"What about the nukes, are they part of this scheme?"

"They're on Luna," I said. "Breuger and Jones took care of them."

"I've had you declared criminals. How do explain that away?"

"Standard disinformation campaign," I said, "we were on a secret mission to draw the pirate fleet out of hiding."

"Sounds familiar," she replied, with a degree of sarcasm that reminded me of my mother. She turned to the First Lady. "Let's say, for the sake of argument, I decided to take leave and spend some time here on Deimos. How much time do you think I should take?"

"We'll start on the modifications immediately," Letitia replied. "They're not terribly complicated. I'd say 15, 20 orbits, give or take."

"Three weeks," the admiral said.

"That sounds about right. Any longer and we miss the launch window," Letitia said.

"What do I do on Deimos for three weeks?"

Becca leaned forward and placed her hand on the arm of the admiral's chair. "Make history," she said.

***

The admiral kept half her ships on station around Deimos to support ongoing salvage operations. She sent the balance to their normal duty stations. It was the first inter-governmental operation since the founding of the fledgling Federation.

The casualties from the battle on the side of the friendly forces were comparatively low. Sixty-one wounded, four dead. The space pirates didn't fare as well. Twenty-one frigates were destroyed. When the butcher's bill was tallied, over three hundred pirates were dead. The battle decimated what remained of the pirate fleet, but once again, Grace Cheng managed to escape.

In the days after the battle, I attended the memorial services for the four Deimosians who were killed. They died because they were given orders to protect our ship, and they followed those orders. It was a debt I did not know how to repay.

I felt a measure of sadness for the pirates as well. I requested a space beacon to carry a message into the cluster of moons around Jupiter, sheltering what was left of their fleet. I did not ask for peace. Instead, I sent my condolences, and my wish for a day when the pirates could find their way back into civilization's fold.

Becca tried to ease my melancholy. She reminded me of our mission, to find a new world, and how it could save many more lives than had been lost. Her words helped me through those dark days.

As the pace of work on the *Ajax* quickened, my spirits began to lift.

When the admiral suggested we rename the ship, I was elated. I was bold enough to defy her, but still craved her approval. Her change of heart was complete. She went so far as to loan several of her engineers to the appropriately named 'Luyten Project.'

The naming of ships was a tricky thing, fraught with political danger, and usually done by committee, after months of careful research. All I had to do was ask Becca.

"Katie," was her immediate reply, "name the ship Katie."

"Katie is perfect," I said, "and next time we make this trip, Katie will be on board the *Katie* – I like it."

While the ship was modified in record time, our launch window was fixed. If we missed it, the next opportunity wouldn't arrived for another 15 Earth months. There was no time for a test flight. We were gambling everything on the Deimosian engineers and our own design. When launch day arrived, we said our goodbyes to the Admiral and our hosts, before boarding a shuttle to the repair dock.

"I'm returning to Luna soon," the admiral said, "but we'll monitor your departure. Remember our agreement, no more than five days over Luyten b, then come back. I'd like to be alive when you get home."

"Thank you," I replied, "we won't let you down."

"No," the admiral said, "I don't believe you will."

I snapped to attention and saluted. She returned my salute and said, "Come back to us, safe and sound, we need you here, no matter what you find there."

"Goodbye, Amanda," Becca said, "thank you, for everything."

"It's time," Letitia said, "we'll go up with you, if it's all right."

"Of course," Becca said.

We boarded the shuttle and left the interior of Deimos behind. The pilot set us on course to our destination, Yard 9, and our ship.

When I saw the ship, my jaw dropped. "It doesn't look like I expected...."

"We made a few modifications, some improvements," Letitia said.

The *Katie* hung within the metal framework of the space dock, lights along the inner axis illuminating her sleek lines and newly refitted hull. The ship looked more than refitted, it looked reborn.

"How did you find the time?" Becca asked.

"We had so many volunteers for this project," President Jay said, "we decided to expand the scope. We might have had a mutiny if we didn't."

The ship barely resembled its former self. The modifications were better than our original design. The changes were integrated into the existing design in a way that gave the ship a streamlined, albeit odd, new look.

The *Katie's* three main thrusters had been replaced with a collection of nine rocket motors, each smaller and more powerful than the originals. The ship's hull sported new exterior panels where damaged thermal plating had been replaced. The flag of the nascent Sol Federation was emblazoned across the bow. The roughed-up ship was new again, beautiful, ready for space, and armed to the teeth. Its lone blemish was the four-spiked frame of the E–R bridge array splaying out from the forward section.

"I don't know how to thank you...," I said, "this is so much more...I don't know what to say."

"Captain Bimmy," Letitia said, "if it weren't for you, our sons would have died on Europa. Consider this a payment on our debt."

Before I left the shuttle, I pulled a memory chip from my pocket and handed it to the President. "We should be back in less than ten Deimos orbits. If we're not, please give this to Reggie, he'll know what to do."

"We'll see you in ten orbits," President Jay replied, "don't make me send him after you."

"Yes, sir," I said, "ten orbits."

Becca and I boarded the ship, and I ran through the pre-flight checks. "Hey, Commander Gorgeous, you ready to go?"

"You bet I am, Captain Handsome," she replied, laughing.

"Here we go," I said, "control nine, this is the *Katie*, ready for departure, requesting clearance to launch coordinates on vector 227."

When the control operator replied, I thought I heard Reggie and Michael laughing in the background, but chalked it up to an echo on the comm.

"*Katie*, you are cleared for departure. The people of Deimos and the Sol Federation look forward to your safe and speedy return."

I engaged the maneuvering thrusters and eased the ship forward. When we were safely beyond the dock I moved the ship into position for launch. I could see the admiral's ships, and many others, holding positions around us to witness the event.

"Control nine, we're in position, give us a marker."

"Twenty-eight seconds to Gateway activation, arm system in three, two, one, ..."

"System armed, powering soliton drive, countdown engaged."

When the wormhole opened, the swirling vortex of color and light took my breath away. The rift in space-time grew to enormous proportions, many times larger than the ship. I tried to focus on the task at hand, but in the final few seconds, I stared into the gaping hole we'd opened in the fabric of the universe. It was a mesmerizing cauldron of motion and light, mostly yellow in color, with a perfect black circle at its center, a field of glittering stars against the backdrop of distant space. I barely acknowledged when the countdown reached its conclusion.

The soliton drive captured and tuned the energy it needed, and the ship moved forward. The framework of the E–R Bridge slipped back, inverted by the pinion movement of the four spines. The nose of the starship made contact with the event horizon, the wormhole took over, and the ship began to glide forward, into the unknown.

From within the ship, the view was bizarre and frightening. Everything was stretched forward, elongated into impossible thinness, swirling in a giant spiral, mixed with the light around us, until my senses failed and all I knew was light and noise and the shuddering of the ship. The sudden shaking and rattling of the ship gave me the overwhelming feeling something had gone wrong. But there was nothing I could do. We had to ride out the experience and hope we arrived...somewhere...when it was over.

# 20

# **Arrival**

To my astonishment, we didn't die. But the jump lasted longer than it should have. Something definitely went wrong, and still we arrived at the Luyten system in one piece. It was an amazing sight to behold. The distant red dwarf star cast a gentle glow, bathing our destination planet in soft light. The planet shone a deep azure blue, the atmosphere streaked with white clouds. We could see two other planets drifting along their orbital paths in the distance, too far away to make out details.

"It's beautiful," I said.

"Bimmy," Becca said, "I think our data was off."

"What do you mean?"

"These two planets," Becca said, pointing at Luyten b's companions, "they're further inside the habitable zone than I thought. I'm reading atmosphere on both of them. The odds of them being habitable have gone way up."

"I thought there were four planets."

"There are. The fourth is on the far side of the sun from us, at the outer limit of the zone, still beyond sensor range."

"Becca, what are the chances of three habitable worlds orbiting one star."

"I don't know," Becca replied, "I don't think anyone can say. We should scan for comm traffic before we drop into orbit. Any one of them could have an advanced civilization."

I activated the sensor array and set the system to alert on any radio frequency traffic. Nothing came up right away. We soaked in the view, recording it to share when we returned home. After an hour with no signals detected I set course to take up orbit around Luyten b.

Nothing happened.

"What's wrong?"

"The drive isn't responding," I said, "standby."

I ran a diagnostic and no data came back.

"The drive is dead."

"We can still get there with the rocket engines…"

"That's not the problem."

"We can't get home," Becca said, "unless we fix it."

"That is the problem."

I couldn't know what Becca was thinking in the moment, but I was thinking about my parents, and Katie. If we couldn't fix the drive, I'd never see them again. It meant we had to make the journey worth it.

"We should go on," I said, "continue the mission, learn what we can. We have limited fuel and supplies. If we can't get back, we need to know our situation here."

"Why not fix the drive first?"

"We could spend days trying to fix it or I could get injured in the process. Or you could. I'll have to leave the ship. The time, the risk, if it prevents us from learning more about Luyten b, then the trip was worthless. The risk is too high. I say we accomplish what we came here to do, gather data. When we're done, figure out what to do about the drive."

Becca didn't say anything. Then she pointed at a tiny dot of light coming into view on the screen, "Luyten b has a moon."

"Good eyes Commander Kiel," I said, "I bet it didn't show up in your data either."

"No, too small, but we should expect planets of any significant mass to have at least one satellite. This one is tiny relative to the planet, its orbit seems eccentric, the trajectory indicates a huge ellipse. Probably exerts no, or at least very little, tidal force."

"What's the significance?"

"It could have implications for coastal erosion, city placement, species migration, all sorts of things. We won't know until we get closer."

"Luyten b is mostly water," I said, "seventy percent surface water. The rest is one big continent. Atmosphere is primarily nitrogen, but I can't be certain of these readings, not from this distance."

"How long before we're in orbit?"

"With standard engines, playing it safe, eight hours, give or take. I'm gonna put us in a geosynchronous orbit over the landmass to start."

We began detailed scans of the planet, each pass delivering reams of data about its surface, its atmosphere, and its ocean. When we arrived in geosynchronous orbit, we were still too far to make out most of the surface details with the naked eye, but our optics revealed a world rich with life. Becca deployed a laser mapping system to create a topographical image of the lone continent. When the mapping was complete, she compare it to the temperature data.

"This is interesting," she said to herself.

"Want to tell me what it is, or should I guess?" I asked.

"Sorry, I guess everything's going to be interesting. It's hard to know where to focus."

"What's the latest?"

"The continent is 28.3 percent of the planet's surface. The planet has a vertical axis, relative to its orbital plane, unlike Earth, which tilts, relative to its plane."

"Does that mean there are no seasons?"

"There's no significant variation in environment across the continental latitudes. The continent has one consistent ecosystem. No deserts, no arid plains, it's a thriving system, loaded with life. There's no sign of volcanic activity on the land mass, no tectonic plate activity. The closest thing to a mountain range are these highlands running north to south in the East. Think small Appalachians, not big Rockies. The temperature is a consistent seventy degrees, it's…"

"It sounds too good to be true."

"Or we've found paradise."

"I think we need to go in for a closer look."

"I'm going to try to get some data on the other two planets," Becca said. "We may not get another chance."

Hours later, we were low over the planet, passing over the continent once every hour. Each time, we took more images and scans. When the land was in darkness, we peered down, looking for lights to indicate the presence of a civilization. With every orbit, we found no indication of civilization, no roads, no cities, no harbors, nothing but vegetation and water.

"It's too perfect to be uninhabited," I said.

"It took millions of years for intelligent life to evolve on Earth,"

Becca said, "it's possible it hasn't happened here yet."

"Don't you think, in an ecosystem like this, something smarter than a plant would evolve?"

"We should expand our definition of intelligent life," she said. "There might be some smart chipmunks, with tiny cities and itty-bitty lights."

"What are you talking about?" I asked, laughing.

"Somebody once said the absence of proof is not proof of absence. We won't know for sure until someone goes down there and explores. I know that wasn't the plan, but our plans have changed, whether we like it or not. I think we need to keep an open mind about what we might find."

"We've been at it too long," I said, "let's get some rest and let the scans run on their own. The chipmunks aren't going anywhere."

"Go ahead," Becca said, "I'll be right there. I'm going to re-target the laser and try to get some topographic renderings of the ocean floor."

"Good idea, you might find some intelligent shrimp to go with your chipmunks."

"I'm not ruling anything out."

***

I drifted off to sleep before Becca joined me. When I woke up, she was curled up beside me, sound asleep. I stayed as still as possible and listened to her breathing. Her slow and steady rhythm lulled me back to sleep.

What seemed like seconds later, we were jarred awake by alarms sounding throughout the ship. I bolted from the room, heading for the bridge, Becca close behind. I jumped into my seat and strapped in, trying to find the source of the problem from the myriad flashing lights.

"What's happening?" Becca asked.

"I don't know, strap in. We've got multiple sensor alerts, a half dozen system alarms, got a hull breach in the starboard cargo bay, a proximity alarm, and we've picked up a some kind transmission."

I was too busy looking at my console to notice what was right outside the portals of the bridge and coming into view on the main screen.

"Bimmy, look," Becca shouted.

Initially I couldn't make sense of the mass drifting toward us. I switched the main viewer to display a closeup of the approaching object. It was many times larger than our ship. Lights flashed along the curved outer edge of a what I knew, in a sudden shock of recognition, was an enormous space station, a giant spindle floating within a constellation of debris.

My training took over and I burned our engines to move the ship to a higher orbit.

"Can you get a reading on it?" I asked.

"No life signs, but there's a signal coming from it, a weak one. It's a repeating pattern, but there's no way I can decipher it. I'm getting crazy readings off its hull."

"We almost crashed into a giant space station, the first proof of intelligent life outside the Sol system. Please be more specific than crazy."

"Based on these readings, this thing could be hundreds of years old, five hundred, a thousand, the isotope decay is all over the place."

"I stand corrected, crazy is the right word."

I shut down the alarms and rerouted critical systems while Becca continued scanning the object.

"Internal bulkheads are sealed," I said, "but the hull breach is now top of the repair list."

"Based on my readings, the station has an elliptical orbit...it matches...I thought this was a small moon," Becca said. "I'm having trouble calculating its orbit."

"How does something stay in orbit for hundreds of years?" I asked. "It should have burned up in the atmosphere a long time ago."

"I don't know, it's another mystery. I mean, who built it, what's it for, what's the signal? The orbital trajectory makes no sense. I'm full up with questions," Becca said. "It seems to be approaching perigee..."

As it grew closer to the planet, a white glow formed around the derelict station, spreading further as the distance closed.

"Thrusters..." I said.

"It's some kind of energy, not propellant," Becca said as she examined the data.

"Maybe some kind of gravity drive, but how does it have power?"

"What does this look like to you, along the perimeter, all these openings? Most look damaged, but..."

"Docking bays," I said.

"If one of those bays is functional," Becca said, "we have to board it.

We have to investigate."

"We most certainly do not have to board it, Becca, no way, it's too risky."

"Captain Bimmy, what does your military training tell you?"

"Captain Bimmy would be happy to blast it out of the sky and be done with it."

"Commander Kiel thinks we should board it and look for anything that might help us repair our ship."

Becca was right. We couldn't miss the opportunity to explore an alien space station. The scavenger in me knew it could be our salvation. But first, some repairs were needed.

I patched our hull breach and re-pressurized the cargo bay, then maneuvered the *Katie* into position to meet the derelict space station post-apogee. I matched its orbit and we tried to work out the best approach. The cloud of detritus drifting around it made it dangerous. After tracking it for 36 hours, Becca noticed a pattern to the movement of the larger objects. More importantly, she noticed a gap in the pattern we could exploit to approach what we presumed was an intact docking bay.

"This is as close as we get," I said, "I'll take the EV suit and use its thrusters to transit over and see if I can find a way in."

"Why do you get to go? This was my idea," Becca said.

"This isn't open for discussion. This is high risk, you need to leave this one to me, I've trained for missions like this."

"What's your plan for getting inside the...what are we gonna call this thing?"

"You remember those old movies we used to watch, where dead people go around trying to eat the living people? We could call it Zombie Station."

"Let's get you suited up while I think of a proper name," Becca said.

We went to the cargo bay and Becca helped me assemble the EV pack and suit up.

"We don't have a lot of time for this. If I can't find a way in, I'm not forcing it. If the interior is pressurized, I could blow the whole thing to bits. Better to back off and try again later."

"Don't you think they'd have a manual override for their hatches?"

"We have no idea what we're dealing with. They could have three legs and four arms for all we know, in which case it would be pretty hard for me to operate whatever mechanism there is."

"You could try knocking."

"Stranger things have happened…no, on second thought, stranger things than this have never happened."

"You should take a plasma torch."

"It could be mistaken for a weapon. Zombie Station might have automated defense systems. Come to think of it, the bay might be automated. You could be right about knocking."

After Becca put my helmet in place, she pulled the tether line from the wall inside the airlock and attached it to the hip of my suit. She tapped my helmet and said, "Go get 'em Bimmy" and left the cargo bay.

When she was on the bridge she radioed, "Comm check."

"Comms good," I replied.

The inner door closed behind me and the airlock depressurized. The artificial gravity switched off, and I activated the outer door. I surveyed the station, making sure I had a clear path through the debris field. When I was satisfied, I pushed out of the lock and used the suit's thrusters to transit to the station.

There were red symbols emblazoned across parts of the upper hull of the station. Some were incomplete where the hull was damaged. There were blue symbols above each of the docking bays, which I assumed were numbers.

When I got closer to the bay, I could see a dim light shining from a window at one end.

"Looks like an airlock, there's light coming from a panel. I'm going in."

"It's not such a zombie after all," Becca said.

The bay was cylindrical, ten meters in diameter and as many deep. Devices protruded from the walls at regular intervals.

"Docking clamps don't look much different from ours, but I don't get this arrangement. It feels too small for a ship to enter."

"Chipmunks, Bimmy, intelligent chipmunks, keep an open mind," Becca replied.

"Understood," I said, "I'm approaching the pressure lock. There's a panel inside. I don't see any…wait, the light is changing."

The soft blue glow of the panel changed to a bright orange, then dim red lights came on throughout the bay and inside the lock.

"Looks like the station sees you," Becca said.

I reached the window to the lock and looked inside. It was larger than the one on our ship but otherwise looked like a standard airlock.

I saw a panel glowing below me. I changed position so I could get a closer look. The panel glowed blue, like the interior panel. Other than the color, the screen had no symbols, but it pulsed slowly, from bright to dim and back again.

"Are you thinking what I'm thinking?" I asked.

"If you're thinking the panel says 'push here,' then yes."

I laughed and pressed the panel.

Through my gloved hand I felt a gentle vibration rumble through the surface of the ship. Two panels moved apart, sliding into the bulkhead to my left and right. The doors opened less than halfway. I wedged my arm between them and shoved. They slipped away and the lock was open.

"Look at you, Bimmy, first day on the job and you've already repaired an alien ship," Becca said.

"Commander Kiel, need I remind you, we are the aliens here, and for the record, I can fix anything."

"I guess we'll see."

"Yes, we will. I'm latching the tether in the bay. If anything goes wrong, jettison the line. This station is plenty big enough to drag us anyplace it wants to go. I'm closing the doors. If I'm not back in 15 minutes, drop the line and get away from this thing."

"Aye, aye, Captain," Becca said.

"What are you, a pirate? Remember, 15 minutes."

Unlike their opening, the doors shut with a rapid movement. The lock ran its pressure cycle and the panel switched from orange to blue. I felt the tug of artificial gravity and the inner door opened. I checked the atmospheric reading on my suit. 1.2 atm and 1.1 G, a notch higher than Earth.

"Artificial G, 1.1," I said, "this place is full of surprises."

The suit's sensor sampled the air and returned a glaring warning. The atmosphere was toxic. "I don't get it," I said, stepping through the door, "if the builders were from Luyten b, wouldn't they breathe the same air?"

"We don't know they didn't," Becca answered, "we have no idea what happened here. There could have been an accident."

"Agreed. I'm reading a lot of nitrogen tetroxide, rocket fuel to us, as toxic as it gets," I said. "It adds up. I'm in a corridor. I can go left, I can go right, care to be my coin toss?"

"There's less damage to your right."

"Right it is."

The corridor was four meters wide, with walls curving outward from the center, and a flat ceiling and floor. The walls were decorated with geometric shapes in red, dark blue, and green. Darkened rectangular panels were spaced at regular intervals along the interior wall. The color of the walls changed as amber lights flickered to life, tracking my progress down the corridor.

A darkened corridor led away to my left, and I could see another airlock further along on the right. Blue lights began to pulse up from the floor, forming a line leading down the corridor toward the interior of the ship. More amber lights came on overhead.

"What do you make of this?"

"Apparently, blue means go," Becca replied.

I followed the blue lights. The curved walls gave way to vertical ones with doors evenly spaced along each wall. Symbols, like those over the docking bays, were placed above each door. The blue lights stopped in front of the last door on my left. When I stepped in front of it, it slid away into the wall. The light within was too dim to see the interior.

"Do not go in there," Becca said.

"I'll be okay."

Before Becca could say more, I stepped into the room. The door slid shut behind me and the lights brightened. When I saw what was in the room, I turned to face the wall.

"Shut off the camera."

"What did you see?"

"Shut off the camera, Becca, please."

"Whatever it is, I want to see it."

"Suit yourself."

I turned back and stepped further into the room. I panned left to right to make sure she saw everything. The room was a large sleeping quarter. There were four beds in the room, two on each side protruding from the walls. A table and chairs sat between them. To one side a door was ajar and led to what I surmised was a washroom.

The beds were occupied.

The bodies, humanoid in form, were locked in contorted positions, twisted in agony, flesh dried and taut against bone. Hands reached out, grasping at nothing, faces frozen in silent screams. Based on the size of the bodies, I was looking at two adults and two children. The scene was as sad as it was gruesome.

"What is this place?" Becca asked.

I didn't answer. I stepped between the beds and looked down at the table, littered with objects. A layer of dust covered everything. The wall beyond the table was transparent, spanning the end of the room. The darkness beyond reflected my image back at me, until red lights began to glow in a grid pattern in the surface beyond, above and below me. Other lights in other rooms were coming on, growing brighter. I stepped backwards, my heart racing. Directly in front of me, someone stared back at me from the facing room across the empty space between us.

"Bimmy, get out of there."

I turned to run for the door. I tripped and landed with a thud. I struggled to stand but couldn't. Something held my leg. I threw my body into a roll, kicked blindly at whatever held me. When I saw what it was, I stopped struggling and tried to slow my breathing.

The hand of a machine gripped my ankle. An android, similar in shape to the bodies. Its eyes pulsed red and orange, its thin lips curled back as if to speak, but the only sound I heard was Becca's scream.

The lights of the android's eyes dimmed, then extinguished, and the grip of its hand loosened. It had been lying under one of the beds, partially assembled. Components were stacked on the floor behind it. I stood and looked through the window again.

The eyes of the 'person' staring back at me pulsed slow and steady, red to orange. I stepped around the table to get a broader view through the window. There were six levels of windows lining the wall across from me. I could see other spaces, other walls and windows, great spokes of a giant wheel, stretched out vertically, rising away from a transparent surface far below.

Light came up from the bottom, at first confusing my vision. Then I realized the light was coming up from the planet. We were going to be closer than I thought. I realized I'd made a horrible mistake. Our ship was going to skim the planet's atmosphere.

"Get back to the ship, we need to reassess…" Becca said.

"How much time?"

"Ten minutes, get moving."

I backed away from the window and left the room behind. I could only guess at the purpose of the station. It was similar to ones in orbit around Earth, but there wasn't enough time for me to learn more. Whatever it was, it had died centuries earlier, taking its occupants with it.

I retraced my steps, running back toward the airlock. I knew I had to be off the station before its thrusters fired. It would take an experienced pilot to avoid disaster if we didn't make for higher orbit over Luyten b before it happened.

I reached the airlock door, pressed the panel and the doors slid open, then closed behind me. When the doors were sealed, the depressurization cycle ran and artificial gravity shut off. When the next panel changed to blue again, I pressed it. The outer doors began to open, moving at a snail's pace. I could feel the ancient machinery straining to do its work until the doors stopped, a hand's width apart.

"We have a problem, how much time do I have?"

"Seven minutes, there's no time to find another way out…"

"Roger that, standby."

I explored the interior of the lock, looking for a panel I could open to reveal a manual mechanism. I noticed a seam at the base of the partially opened doors, then pulled myself down for a closer look.

I ran my glove over the surface and found a small depression, about the size of my thumb. I pressed it and a panel opened. Inside were two orange rods, arranged opposite one another. One was raised, while the other was lowered. I pushed down on one but couldn't make it budge. I pulled up on the other with the same result. I grabbed the first lever again, then grabbed the edge of the door with my free hand and pushed with all my strength and still the lever wouldn't move.

"Bimmy…," Becca said.

"I don't need a countdown."

"Listen to me," she said, her voice calm, "try working both at the same time."

I stabbed my free hand into the compartment and gripped the second lever. I pulled and pushed as hard as I could with both hands, expecting the same resistance I'd already met.

This time, the levers moved with sudden ease. My hands slipped off, and the energy I expected to expend on the levers found its way into my body. I flew up and away from the mechanism, slamming back against the inner door.

"Bimmy, what's happening?"

"I'm learning to fly," I said and pushed myself back to the levers. I took hold again and moved them up and down, watching the doors open a few millimeters with each pull and push of the levers.

"Time check," I said.

"Four minutes."

"If I'm not on the tether in two, jettison and get out of here."

"You know I can't fly this ship. I can't come back for you, you have to get off the station."

"Then don't come back for me."

"Shut up and get the doors open."

"Working on it."

When the gap between the doors was wide enough, I tried the same approach I used when I entered from outside. I wedged my arms into the gap and shoved the doors with all my strength.

The mechanism gave way, and the doors flew apart, sending me tumbling through the docking bay, towards open space.

I flailed my arms and legs grasping for anything to stop my motion. I saw the tether stretching through the bay and stopped struggling. I was about to exit the bay, then reached out and grabbed the line.

"Time check," I said, pulling myself back into the bay.

"Two minutes. You can do it."

I threw caution aside and blasted the suit's thrusters, catapulting back toward the interior. I crashed into the bulkhead next to the open airlock doors but kept my grip on the tether. I pulled myself around to face the latch, steadied my body, then released the line from the bulkhead and attached it to the locking ring at my hip. I aimed for the open end of the bay and activated my thrusters again.

They didn't fire. The impact had damaged the system.

"Thrusters out, I'm on the tether. Once I exit the bay, fire maneuvering thrusters, we need altitude."

I aimed for the open end of the bay and pushed off the bulkhead behind me.

"Becca, acknowledge, I'm exiting, prepare to burn thrusters and get us out of here."

Becca would never leave me in the dark. My collision must have damaged the comm as well. Everything that could go wrong, was going wrong. If she didn't fire the thrusters soon, the *Katie* was doomed.

I flew out of the bay as the base of the station began to glow. I looked beyond the light at the sparkling blue sea below, so close I wanted to reach out and touch it. I saw the maneuvering thrusters of our ship fire and pulled on the tether with the last of my strength, hoping I could make it to the cargo bay airlock.

A piece of debris from the station struck my leg, tearing a hole in my suit. My air began to jet out, changing my trajectory. I screamed in rage and frustration and slammed my fist into the gel pack at my thigh, filling the leg of my suit, sealing the leak.

A sudden jerk against my hip told me Becca had activated the tether coil and was pulling me back to the cargo bay. I landed face down in the *Katie's* airlock, unable to move. The outer door closed and when the cycle finished, Becca stepped inside and tried to roll me over. I waved my hand at her and slapped at my helmet. She unlatched the locking ring and pulled the helmet away. I was yelling before it was off.

"Kill the grav-plates, I have to get out of this suit, hurry!" I shouted.

"We're OK, we're gaining altitude, it's OK."

"We're too low, the planet's already got us, we're gonna burn up in the atmosphere, kill the plates!"

Becca deactivated the artificial gravity in the bay, then braced herself against the hatch and pulled me inside. We had practiced the suit removal procedure, but never had to deal with a leg full of sealant. Becca latched me into a rack and pulled at my gloves. Once my hands were free, she uncoupled the lower section of the suit and pulled me down out of the upper section. I held onto the rack and Becca pulled the lower portion. The gel had begun to deactivate with the change in pressure, allowing the the suit to come away with a disgusting gurgle.

I was spent. Becca turned the gravity plates back on and looked down at me. She ripped a med kit from the wall and dug through its contents. She found what she was looking for and came back to me.

"I love you," she said, "but this is gonna hurt."

"What is it?" I gasped.

She drove the syringe into my thigh and said, "Adrenaline."

***

Sixty seconds later we were back on the bridge, strapped into our seats.

We didn't have enough fuel to break free from the planet's pull. We'd burned most of it on approach to the planet, and on our expedition to the dead station. We had saved enough to break high orbit, but it wasn't enough to resolve our dilemma.

"We're going in," I said, "there's no way out of this."

"How can you land without fuel?" Becca asked.

"Let's call it another first for us."

We had time before the hull of the ship would superheat. I risked everything on a desperate gamble. We were approaching the terminator, about to enter the dark night side of the planet. The continent wasn't in sight.

"Bring up the topo-map, put it on the main viewer," I shouted over the growing noise.

Becca's hands rushed over her console and the screen filled with the false-color image of the planet's surface. Nothing but a flat expanse ahead and all around.

"Can't we land on water?" Becca asked.

"We'll sink like a rock. We make landfall, or we're swimming. I'm gonna buy us some time. Here we go."

I fired the ship's nine engines and the *Katie* tried to return to space. Once the fuel was exhausted, we had gained altitude but soon began to fall back toward the planet. I used the remaining thruster propellant to place the ship at a sharp angle relative to the atmosphere. I needed the ship to last as long as possible before jettisoning the majority of its mass.

The view screen flickered as the portals lit up orange and black from friction burning away the ship's skin. The flames intensified and the ship shuddered and groaned. Becca grabbed the arms of her seat. I held our angle of approach as long as possible, waiting for the right moment.

"If this works," I shouted, "you're gonna have to come up with a name for this planet."

"Why me?"

"Because I came up with Zombie Station."

Becca started laughing, as I hoped she would.

"Hold on tight," I shouted.

I tapped an icon on my screen, firing the explosive bolts holding the forward compartment to the rest of the ship. The bridge and a section immediately aft were designed to blast away from the ship together, as an oversized escape pod, but for use in space, not on reentry. I struggled with the controls in an effort to minimize the distance between our lifeboat and the body of our dying ship. I wanted to use it as a heat shield as long as possible. I looked over at Becca. Her eyes were closed.

"Becca," I shouted, "look."

She opened her eyes, "Can we make it?" she shouted back.

The coastline of the planet's lone continent was approaching on the view screen as the fire around the ship diminished and the noise dropped with it. The bulk of the *Katie,* having saved our lives for the last time, dropped away toward the sea.

There was no propellant left for thrusters. I held off as long as I could, then fired our solid fuel retro-rockets, reducing our speed. Our altitude and basic control surfaces enabled me to place the ship into a wide spiral to lose more speed.

Becca pointed at an area of open terrain on the topographic map. "There," she said, "between the tree lines, can you bring us around?"

I lined the ship up, then pulled back on the controls. "Can't make it, brace for impact!"

The landing wasn't even close. I overshot the open terrain and hit the trees, shredding everything in our path. Our lifeboat ripped through the treetops, snapping them apart, setting some on fire, until the ship cratered into the ground, coming to rest in a flaming-hot heap and cloud of smoke, throwing debris up into the sky.

I switched off the clanging and buzzing alarms until all we heard was the ticking sound made by what was left of the hull plating as it cooled.

Becca had closed her eyes again.

I reached out and touched her arm. "You okay?"

She opened her eyes, unstrapped from her seat and stood at the starboard portal, staring out at the smoldering scene. She moved to the port side, looked out, then turned to look at me. "You have to see this, get up, look," she said.

I stood beside her and looked out at the forest, expecting to see only darkness. Our immediate surroundings glowed orange from the fire our crash had ignited, but beyond that, the forest was anything but dark.

A raucous collection of color filled the space beneath the treetops, generated by what seemed to be an endless mass of bioluminescent vegetation. What had been, from space, a land of varying shades of green by daylight turned by night into a show of light and motion in the undergrowth, presenting every color imaginable, and some I could not begin to describe. It was an iridescent feast for the eyes.

As we stared at the world around us, plants on the edge of the burn zone began to move, swaying back and forth, leaning toward, then away from our ruined ship.

"They're moving," Becca said.

"I see that," I replied, "it's like a dance…"

"No," she said, "not a dance, they're moving toward us."

I looked away, rubbed my eyes and looked back. Tendrils of vines, as well as branches of shrubs and small trees, began to glow a uniform dark orange and reach out toward the ship. Where embers glowed or flames burned, the orange vegetation fell down onto the fire, sending jets of steam skyward. We watched for an hour, moving from one side of the ship to the other, as the plants extinguished all traces of the fire we had caused, until the forest floor, once burning in the night, finally turned to black.

I sat down and stared at my console, its lights a pale semblance of the scene outside. I thought about updating the ship's log, but didn't. Exhaustion was overtaking me. Becca remained at the portal, gazing into the night.

"What are you thinking?" I asked.

"How much time do you have?"

"In the grand scheme of things? Lots and lots. But right now, I'm done, the tank is empty, I need some rest."

She stepped in front of me and placed her hand on my cheek as she'd done a thousand times before, a touch I knew I could never live without.

"Avalon," she said.

"What…"

"That's what we'll call this world," she said, looking down at me, "Avalon."

***

The bridge of the ship was designed to maintain its attitude relative to the angle of flight. It had done the same during our crash, even though the ship had rolled ninety degrees after impact.

I opened the hatch and stepped through. "Looks like the bulkhead is the new floor," I said.

"That's what happens when you crash," Becca said.

"If you live, it's a rough landing, not a crash."

"A rough landing precipitated by the sudden disassembly of the primary vehicle?"

"Exactly," I replied.

Our quarters had gone down with the bulk of the ship. What remained was a bunk room, intended for use until surviving crew could be rescued. The bunks folded up against the walls but were useless in the current orientation of the ship. I pulled all the bedding off the bunks and used what was once the floor as the headboard. It was comfortable enough, and we drifted off to sleep. It seemed liked my eyes had just closed when I woke up with Becca kneeling beside me.

"What time is it?" I asked, rubbing my eyes,

"Who can say?" she said, smiling. She placed her hand on my chest, "It's almost dawn, that much I can tell you."

"How long have you been up?"

"Less than an hour, running some scans, watching the world wake up."

"And now you're watching me...."

"Yes, and you need to get up. There's something I want you to see."

"I was dreaming about a cheeseburger, I was about to take a bite..."

"When's the last time you ate a cheeseburger?"

"That's my point, you woke me up too early, you owe me a cheeseburger, and no pseudo-beef, the real thing."

"This is better than a cheeseburger. Get dressed, come see," Becca said, then left the room.

I joined Becca on the bridge and looked outside. "You're right, this is better than a cheeseburger."

As the sky changed from night black to shades of blue, and sunlight began to filter down to us, the forest changed with it. The illumination of the night transitioned to greens and browns, punctuated by colorful flowers, opening to greet the sun. In the places not yet touched by the light, the plants remained iridescent hues of blue and yellow, white and glowing green. They swayed and shook, dancing as they had when we first looked out at them. This time, the undergrowth wasn't moving on its own, but was being tossed, tugged and brushed about by animals, feeding on the vegetation.

"They look like baby deer," Becca said.

"An entire herd of baby deer? That doesn't seem right."

"No, but what they're doing does. It took me a while to figure it out. See the pattern?"

"I see little creatures, possibly dinner, eating their breakfast."

"We are not eating the baby deer, don't even joke about it."

"We'll see how you feel in a month. I don't see a pattern here."

"They only eat the green and blue plants."

"Interesting, is it useful?"

"It might be. One way to know what's safe to eat is to watch what the animals eat. If there are any primates here, something more like us, it could be helpful to observe them. Hopefully we won't be stuck here long enough to worry about it."

"You know the admiral's favorite saying...?"

"Hope is not a strategy."

"Yeah," I said, "that's the one."

"How long will the power last?"

"Longer than the food."

"I have a feeling there's plenty to eat out there," Becca said, pointing at the forest. "It looks so much like Earth looked when it was still alive."

"We have to be cautious. We have no idea what's out there."

"We have to explore it sooner or later, I say sooner is better."

"If sensors are working, we can check the data, then we'll see about going outside."

"Some are, most aren't. What about a distress signal?"

"Automated, but I doubt anyone's around to hear it."

"Why?"

"Zombie Station. If there were other people, they would have sorted that mess out a long time ago. Our one shot is for Deimos to send another ship, a crewed ship, and send down a lander."

A light began to pulse on the console in front of Becca. "Atmospheric readings," she said. "This looks good, I'd say exceptional. 78% nitrogen, 21% oxygen, some carbon dioxide, some trace elements. It's better than Earth."

I pointed at a reading on the console, "What's this all about?"

"Unknown element, but the system hasn't tagged it as toxic, nothing to worry about."

"And you say I'm the optimist. I don't like unknown, toxic or not."

"Bimmy, look around, everything outside this ship is unknown. Get used it."

"If you trust the scans, I think a scouting trip is in order."

"I'll go, you stay here in case a miracle happens and a rescue ship shows up while I'm gone."

"This is a lot different from visiting a dead space station."

"It's less risky. Besides, we've already crashed the ship, how much worse can it get? We've got a breathable atmosphere, nominal gravity variance, there's…"

"I'll agree on one condition," I said.

"No conditions, take it or leave it."

"You should hear the condition first."

"I'm listening."

"We get to count this as our honeymoon."

Becca smiled and put her hand on my shoulder, "You really know how to show a girl a good time Captain Bimmy. It's a deal."

I pulled together enough material to fashion a backpack from some cloth and strips of wire, then loaded it with a canteen of water, a thermal blanket, and some protein bars.

"Do I need all this? I'm not planning to be gone long."

"Just in case," I said. "You can use the pack to bring back anything you think is edible. Get a water sample, too, if you can. We'll probably run out of water before we run out of food."

After she slipped the makeshift pack over her shoulders, I placed a comm-bud in her ear. "We'll do a comm-check when you're outside, then check-in every ten minutes. If you miss a check-in, I'm coming to look for you. If you're not back in an hour, I'm coming to look for you. Getting the picture?"

"Yes sir, Captain sir," Becca said.

"No joking around, no taking chances. Don't trust your compass. Maintain line of sight with the damaged trees. I don't want you to get lost."

"I'm a big girl, I got this, try to relax."

"I'll relax when you get back."

Becca crouched and entered the airlock. The pressure outside the ship and inside were similar, there was no need to pressurize. We decided to use the lock in the short term to avoid mixing the interior and exterior atmospheres. It didn't count for much without pressure suits, but it mitigated some of the risk.

I closed the inner door and Becca opened the outer door. She took a deep breath, then stepped down to the forest floor. She looked around, then turned and waved at me.

"Every ten minutes, one hour max," I shouted through the door.

Becca gave me a thumbs up, then walked out of sight along the path of destruction our landing had created. I returned to the bridge and radioed Becca, "Where's my comm check?"

"Comm check," she replied.

"Comms good," I said.

"You won't believe this air. It's like drinking cool water, it's… energizing is the best word I can think of."

"Any air is nice after you've been on a starship long enough. Talk to me about insects, anything buzzing around you?"

"No, but I've been out here for all of two minutes."

"Are you telling me to be quiet?"

"Yes, but I'm being nice about it."

"Message received, next comm check in…seven minutes and twenty seconds."

A few minutes shy of our next check-in, Becca called back.

"Bimmy, I'm at the tree line. When we flew over the open terrain, I thought it was tall grass, but it's not. It's millions and millions of tall… ferns, I guess. Some are two, even three meters high."

"Remember, line of sight," I said.

"I have no interest in getting lost. The ship may be wrecked, but it's home. I think I hear running water, I can't gauge the distance. I'm gonna see if I can find it."

A moment later, the sound of Becca gasping for air echoed over the system.

"Becca? What's wrong? What's happening?"

"Bimmy…" she said, her voice a choked whisper, "Bimmy…"

"Becca, talk to me," I shouted, "Becca!"

I heard her choking and gasping, then something like a growl, as if she tried to scream. Then silence. I fought the urge to bolt from the ship. I activated the bridge recorder and began to speak, straining to keep my voice calm.

When I finished, I shut off the camera, grabbed a transceiver, and ran to the airlock. I jumped out of the ship and raced in the direction Becca had gone, squeezing my radio into place over my ear. By the time I reached the tree line, I was gasping for air.

I saw a few broken ferns and moved forward slowly, scanning the ground. It was carpeted with layers of vegetation in varying degrees of decay. I found a partial footprint in a patch of exposed soil and began running. I was approaching the tree line again when my breathing became labored. I knew I couldn't sustain my speed, unless I could get more air into my lungs. Then my throat abruptly closed, as if a hand clamped around my neck. My lungs were closed off to any more air. I stumbled and fell to my knees. My vision became blurry.

I tried to call out but managed nothing more than a croaking sound. My lips began to dry, it felt like they were splitting apart. I forced my body to stand, then the light dimmed around me. I fell to the ground, the thick ferns softening my landing as I reached into the fading light, until all that remained was silence, and the dark.

# 21

# **Jackpot**

I woke up on a bed of ferns, enveloped in silence, the sun shining in the clear blue sky. I tried to stand but fell back. My mind was fog and shadow. I stayed on the ground and considered my situation. I could not recall my name, where I was, or why I was there. I felt panic setting in.

Then a sense of calm swept over me. The air was cool and crisp, it grounded me. "Bimmy," I remembered, "I'm Captain Charles Bimmy." A lightning bolt of a memory brought a measure of clarity. "Becca," I thought, "I need to find Becca."

I sat up and looked around. I was surrounded by giant ferns. I looked down at my body, confused by what I saw. The fabric of my uniform shimmered with an iridescence I hadn't seen before. I looked at my comm and found barely an hour had passed since I left the ship.

I saw the broken trees, the tops now sprouting new growth, the wounds inflicted by our landing already beginning to heal. The silence lifted and I was overwhelmed by a cacophony of noise emanating from the forest, as if I could hear every living thing all at once. I forced myself to focus. I had to find Becca. I stood, found my balance, and entered the forest. The noise around me fell to a whisper, slipping to the periphery of my awareness. The sun-lit forest had been a collection of greens and browns, but was now a glittering and glowing wonderland of color and light, sound and smell.

I returned to the burnt and broken remains of our ship. Vegetation had crept closer, covering the charred ground. Vines curled upward, reaching for the open airlock. A pulsing light inside the airlock begged to be pushed. I ignored it and turned to the forest. I called out, "Becca…"

"Bimmy," I heard her reply.

She was close. I ran toward the sound of her voice, calling out again, "Where are you?"

"Right here," she said.

I pushed through the underbrush and found her standing next to a stream. I wrapped my arms around her, overwhelmed by emotion. "I thought I'd lost you."

"I'm okay, something happened, I'm not sure…"

"Me, too," I replied, "I thought I was dying, I thought you were dead…"

"I woke up by the stream, I was confused, I thought…I don't know what I thought, but something is different, I can't say…"

"Everything is different," I said, "the forest, my uniform, they're not the same…"

She pushed away from me, "Come with me," she said, "I have something to show you," she said.

"What is it?" I asked.

"A city, beside a lake."

"Why didn't we see it before?"

"I don't know, but if we want answers, I'm betting the city is where we'll find them."

I felt parched and knelt by the stream to scoop water into my cupped hands. I slurped it down, making her laugh. I did it again, so I could hear her laughter again, then we made our way along the bank of the stream. The stream rounded a bend, then cut through the edge of a white sand beach before entering a long narrow lake, stretching off into the distance.

On the far shore of the lake, the towers of a city sparkled in the sun.

"Look," she said, pointing at a small boat crossing the lake, approaching the beach. When it got closer to us, it spun around, then backed up onto the beach, aiming its bow at the city. It had four seats in two rows, with no obvious means of propulsion. A blue light pulsed softly on the stern.

I looked at Becca, "What do you think?"

"If there's one thing we've learned, blue means go." She stepped aboard and took a seat in front. "Give us a push."

I slid the boat off the beach then climbed in. Some hidden

mechanism propelled us across the water, toward the city. I looked down into the clear water, watching until the rocky bottom of the lake slipped away into deep blue darkness. We reached the opposite shore and the boat rounded an artificial peninsula, an organized mass of giant cut stones in shades of rust red and brown.

"Look at the boats," Becca said.

Inside the harbor, we passed between marinas populated by sunken, decaying vessels. Some had portions visible above the surface, with more visible in the depths of the clear water. A handful remained intact, floating peacefully at their moorings.

We approached a set of stairs set within a series of stone terraces marching from the water up to an open area above. A line of lights glowed soft blue, leading up the steps. The boat entered a notch cut into the lowest terrace, next to the row of lights. There were similar notches spaced along the water's edge, each with a boat like ours. A platform rose up beneath us, lifting the boat until the gunnels were level with the flat area on either side.

At the top of the stairs, a park spread out before us. Broad expanses of trimmed grass were divided by paved paths from each corner and from the midpoint of each side. The paths converged on a circular plaza, ringed by benches. A tall sculpture dominated the plaza, made of polished stone adorned with metal and stone figures of animals and children playing together, stacked in successive rings which grew smaller as the structure grew taller. It was crowned with a gleaming metal sphere with three rods of different lengths protruding from it.

The pulsing blue lights encircled the sculpture. We stepped inside the circle and the structure came to life. The sphere turned on its axis and water began to flow from openings dispersed around the lower rings of stone. It poured onto the surface of the plaza, then disappeared down drains embedded in the pavement. In several places, water arched out from the fountain, splashing into circular designs in the masonry.

"This could be fun," I said.

"Maybe later," Becca replied, smiling.

"Wait," I said, "look at these figures, this one looks like us, human. These other two are similar, but not the same. Are we looking at three different humanoid species on one planet?"

"I'm still in the 'anything is possible' mindset."

We rounded the fountain and continued toward a wide, mid-height building dominating the far side of the park. A three-story-high colonnade stretched across the front. A series of doors were set low in the facade behind the colonnade. We followed the path of lights to one set of doors in the center of the building. When I reached out, before I touched the surface, the doors slid open.

A wave of warm air cascaded over us. We passed through the door and were met by another set.

"Look," Becca said, pointing at the door that closed behind us, "I can read this, can you?"

I looked at the markings on a plaque, every outer door had the same message, written in the same script we'd seen on the space station hull.

"People of the three," I read, "go…something…in harmony."

"Forth," Becca said, "People of the triad, go forth in harmony. Are we coming in through the out door?"

"We're reading an alien language, and that's your question?"

Before she could reply, we heard a loud click as the outer door sealed, after which the inner door began to open.

"We're in an airlock," I said, "a really big one."

"Yes," Becca replied, "but why?"

Once the door was fully open, we entered a grand hall, as tall as the building, but not as wide. Soaring rows of ornate stone pillars marched along the flanks of the hall, rising up to an arched ceiling far above, painted with white clouds and a sunburst shining over a bucolic landscape. Light poured in from elliptical windows evenly spaced across the width and length of the ceiling. The floor was inlayed with repeating rows of the same blue lights in lines connecting the doors to the far end of the hall. More doors, all of them closed, dotted the walls beyond the columns.

A yellow light glowed in the distance, revealing an arched opening, five meters wide, in the far end of the hall. As we approached, more lights came on, illuminating the corridor beyond.

We passed through the corridor and into a broad, glass-enclosed courtyard, larger than the space we'd left behind, filled with lush gardens, fruit hanging heavy from low branches of trees. Thick vines, laden with red and blue berries, engulfed trellises made of wood and stone, flowers bloomed in planters set next to benches placed around tables carved of the same stone we'd seen in the park.

The courtyard gave way to a tree-lined cobblestone path, wide enough for several people to walk abreast. The trees met in an arch over the path, pressing up against the curved glass ceiling ten meters above us. Smaller paths at regular intervals led away to more courtyards. These fronted buildings with polished stone facades and windows of various sizes and shapes, large metal doors set in the center of each. Their designs made me think of the neighborhoods of Arcadia and the rows of homes behind neatly kept lawns.

"Where is everyone? Why aren't there other people here?" Becca asked.

"Someone has to take care of all this, but it may not be people," I said. "Remember the androids on the station?"

"If there are no people, why maintain it?"

"Maybe they're expecting someone…"

"Bimmy, if the door was an airlock, what's different here versus out there," she said, pointing at a patch of sky beyond the glass ceiling, visible through the canopy of trees.

"I've got nothing but questions, questions, and more questions. Let's keep going. If we came in through the exit, I say we find the front door and see if that tells us anything."

We continued on and soon the trees ended and the path opened into another park, a smaller version of what we found at the harbor, enclosed in glass like the area we'd left. A metal structure stood at the center, a dome, with wide arched openings around the base. A light shone blue over each opening.

"This looks promising," Becca said.

When we entered the structure, recessed fixtures filled the space with light. The ceiling was decorated in a similar fashion to the round corridors of the space station, large geometric and organic shapes in rich hues of blue and green and red.

The dome covered a circular auditorium, concentric rings lined with seating descending to a platform at the base. The chairs along the upper four levels were large and comfortable, situated in pairs. The chairs on the four levels below were much smaller, and equally spaced around each level.

"Looks like a theater," I said.

"Or a classroom," Becca replied.

More blue lights in the floor directed us to two seats on the lowest of the upper four levels. When we arrived, the lights at the base of the chairs switched to green.

"Looks like green means 'have a seat'," she said.

"I'm not ready to stop," I said, "let's see what happens if we keep going."

We exited the opposite side of the dome and could see what had been hidden from our approach. The glass ceiling descended to a massive wall of black stone, a dozen meters high and twice as wide, another arched opening cut into its center. We crossed the park and entered the corridor, which illuminated as we passed the threshold. The corridor was a tunnel. A short distance inside, the floor inclined and the ceiling curved up and away.

"Notice anything different?" Becca asked.

"Where do I start?"

"This space, it's not like all the others. There's no decoration, nothing ornate, no splashes of color. It's utilitarian, form and function."

"Every colony I've been to is divided into functional sections; residential, maintenance, recreation. We could be leaving one and entering another."

We walked for several minutes more until the upward curving floor transitioned to stairs leading out of the tunnel. The stairs weren't steep, but rose away from us for 30 meters. At the top, natural light invaded the inner space. We stepped into another large glass atrium, with a set of doors, an airlock, positioned in the far side, similar to what we encountered at the harbor. When we saw what stood beyond the atrium, outside the glass wall, I heard Becca gasp and felt my heart race. We ran to the doors of the lock, passed through the chamber, and stepped into another transparent tunnel, still sealed off from the air outside.

"Jackpot," I said, and began to laugh.

"Bimmy," Becca said, "how did we not see any of this from orbit?"

"I don't know, but we're seeing it now, that's all I care about."

To our left, a partially constructed spacecraft, larger than anything in the Federation fleet, rested in a hangar embedded in a hillside. An empty hangar of equal size sat next to it. In front of us, our path led to a gleaming white tower rising several stories into the sky. The top of the tower was wider than the base, and encircled with reflective glass. Three gantries extended out from the midsection of the tower, each of them connected to a spacecraft. The ships were identical, each as large the *Arcturus*, but much smaller than the unfinished ship in the hangar. They looked like they were ready for boarding and launch, or for passengers to disembark. Their hulls shone silver in the sunlight, adorned with an image, a sphere with three lines emanating from it.

"There's a reason this is hidden," I said. "Think of the power required to shield all of this, the city, the spaceport. And all of it looks like it was built yesterday. Something is not right here, we're missing it..."

"Agreed, but nothing here has tried to harm us, or stop us. We came here for answers. We have to keep going."

"Can't argue with you."

We walked into the tower and found a lobby filled with armchairs and sofas, arranged into groups throughout the interior. Water splashed softly down one wall of rough stone. A cylinder at the center of the structure disappeared through the ceiling. Transparent doors covered openings several meters across, ringing its base.

"Does that look like a lift tube to you, an exceptionally large one?" Becca asked.

"One way to find out."

The doors opened before us, and we stepped through. There were circles arranged in a pattern on the floor. When we each stood in a circle, we began to rise. On the first levels we passed, we could see walkways around the tube and walls lined with doors. The lift stopped at an open floor, dotted with chairs and small tables. Portals lined the exterior wall, three of them open. Along one section of the wall, a staircase curved up and out of sight.

When we exited, the doors slid shut and the lift dropped away.

"We know where those go," I said, indicating the open portals and their gangways to the waiting spacecraft, "what say we see where the stairs take us."

"After you."

As I suspected, the stairs led to a control room. Banks of consoles lined the outer wall with chairs placed at each, overlooking the spaceport. A round flat console on a raised platform stood guard over the room.

One section of windows, facing the city, ran floor to ceiling with no equipment in front of it. Becca stood staring out at the city below and the lake beyond. I went to the central console and touched the smooth surface. Nothing happened until I raised my hand and inadvertently waved it over one edge. A holographic image of the tower and the three attached ships rose up from the surface, data scrolling in a loop next to each. As with the sign on the door, I found I could read the information. As surprising as this was, I was more surprised to learn the status of the ships. "All fully fueled," I said, "they're ready to launch. But who's gonna fly them?"

Becca looked over her shoulder at me, then back out the window. I left the console and joined her.

She looked at me, her eyes bright, her face the essence of calm, then looked out the window again, gazing down on the city spread out below, nestled against the deep blue of the lake beyond, verdant land all around. I glimpsed the ocean on the distant horizon. The sun had passed its zenith, casting short shadows across the world. Becca reached out and took my hand, gave it a gentle squeeze, then let go.

"What do you see?" I asked.

"Home. I see home."

"What about our families, our friends…"

"We made it here," she said, "so can they."

I thought about my parents, Katie, the journey Becca and I had made, what we'd found and what we'd left behind, all we knew, and all we had yet to learn. She leaned into me and I draped my arm over her shoulders.

"Fair enough," I said, "fair enough."

# About the Book

I wrote this book first and foremost because I love the genre. The library at my middle school had a substantial science fiction collection, and I made it a point to read as many of those books as I could. Which in the end was all of them. Books written by the likes of Issac Asimov, Arthur C. Clarke, Robert Heinlein, Ray Bradbury, and others.

In retrospect, that which connected my favorite science fiction books and stories then, has not changed over the intervening years. I prefer science fiction that is firmly rooted in science, whether known, hypothetical, or theoretical. I much preferred, and still do, stories and novels which connect the future state of science to the current state. Robots, artificial intelligence, space stations, even advanced forms of communication, held a special fascination for me. If I could read about such things, and know they had a basis in fact, I could relate to them and have hope for a better, and more technologically advanced future.

At the same time, subjects like alien species, interplanetary and interstellar travel, ancient civilizations on distant worlds; these concepts, while not supported by the science of the day, were equally fascinating to me because there was no evidence they couldn't be possible. We, as a species, simply hadn't advanced our understanding of the universe far enough to lend credence to the more fantastic conjurings of our imagination.

More than anything, *Beyond Tomorrow's Sun* is a story of hope, courage, and love, that never loses sight of the increasing dangers of our possible future.

# About the Author

Ronald McGuire writes stories about change—how it arrives, how it reshapes us, and what remains in its wake. Blending literary and speculative elements, his fiction explores identity, memory, and the moments that define and redefine who we are.

He is the author of the novels *Beyond Tomorrow's Sun* and *Beyond the Rivers of Time*. *Pax Liminalis* is his second collection of short fiction, following *Nightmares & Lullabies*.

Ronald's work spans fiction, essays, journalism, and scriptwriting, with publication credits including Flash Fiction Magazine, Drunk Monkeys, The Dead Mule School of Southern Literature, Winning Writers, and CNN.com.

Learn more at ronaldmcguire.com or beachbookpress.com.